WHITE GOLD

A DAN TAYLOR THRILLER

RACHEL AMPHLETT

SAXON
PUBLISHING

For the real Harry

PROLOGUE

JANUARY 2009

Somewhere in Iraq

Dan Taylor pulled at the padded vest, reached underneath it, and flicked another shirt button open.

Sweat poured down his face as the armoured vehicle bucked and swayed along the pot-holed road towards their target. He turned to the man seated beside him. He had to shout to be heard over the roar of the engine. 'Who called it in Terry?'

The other man shrugged. 'Some woman walked up to one of the patrols – said her boy had seen a couple of blokes running away from the house opposite and it looked like they'd buried something in the road there.'

Dan nodded, lowered his gaze to his feet and sat, trance-like, waiting for the vehicle to arrive at their destination. He shuffled, trying to work the cramp out of his legs in the tight, confined space. The man opposite kicked his foot. Dan looked up and took the proffered chewing gum with a grunt of thanks.

'Cheers H.'

Not that a stomach ulcer is a major cause of concern right now, he thought. He pulled at the strap under his chin which held his helmet in place. He felt a headache materialising, the helmet squeezing his skull in the heat.

The armoured vehicle continued to power along the dirt road between dilapidated houses. Most bore battle scars – bullet holes, missing roof tiles. In some places, rubble and twisted metal were the only clues where buildings had once stood.

Dan closed his eyes and let his body move with the twists and turns the vehicle made along the road. The tiredness and exhaustion consumed him. Three months added onto an already extended tour in the desert, the team were struggling to keep their wits about them. Every day, more explosive devices were being detonated by the unit. Just as they safely disposed of one bomb, another two were discovered, lying in wait for them.

Dan opened his eyes and glanced at his watch. They'd been out of the compound for six hours straight, driving from one emergency to another. He tilted his head back, stretching his neck muscles.

A shout from the front seat made him jump. 'Hang on!'

The vehicle veered around a sharp left-hand bend and the road widened out. Dust whipped across the road as small pebbles spat out from under the wheels of the vehicle. They'd left behind the suburban sprawl of the rocket-shelled town. The houses left standing along the road stood sentinel as the vehicle followed in the day-old tracks of a supply convoy. The main road in and out of the town was a popular target for terrorists. The armoured vehicle accelerated, swinging left and right to dodge the larger craters and pot-holes.

The men sitting on the back panel seats held on to straps hanging from the ceiling of the vehicle and swayed with the motion.

'Dicko, could your driving possibly get any worse?' yelled H.

Dan didn't hear the reply but from the grin across H's face, he could tell it wasn't polite. Dicko had once told him he'd been a courier driver in London before signing up – Dan often wondered how temporary that career would have been if Dicko hadn't suddenly decided on a change of direction. He felt the vehicle slow to a crawl. Dicko spun the wheel and stopped.

A voice called back to them from the passenger seat. 'Everybody out!' David Ludlow, a young ambitious captain, shouted over his shoulder. 'Dan, Mitch – you're on the robot.'

Dan waited while H leaned over to the back of the wagon and released the door. The team crawled out into the glaring heat. Dust devils whipped up small clouds of dirt and grit. Dan stretched his large frame, and then walked to the passenger door. He leaned against the vehicle while David radioed in their position from the GPS coordinates.

The scenery had all started looking the same after a couple of months into the tour. Dust, sand, dust, and more dust. A burst of static was followed by a faint confirmation from their base.

David replaced the radio and turned to Dan. 'Let's do it.'

Dan walked to the back of the vehicle. A breeze off the desert swept the sweat from his face. He held up his hand to shield his deep blue eyes from the sun's glare and stared down the road ahead of him. A thick haze clung to the afternoon horizon. On the left, further down the road, two burnt-out cars had been pushed out of the way and over to the side, to not to slow yesterday's supply convoy. Dan blinked and pushed his sunglasses tighter to his face. He turned to help Mitch unload the bomb disposal robot from the wagon.

A small machine, supported on large tracked wheels with two claws at the front and a camera mounted onto the top, the robot enabled the team to get closer to the suspected IED without endangering their own lives.

While the other man went to gauge the terrain, Dan reached into the back of the wagon and pulled out a reinforced case. He opened it, and then unfolded a small laptop and joystick controls. He switched on the computer and was soon relaying commands to the robot on the floor.

It twitched on its tracks, the cable attached to the back of the camera playing out as the robot began to roll away, relaying live pictures back to the computer.

Dan looked up and saw Mitch walking back towards him. 'All clear?'

Mitch nodded. 'Terry's gone to take a look around that house over there, just to make sure no-one sticks their heads out while we do this. There're hardly any buildings around, which helps. H says there's not enough cover for snipers.'

Dan looked where Mitch was pointing. The house stood on the left side of the track – mud and bricks, with a low stone wall which hemmed in a goat and some chickens. An old couple stared at them from a front doorway. He watched as Terry approached the building, shouted to the old lady in the doorway and gestured to her they should move away.

Dan turned as David called out commands. 'Dicko, H – make sure this area is cleared. One-fifty metre boundary. Take a look at those dunes on the perimeter. Keep your eyes open.'

Dan watched as the two men left the sheltered side of the vehicle and strode out into the bright sunshine, their heads swivelling from side to side as they scanned the landscape for any threats to the team. David kept watch from the rear of the vehicle, his eyes flickering over the small crowd of people staring at them from the opposite end of the road.

Dan jumped as Mitch slapped him on the back.

5

'Come on posh boy, stop daydreaming. Let's go play with a bomb.'

Dan shook his head and smirked. After two years working together, Mitch still took the piss out of his Oxfordshire accent. 'Better still, send the robot. It's too hot for the suit today.'

He glanced down the road and stopped. 'Christ – where did *he* come from?'

Mitch looked up to where Dan pointed.

A young boy had appeared from the side of one of the houses to their right, about fifty metres away. The boy pedalled happily towards the road on a small beat-up green tricycle. He smiled and waved at Dicko and H as they approached. Unaware of the danger he was in, the boy began chattering loudly to them as he cycled faster into the middle of the road.

The two soldiers ran to him, oblivious of their own safety, and waved their hands at him to tell him to stop.

Dan could feel his heart hammering in his chest as he watched H bend down to talk to the boy. He couldn't have been more than three years old. Dan watched, his throat dry, as the child was sent running back in exactly the same direction he'd cycled from.

As he got to the house, a woman snatched him up in her arms and scolded him. A man held his hand up in thanks. Dicko and H waved at him, indicating the family should go inside and shelter, before they continued their patrol, walking past the discarded tricycle and away towards the dunes.

Dan swallowed and wiped the sweat from his eyes. He breathed out slowly, trying to stop his voice from wavering. 'Where did the report say the IED was?'

Mitch stood next to Dan and pointed. Dan ignored the fact he could see the other man's hand shaking. They'd both been scared for the kid. 'Check out the tyre to the left of the road, about eighty metres away. Got it?'

Dan nodded.

'Okay – now look to the right of it. You can see where the surface has been dug up and replaced. It's just a pile of dirt with a bit of debris around it, yeah?'

'Yeah, okay – I see it.'

Dan moved closer to the laptop and took hold of the small joystick between his finger and thumb. He glanced up at the screen, checked the camera was working properly, and then sent the robot rolling down the road towards its target.

As the robot bumped over the rough surface, Dan moved the camera left and right, testing the camera angles and making sure the picture on the laptop was clear. The last thing he needed was a dodgy signal, especially if he was going to have to use the robot to cut any wires to timing devices.

He looked across at Mitch who was standing at the side of the armoured vehicle, watching the robot as it trundled over the rough terrain.

'How are they doing?'

Mitch's gaze changed slightly, taking in the road and H and Dicko walking up over the sand dunes. 'Looks okay.

As long as they keep that perimeter, they'll be fine.' He clicked his radio microphone. 'How's it going you two?'

Dan heard a burst of static over Mitch's earpiece and kept his eyes on the computer screen.

Mitch guffawed. 'Dicko reckons he's actually found a sand dune dirtier than the ones back home in Pembrokeshire. Amazing.'

Dan smiled. 'Just tell them to watch where they're walking. It won't be dog shit that gets them into trouble here.'

Mitch grinned and relayed the message.

Dan slowed the robot as it drew near to the pile of debris in the middle of the road. He took his hand off the joystick and turned to David. 'I'm ready when you are,' he called.

David nodded and clicked his own radio microphone. 'Okay everyone. Here we go. Keep your eyes and ears open.'

Dan peered around the back of the vehicle and saw Dicko and H taking up a defensive position on the sand dune in the distance, their rifles swinging as they panned round, taking in their surroundings. Behind him, David covered his back, glaring at anyone who looked like they were going to approach the vehicle, occasionally shouting to make sure the small crowd stayed back.

Dan took hold of the joystick and began the robot's final approach. Bringing it to a stop next to the debris, he stopped the machine and used one of its claws to gently lift a discarded piece of blue cloth. He tapped a series of keys on the laptop and the camera angle zoomed into the space underneath the cloth. He held his breath. Underneath the cloth, the tell-tale signs of an IED were just visible.

Mitch peered over his shoulder. 'Bastards.'

Dan nodded. 'There are plenty of them around here.'

'Can you lift that cloth out of the way?'

'I can try – it doesn't look like it's weighing on the device.'

Dan touched the joystick and gently pushed it forward. The robot's claw began to lift the material slowly away from the bomb.

'Lift it straight up,' said Mitch. 'You don't want it dragging across otherwise it could catch on the IED and set it off.'

Dan blinked as sweat ran down his face. He paused, wiping his eyes, trying to stop them stinging and rubbed his hands down the front of his trousers. He took hold of the joystick once more and the robot trundled backwards, carrying the bundle of cloth with it. He waited until the robot was a couple of metres back from the bomb, then hit a series of keys. The robot's claw opened and the cloth fell to the ground.

'Okay, now let's get back in there and see what we're dealing with,' said Mitch, as he leaned against the back door of the vehicle and peered at the laptop screen.

Dan steered the robot back up to the bomb. He swung the camera left and right, recording all the angles, then stopped. 'Here.' He pointed at the screen. 'The wires are exposed just there, look.'

Mitch bent down and peered at the relayed image. 'Can you get to them?'

Dan nodded. 'I reckon so. Standard configuration.'

Mitch grunted. 'Yeah, looks like it. Can you get the cutters under it?'

Dan hit a series of keys and the robot's claw swung into the camera's view. The pincers snapped together twice and Dan eased them steadily towards a set of three wires. He lowered the claw until its lower edge was touching the dirt road. He stopped, took his finger and thumb off the joystick and wiped his hand on his padded vest. He then rubbed his finger and thumb together, trying to lose the grease, then took hold of the controls once more.

'Any time today will do,' murmured Mitch.

'Fuck off.'

In spite of Dan's response, he had a lot of respect for the other man. After joining the team following extensive training at Vauxhall Barracks in Oxfordshire, Dan began his first tour in the Middle East and Mitch had spent a lot of time making sure Dan's training continued.

Dan twitched the robot forward. The claw scraped the dirt as it eased under the bomb's wiring. He punched a key on the laptop and the picture zoomed in.

'Child's play,' commented Mitch.

Dan glanced sideways at him. 'Don't you have to be somewhere?'

Mitch chuckled. 'No.'

Dan rolled his eyes and then concentrated on the picture in front of him. Despite being annoying, Mitch's observation had been right. The construction of the IED was deceptively simple. Deadly, but simple. A set of three wires connected the explosives to a trip switch.

'No sign of a remote detonator,' he reported.

Mitch slapped him on the back. 'Good, get on with it then.' He turned and called to David, relaying the message. David nodded and turned his attention back to the small group of bystanders.

Dan lined up the robot's claw and began to gently lift the wires apart. He hit another command on the computer, which sent a telescopic tube out from under the robot, a set of wire cutters protruding from the end.

He breathed out slowly and willed his heart rate to calm down. He closed his eyes, replayed in his mind what needed to be done, then opened them, focused and ready.

As he typed in the final sequence of controls, the robot's claw gently pulled a blue wire away from the other two. When it drew close to the wire cutters, a single keystroke sent a message to the robot and its blades drove through the wire.

Silence.

Dan breathed out, and turned to Mitch. 'Job done.'

Mitch nodded, called to David and gave him a thumbs up.

David radioed the message to the others. 'We're clear.'

The small crowd lost interest and began to disperse across the road. Dan looked up and saw the old couple next to the house. They were arguing by the look of it, the woman gesturing wildly to her husband before storming into the house and shutting the door behind her.

David walked past and gave Dan the thumbs up. 'Good work Taylor. Get that robot back and packed up quickly, otherwise the kids will have it dismantled for parts before we know it.'

'I'm on to it.'

Dan pulled the joystick backwards on the laptop and the robot began its slow reverse journey back to the armoured vehicle, the relayed picture jumping as the on-board camera shook over the rough surface.

David signalled to Mitch. 'Don't stand around – go and grab that gear. We don't want them recycling it for the next one they plant for us.'

Mitch nodded and jogged off towards the defused bomb. Dan glanced round the back of the vehicle and watched as he collected the parts while Dicko and H began to stroll back from the roadside dunes, their laughter carrying across the breeze.

David followed his gaze and sighed. 'Anyone would think those two were on a bloody holiday,' he said and shook his head, before walking round to the front of the vehicle to radio in their progress.

Dan looked up as Mitch jogged back to the vehicle, various wires, timers and parts cradled in his hands. He set them down in the back of the vehicle where they began to sift through them, looking for serial numbers or identifying markings – anything to provide information about who had supplied the pieces.

David appeared from the side of the armoured vehicle, a puzzled look on his face. 'Have you seen Terry?'

Dan and Mitch shook their heads.

'Last time I saw him, he was talking to a couple by that house over there.' Dan pointed.

David glanced over. 'His radio might have packed up. I'll keep trying. If you see him, wave him over – we want to get back to the compound for some rest before we drop from exhaustion.'

He disappeared round the back of the vehicle, talking into his radio.

Dan turned a piece of the blue wire between his fingers as he monitored the robot's progress on the laptop.

'This is weird,' said Mitch.

'What is?'

'It doesn't make sense.' Mitch held up the pieces, and pointed to a single wire protruding upwards. 'There's nothing attached to it. Did you cut it by mistake?'

Dan shook his head. 'No.'

He watched as Mitch stepped away from the back of the vehicle to watch Dicko and H's progress. Terry was waving his goodbyes to the old couple outside their house.

Mitch turned to Dan, his face pale. 'This isn't the one – it's a decoy.'

Dan looked at Mitch. 'What? *What*?'

Mitch had turned back to the road, running his fingers through his hair and turning his head from side to side, desperately surveying the landscape. His eyes fell on the abandoned green tricycle standing in the middle of the road. *It was the real bomb.*

'This isn't the one Dan – we've fixed the wrong one!'

Then H yelled, his shout carried away by a blast before Dan could register the warning. The robot tipped sideways in the shockwave, the camera blinked once, then continued recording. A red light on the camera flashed silently and, as the dust began to settle, the screaming began.

ONE

'Gold has long been valued in ancient cultures around the world. One must question exactly what was so special about gold that men would wage war with each other for years, far from their own lands.

Maybe, just maybe, it was not so much about the gold itself, but rather the power it contained...

The power harnessed from the processing of gold in the ways I shall describe will show beyond doubt it is a cleaner, more stable alternative to nuclear fuel while surpassing the output we are told to expect from solar or wind energy.

As usual, however, the polluting industries of oil and coal hold sway over governments around the world and continue to block extensive research and exploration into the mass manufacture of this potential wonder-fuel...'

Extract from lecture series by Doctor Peter Edgewater,
Berlin, Germany

JANUARY 2012

Oxford, England

Dan Taylor woke up in a sweat. The same nightmare
punctuated his sleep, night after night – dust, sand,
screaming, blood. He rubbed his eyes. He'd been crying in
his sleep again. He knew the army shrinks said the
memories would fade in time but he didn't believe them.
He'd spoken to enough people who had been caught up in
combat before to know the dreams never left. He could
almost hear the ringing in his ears from the explosion.

He tried to roll over and discovered he couldn't. He
opened his eyes, slowly. He'd passed out on the sofa.
Again. He eased himself up onto his elbows and turned his
head to survey the damage, wrinkling his nose in disgust at
the stale odours in the room.

The remains of a Chinese takeaway littered the small
coffee table next to him. He blinked in surprise. He didn't
remember eating last night. He reached down towards the
floor and felt about until his fingers connected with a
familiar glass surface. Clutching at it, he drew it up level

until the whiskey bottle was in front of his face. He glanced at it and winced. Empty. He stood it on the coffee table.

He looked up and saw the television flickering on in the corner of the room. Some sort of daytime television talk-show rubbish. He reached between the sofa cushions underneath him. He pulled out the remote control, aimed it at the offending broadcast and hit the off switch.

He closed his eyes. He remembered thinking he'd have just one drink to help him get to sleep, to ward off the nightmares. He looked at the bottle accusingly. It had let him down. It no longer worked. He opened his eyes and blinked, trying to focus so the tears wouldn't start.

He swung his legs off the sofa and sat with his head in his hands until he felt he could stand without falling over. Slowly, he straightened up and groaned.

Coffee.

He picked up the empty whiskey bottle and takeaway cartons and staggered towards the kitchen. He swore profusely as he stubbed his toe on one of the bags littering the hallway. A steel-capped boot fell out on to the floor and he stared at it accusingly. He'd arrived back in Oxford two days ago but couldn't face the depressing task of unpacking. He yearned to be travelling again, even if it only meant returning to his old career of collecting more soil samples for yet another mining exploration company. It stopped him thinking too hard about the past. Or the present. Or the future.

He shook his head and shuffled into the kitchen. He

opened the back door, swung the rubbish into the bins outside and blinked in the bright sunshine. He belched and watched in mild amusement as the hot emission turned to steam in the cold morning air.

He stepped back into the kitchen, left the door open to help air the house and switched the kettle on. As he turned and reached up to a cupboard over the kitchen bench for a coffee mug, he noticed his mobile phone blinking.

New voicemail message.

Dan grunted, picked up the phone and put it in the back pocket of his jeans. He got a coffee mug, organised the first caffeine shot of the morning and sloped back to the living room.

He grimaced. The room stank.

He pulled open the curtains and opened the windows. Cold air filtered through. He shivered. At least it would freshen up the place. He sat down in an armchair and winced. He reached behind him and pulled the mobile phone from his pocket. He glared at it, then dialled the voicemail service and put the phone to his ear.

He took a sip of coffee while the mobile service went through all the options available to him. According to the mobile service, the message had been left the previous night. He waited, and then the message began.

'Dan, hi – it's Peter Edgewater here. Listen, I'm in a bit of a rush but you're the only one who will really appreciate this – I've done it! I know who's managing to produce white gold on a commercial basis! Listen, I'm just finishing a lecture tour in Europe at the moment but I'll be back in a few days. I'm organising drinks with a few people I haven't seen for a while so I can tell you all about it – let's catch up, yeah? Give me a call and I'll…'

Dan hit the button to hang up the call and threw the phone on the coffee table. He wondered why he bothered to have one. He really wasn't interested in catching up with old friends so they could tell him how successful they were. It just reminded him how low he had sunk.

He leaned forward, picked up the phone and deleted the message. Dan glanced at his watch and grunted in satisfaction. The pub would be open in another hour.

Berlin, Germany

Peter hurried along the pavement in the direction of the hotel, his breath turning to vapour in the chill of the air. He shrugged the backpack further up his shoulder and thrust his gloved hands deeper into his jacket pockets, seeking out the last of the warmth from his body. 'Note to self,' he murmured, 'next time, arrange lecture tours in the summer.'

Broad-shouldered, the man was athletic in build, tall and sinewy. He shivered in the bitter night though, and wished he had a few more natural layers of padding to cope with the cold German winter.

His attention was drawn to the familiar white and red

of a Stella Artois sign protruding from the building on his left. Slowing down, Peter climbed up the two uneven narrow steps to an ornate hardwood door and pushed it open. Immediately, the cold of the night was forgotten as the warmth from the hotel's reception area enveloped him.

A small, but effective, log fire burned in an elaborate fireplace set into the wall on his right, throwing out its heat across the room. To his left, a narrow doorway led to the hotel bar, which resonated with the sound of laughter and the soft clink of glasses as patrons eased out the creases of another day. Peter glanced at the bar, then made his way to the reception desk at the back of the foyer and let the backpack slide down his arm to the floor.

The receptionist, dressed in a blue suit with a white blouse, caught his eye as she took a booking over the telephone and motioned to him to wait. She finished the call and smiled.

'Any messages?' Peter asked as he removed his gloves.

'One moment *bitte*.'

The receptionist turned to the computer and keyed in a command. She absently pushed her glasses up her nose as the screen refreshed.

'A man was here asking for you earlier sir,' she read from the screen. 'He told the receptionist on duty he would telephone you. He didn't leave his name.'

Peter frowned. The phone call was unexpected but, he reasoned, he'd met a lot of people over the past few weeks who would want to discuss his theories in more detail. He'd run out of business cards two days ago and had resorted to scribbling his name and phone number on catering napkins and beer mats to keep up with the demand of journalists, researchers and, he smiled, the occasional nut case.

He thanked the receptionist as he collected his electronic room key and shouldered his backpack once more before heading across the foyer to the elevator.

Stepping out on to the fifth floor, Peter walked across the hallway and inserted the swipe card to his hotel room, waited for the green light and the soft click of the lock, and opened the door. Reaching to his right, his hand automatically seeking the light switch, he yawned, closed the door behind him and ran his fingers through his hair.

The room was stuffy, the heating turned up high by the cleaning staff. He dropped the backpack to the floor, his shoulder aching with relief as the weight of the laptop and documents subsided. He closed the door behind him, tossed his swipe card onto the hardwood dresser and kicked off his shoes. He threw his jacket onto the bed, made his way over to the balcony door and pushed it open a little, letting the cold fresh air wash over him. Turning slightly, he reached down to the small refrigerator in the corner of the room and grabbed a cold beer.

'Cheers,' he said to the empty room, tearing off his tie.

Bending down to open his backpack, he noticed the answering machine light blinking. He punched in the access code and tucked the phone between his ear and shoulder while he gathered up his notes. The message began to play, the soundtrack a busy street, before a heavily accented voice cut through the static.

'Doctor Edgewater, you know who I represent. If you continue to insinuate that my employer's organisation is in any way involved in matters pertaining to white gold and super-conducted precious metals, we will be unable to guarantee your safety on this lecture tour. We *will* harm you and your family if you persist.'

The message ended abruptly.

Peter slammed down the phone in disgust and disbelief. He had expected a few idiots on the lecture tour, but not threats – not yet. He hadn't even discussed the really controversial claims as he found himself still debating whether it was worth the trouble he could cause for himself. Now this. Someone was actively watching him and his research.

He shivered. He'd be glad to get out of Berlin tomorrow. Travelling to Paris meant being a little closer to home. Living out of a suitcase lost its appeal after a few weeks on the road.

Peter walked across the room and slid the balcony door shut, sweeping the curtains closed, though not before he'd glanced nervously at the windows in the building opposite. How long had he been followed? Had he spoken to the person who had phoned? Had he been approached after the lecture today without realising who he was speaking with?

Peter realised he no longer knew who to trust.

The university had threatened to cut his funding last month – the lecture tour was devised by Peter to create an awareness of the clandestine demand for super-conducted precious metals, particularly white gold, so the research couldn't be ignored. He was sure the university was under pressure from the UK government to stop him before he uncovered anything it was experimenting with.

He wandered back to the bed, sat down and swung his legs up, grabbed the television remote and flicked to the 24-hour news channel. His flight to Paris was scheduled to leave mid-morning, with the lecture taking place in the evening. Hitting the mute button, he reached for his notes.

He took a long swallow of the beer and absently contemplated the label. Maybe it was time to ramp up the lectures now he was heading home, to see who came out of the shadows, he thought, then turned the page.

Despite the warning, he couldn't quit, not now – he was too close. There was too much at stake.

TWO

'The increasing price of oil is just the start. Consider the fact that when oil prices rise, so do gold and platinum. Many reasons are given – the weak dollar, global inflation ... except oil prices fluctuate depending on what's going on in the world. Gold, however, has continually increased in price and shows no sign of stopping ...'

Extract from lecture series by Doctor Peter Edgewater,
Paris, France

Paris, France

Peter stood in the doorway leading out of the lecture theatre, elated and high on adrenaline after another successful presentation. *The risk was worth it.* The audience took a while to file past, some shaking his hand, others stopping to chat as they went.

Peter excused himself from the throng and began to walk back to the podium for his water glass. He took a sip, and then started to gather up his notes, snapping his briefcase shut before stepping off the small dais.

'Doctor Edgewater?'

Peter turned to the man on his left. 'Yes?'

The man stepped forward, and offered his hand. 'An impressive lecture Doctor Edgewater – I see it's proving popular.'

Peter put the glass down and shook the proffered hand. 'Thank you – yes, it seems to be; although I'm not sure how many audience members see this as another conspiracy theory instead of what it really is.'

'And what would that be?' asked the man. He fell into step with Peter as he walked out of the lecture theatre and through the ornate hallway.

Peter stopped in his tracks and considered the question briefly before answering. 'An organised takeover of the world's precious metal resources by large conglomerates who have failed to disclose their interests and ulterior motives would be a good start... sorry, have we met before?'

'No, sorry, forgive my rudeness. My name's David Ludlow – I've been following the reviews of your lecture series with interest. You seem to have stirred up a hornet's nest in high places.'

'Is that so? Would you care to elaborate?'

David looked down the hallway, before taking hold of Peter by the elbow and steering him to a small alcove. 'Here – where we can't be overheard.'

Peter followed, puzzled. 'Who did you say you worked for?'

'I didn't,' said David dismissively.

Peter folded his arms across his chest. 'Then why should I listen to you?'

The other man looked at him closely, appraising him. 'Because your life is at risk.'

'So you're threatening me?'

'No, Peter, no I'm not.' David checked the hallway before continuing. 'I work for an agency which, let's just say, advises the government about threats to national security.'

He held up his hand to stop Peter interrupting.

'Hear me out. Twelve months ago, we started looking more closely into an organisation which had been actively purchasing or forcibly taking over gold mining operations over the space of two to three years. Australia, South Africa, Eastern Europe, South America – you get the picture. For a while, we couldn't work out why – it wasn't the usual mergers and acquisitions strategy of a normal mining company, neither was it money-laundering activities we'd associate with either drugs or terrorism. Still, we added it to our watch list.'

'Then you began your lecture tour in Europe. The communications traffic increased dramatically – particular phrases kept cropping up – white gold, super-conducted precious metals.'

Peter frowned. 'Well, without sounding like I have a huge ego, I would imagine that would be because a lot of what I've been presenting has been highly controversial – I'd expect a flurry of activity on the internet,' he said.

David shook his head. 'What I'm talking about couldn't be described as a 'flurry' Peter. We're talking a snowstorm of incredible proportions – some of it covert, and not ours.'

'I still can't see how all this means my life is in danger,' said Peter, exasperated. 'All I'm doing is raising people's awareness about what's going on – same as any journalist would.'

'And how is Sarah these days?' asked David.

'What?' Peter was taken aback. 'What do you mean?'

'Well, she's a journalist – with a deserved reputation for digging up stories like this. What does she think about your lectures?'

'You leave her out of this – we've been separated for the last eighteen months, as you're probably aware, given you've been spying on me – and she knows nothing about this research.' Peter stepped closer to the other man and lowered his voice. 'And if you're going to threaten me or my family, then you can piss off.' Peter began to turn away.

'Doctor Edgewater, I'm sorry you feel that way inclined,' said David. He took hold of Peter's arm. 'I've been asked to convey the message that you tread very

27

carefully. Some of the comments you've been making during your lecture tour could be construed by others as being inflammatory, at least.'

'That's the idea.'

'Have you received any threats in recent weeks?'

Peter shrugged the other man's grip off his sleeve. 'Apart from the one you just gave me? No.'

David looked at him. 'I hope you're telling me the truth Peter. I am not a threat, and I don't like being lied to – my superiors are actually very concerned for your safety. If you get yourself into trouble before we're ready to make a move against this organisation, you're on your own – I certainly can't vouch for your safety. We'd much rather work with you than against you.'

'Thank your superiors for me David. Now, if you'll excuse me, I've got a meeting to go to.' Peter brushed past the other man and walked down the ornate steps to the door, heart racing.

He pushed the door open and stepped out onto the busy street. He looked both ways, willing himself not to start panicking. The lecture notes and research were in an envelope in his briefcase.

Call it instinct, but he'd decided from the outset of his lecture tour in Europe he'd need a back-up plan. He expected the conglomerates and organisations involved in blocking the research would sit up and take notice, but this was suddenly becoming more extreme than he'd bargained for.

As he hurried along the street, he raised his umbrella

and pushed past commuters heading out to lunch. He turned left at the intersection, careful not to slide on the wet pavement. He spotted the post office on the other side of the road and tapped his foot while he waited for the traffic lights to change. He stepped back as a bus splashed past him. He couldn't help a surreptitious glance over his shoulder.

He was convinced he saw David Ludlow standing with a woman, watching him from a distance, but the crowd shifted and he lost sight of them. An electronic *zap* brought him to his senses as the pedestrian crossing lights flashed green and he hurried across the street. Increasing his pace, he hurried along the street to the post office and pushed the door open, lowering his umbrella and nearly knocking over a young mother and her child. '*P-pardon, Madame,*' he stuttered as he held the door open for them.

The woman glared at him with the child's face echoing hers. Peter closed the door and turned to the counter. He breathed a sigh of relief – the lunchtime rush hadn't yet started.

He opened the briefcase against his leg and slid out an envelope. After checking the seal was secure, he took a pen from his jacket pocket and scribbled an address on the outside.

As he paid the postage to send the package, Peter turned and glanced up out the post office window as a woman passed by. He was sure it was the same person he'd seen standing with David Ludlow.

He swallowed, and felt a drop of sweat streak down the

side of his face. This was real. It was really happening. A thought raced through his head – *I was right*! It did nothing to calm him. If people really were following him, it meant his research was correct and he had to protect that.

Peter moved over to a corner of the room, away from the growing queue and took out his mobile phone. Scrolling through the contact list, he glanced outside the window again. No-one there. He found the name he wanted, hit the send button and waited for the connection.

Dammit! It went straight to voicemail.

'Dan, it's Peter here. I think I'm in trouble. I-I don't know who else to call. I'm in Paris at the moment. I'm going to get a train back to Ashford this afternoon then I'll drive up to Oxford to do the last lecture tomorrow. I'll call you after the lecture. I've no idea where you are these days so I've sent some information to Sarah – it'll explain everything. I don't know if I'll be able to. If I don't make it, please go to her – and be careful who you give the information to or discuss it with. I've already received some threats I didn't think were serious, but after today, I'm beginning to think my life's in danger. I'll call you as soon as I can.'

Hanging up, Peter realised his hands were shaking.

THREE

'Events continue to prove the rush for precious metals is real. People continue to struggle against multi-national takeovers of their gold mines, with more and more control of these resources being lost to foreign organisations. Further, takeovers are little-publicised affairs, despite the size of the organisations involved. More importantly, it would seem it is the coal, oil and gas companies seeking to control the precious metals market.'

Extract from lecture series by Doctor Peter Edgewater,
Paris, France

Brisbane, Australia

. . .

Morris Delaney stood with his hands clasped behind his back, and looked out of the smoked glass office window. Below, he could see people dashing backwards and forwards across the busy intersection. *Ants*, he thought. *No – cockroaches.*

Tall, broad shouldered, a slight limp was the only indication of his old rugby-playing school days. He ran his hand through his white hair, still thick after all these years and cut slightly longer than his contemporaries. He tipped his head backwards and heard a satisfying crack as a muscle stretched. He grimaced, conceding that over the past few years he'd spent too much time in an office instead of being outside, getting his hands dirty.

He glanced down at the reproduction paddle-steamer going up the river, the late afternoon sun casting its shadow along the embankment as it went along, full of tourists clamouring for a three-course buffet dinner. He snorted with amusement.

His gaze shifted to the plaza below, where a small group of protestors gathered around the entrance to the building, their sad placards flapping in the breeze coming off the river. *Down with Delaney. Wind not Coal. Coal Equals Global Warming.* Apparently the London office was attracting the same sorry bunch of misinformed members of the public.

Delaney didn't mind protestors – any publicity was welcome as far as he was concerned – it gave him an opportunity to go to the media and explain to the masses

32

why the environmentalists had it so wrong and then publicise his latest mining acquisition.

He glanced down at the newspaper on his desk and smirked. The *Mail* always misquoted him. He tossed it into the bin. He knew his facts, even if the journalists didn't.

Only three years ago, the UK government had received information from one of its key advisors that the country would be facing blackouts within the next five years as the old coal-powered power stations were decommissioned, because the wind and solar plants wouldn't be operational in time and gas was so expensive. Delaney shook his head in wonder. The public always wanted renewable energy – as long as the wind farm or solar array wasn't built next door. It made it so much easier for organisations like his to continue touting coal as the fuel of choice. Dirty, yes, but so what? Coal was still cheap, it was safe – and there was plenty to go around, not to mention export opportunities.

He noticed the reflection in the glass of his office door opening as his secretary knocked and entered the office, her high heels silenced by the thick carpet.

'What is it?'

'A new report from the mine – it just came through.' She held up an envelope and stood in the doorway, hesitant.

He nodded to his desk. 'Leave it there; I'll get to it in a minute. Any surprises?'

'I- I didn't read it.'

'Good,' he growled. He knew how secretaries in the small city networked and gossiped; it was a strict policy at the organisation that access to senior managers' post and emails was never provided to administration staff. Still, he figured it didn't hurt to check and keep them on their toes on a regular basis. 'Leave it and get out.'

The secretary placed the package where he indicated then turned and quickly walked out of the office, closing the door quietly behind her. Delaney wandered over to his desk, ripped open the envelope and scanned the pages of the report.

The equipment development had been going well. Now the extraction method had been perfected and scaled upwards, the schedule was going smoothly. Building the entire operation near the existing coal mine had ensured the process hadn't raised suspicion.

A piece of notepaper protruded from under one of the reports. Removing a fountain pen from his jacket pocket, Delaney drew out the notepaper carefully with the nib of the pen. He had a team of security agents which monitored all reporting about his company. More diligent than a typical press agency, his agents also monitored conferences, lectures and government campaigns. If anything threatened the reputation or success of his organisation, it was brought to his attention.

A vein on the side of his head began to pulse as he read the message. His fingers tightened on the file cover. Pulling out the notepaper completely, he read it again before he picked up his phone, dialled a three-digit number then slammed the receiver back down. No need to say anything – his number would be displayed at the other end.

No-one asked questions. They came when they were summoned.

A minute later, a knock on the door preceded a small man, buttoning up his jacket and straightening his tie.

Delaney waited until the door was shut. Glaring at the other man, he walked around his desk and sat down, the chair creaking under his weight. He left the other man standing nervously in the middle of the room, shuffling uncomfortably on the carpet.

'Who have we got in Europe at the moment, Ray?'

The other man visibly sweated as he wracked his brains. 'Um, that would be, um, Charles, Mr Delaney. That is, er, if we're talking about someone you need to *kill*.'

Delaney pressed his fingers against his lips. 'Shhh, Ray. Never mention that word in here, or anywhere else in my presence.'

Ray nodded, sweat patches beginning to show under his arms, despite the air-conditioning. 'Right, Mr Delaney. Of course.' He changed his weight from leg to leg.

'Where is Charles at the moment?' asked Delaney.

Ray pulled out a palmtop computer and ran a sequence of numbers. 'London. Just arrived from Berlin.' Ray put the device away and nervously played with a ring on his left hand. 'He's the source of the information you've just received from us,' he added.

'Is he trustworthy?'

Ray nodded again, more enthusiastically. 'Oh yes. Loves his work. That is, he's very dependable. Tidies up nicely too.'

Delaney smirked. 'Perfect. Tell him to get to Oxford. There's a conference there I want him to attend tomorrow. One of the presenters is starting to become a bit of a pain. Tell Charles to get a feel for what this guy's movements are.' He scribbled on a piece of paper and handed it to Ray. 'Tell him to phone me on this number once he's had a chance to speak with Doctor Edgewater and be ready to accept orders directly from me.'

Ray almost ran across to the desk and took the note from Delaney. Retreating to the middle of the room, he opened his mouth to speak then thought otherwise.

'What is it Ray?'

The other man looked at the piece of paper, then at his boss. 'There's a ten-hour time difference between here and London at present, Mr Delaney.'

Delaney glared at the small man. 'Wake him up.'

Ray nodded and retreated as quickly as he could from the room. As the door closed, Delaney got up and turned, looking out the window. He closed his eyes, replaying the plan in his mind.

Nearly three years of extensive research in a remote area of central Queensland followed by six months perfecting the sequence. Only two months remained until everything fell into place. He opened his eyes and glared down at the protestors.

It couldn't come soon enough.

FOUR

'Someone is buying and, moreover, stockpiling the world's gold supply. In the current climate and demand for oil, gas and uranium, the sale and purchase of this valuable commodity is overlooked by analysts again and again. We must ask ourselves, why? Why is this not being highlighted, pursued, or investigated? Here, today, we seek to rectify this.'

Extract from lecture series by Doctor Peter Edgewater,
Oxford, England

Oxford, England

· · ·

Peter closed his eyes and tilted his head back, stretching his neck muscles, glad to be home. He felt he could smell the history of the building surrounding him while, in the next room, he could hear the audience finding their seats, the soft clink of wine glasses as they greeted colleagues, calling to each other, laughter.

'It never loses it, you know.' The voice broke his reverie.

'What?' He opened his eyes, and looked around for the source of the interruption.

'Sorry – didn't mean to startle you.' A man leaned against one of the pillars, smiling. 'I meant the atmosphere of the place – it's always here.' He walked towards Peter and held out his hand. 'Charles Moore.'

Peter shook it, then looked around him once more. 'You're right.'

'I take it you were a student here?' Charles enquired. He took his glasses off and began to polish them.

'Yes. Although it seems a lifetime ago these days – you?'

'Cambridge I'm afraid,' Charles smiled apologetically, put his glasses back on and wandered over to the archway which led to the lecture theatre and peered through.

'Are you planning on talking to this lot today?'

Peter nodded, joining him. 'Yes. I've just completed a small lecture tour around Europe and the college asked me if I'd like to take part in the inaugural New Year lecture series before the university term begins. It seemed a fitting way to finish my tour.'

Charles turned to him. 'Has the lecture tour been well received?'

'Not bad. I enjoy the conversations afterwards actually – travelling can be a bit monotonous. I got the opportunity to talk with quite a few people about my research. You know, compare facts and the like. Always good to know what other academics think – and some of the students. It helps to gauge what reaction the published article will have.'

Charles' face visibly hardened. 'Published article?'

Peter nodded enthusiastically, not noticing the man's changed demeanour. 'Yes – the feedback from the lecture tour has been so good, I'm discussing publication of the research and lecture notes with a few people, the press included.'

A figure appeared in the entrance to the lecture hall. 'Doctor Edgewater? You're up next.'

Peter nodded. 'I'll be right there.' He turned and offered his hand to Charles. 'Nice to meet you – I'd better go.'

Charles shook Peter's hand and stepped back. 'Good luck with the article Doctor Edgewater. I'm sure it'll be a fascinating read.'

Charles watched Peter enter the lecture hall, then turned and walked down the hallway to the exit. As he left the building and walked down Parks Road, he pulled a mobile phone from his jacket pocket and dialled a sequence of numbers.

Brisbane, Australia

The city lights cast an orange glow over the river, as ferries and high-powered catamarans carried the last of the late-night diners home. A faint breeze moved through the humid air while the occasional frustrated car horn or siren broke the enveloping silence across the business district.

On the eleventh floor of the skyscraper, Morris Delaney opened the door to his office and ushered in his guest.

Stephen Pallisder was a tall, broad man. A self-made millionaire, the chairman of a large national rail organisation, he had few friends, but had many politicians on his payroll and enormous influence nationally. He also had a reputation for a short temper and an unforgiving fury. Overweight, the product of too much fine wine and dining and very little exercise, he eased himself into one of four leather armchairs, sighed, loosened his tie and put his feet up on the low coffee table in front of him.

'Jesus, Morris, when did it become so fucking fashionable to be a tree-hugger?'

'Blame Al Gore – I do,' said Delaney, 'I even had one of Helen's nieces lecturing me at the weekend about clean coal technology being the equivalent of a low-tar cigarette.'

Pallisder laughed. 'I hope you wrote her out of your will first thing on Monday.'

Delaney grinned. 'Well, her university fund just mysteriously stopped being paid. Not that I ever understood what she hoped to achieve with a degree in bloody drawing. Surely it can't be that hard.'

Delaney pushed a brochure across the table to Pallisder.

'There you have it. With my new mine coming on line and your railway commissioned last month, the shareholders will be happy and we'll blow away the competition at the conference. I expect we'll have quite a few offers for new investment by next week.'

Pallisder nodded as he looked at the glossy presentation promoting the joint venture between the two men. 'Good work. I'll have my marketing team send you some up-to-date material for that promotional film too – we sent a film crew up there last week to do some aerial shots from a helicopter, you know, the sweeping camera angles over a fully loaded coal train – good for the Australian economy, the usual messages.'

Walking over to a mahogany cabinet, Delaney picked up two crystal tumblers and a decanter. 'Drink?'

'Make it a large one. Apparently the traffic's backed up all the way to the Bribie exit so there's no point leaving town for another hour. Lucy will kill me for being late again,' said Pallisder.

Delaney carried the drinks over and sat in the opposite armchair. He chuckled. 'I do believe you're officially under her thumb.' He handed a glass to the other man and raised his in a toast. 'To plans going well.'

Stephen raised his glass in salute and took a large sip. 'Is my investment safe?'

Delaney nodded. 'Just checking on that academic pain in the ass, Peter Edgewater, over in the UK – remember I said he was doing that lecture tour and starting to point the finger our way?'

Pallisder nodded and gestured for Delaney to continue.

'I've got someone having a word with him today. The previous warning we gave him didn't work so we're putting the pressure on.'

'Perhaps I could get your man to do some work for me.'

'How many coal trains were stopped this week?'

Pallisder glowered. 'Three. If I could tell the drivers to run the fuckers over, I would, but the press probably wouldn't report it sympathetically.'

Delaney laughed ruefully. 'True. I'll let you know when he's back here.'

Pallisder lowered his feet, leaned forward, and picked up the brochure from the table in front of him. 'Who's going to be at this conference?'

'The usual suspects. I've spoken to our marketing team at length and they're fully aware of what we expect from them. A good, concise counter-offensive against those idiots.' He nodded over his shoulder in the general direction of the protestors outside. 'We'll hit them hard with our protestors campaigning *against* emissions trading

– the usual message, it's a stealth tax, jobs will be lost, clean coal technology is a better alternative, blah, blah, blah.'

Pallisder leaned back and looked hard at Delaney. 'I had a phone call from another Federal minister yesterday. I've agreed to maintain my campaign contributions to him on the understanding he continues to lobby for the coal industry here in Australia.'

Delaney nodded. 'That's good. Most of them don't understand the science of it all anyway – as long as we keep lining their pockets, they'll do as they're told.'

Pallisder laughed. 'Yeah – heaven forbid they lose the vote and have to get a real job.'

Delaney looked up as the phone on his desk began to ring. Standing up, he glanced at Pallisder. 'Excuse me.'

Pallisder shrugged and gestured to Delaney to take the call. The men had few secrets between them – both had built up their empires over the years through hard graft, hard-fought deals and a close relationship between a mining empire which spanned Australia, the UK and Eastern Europe, and a railroad organisation which owned and leased half the routes in Australia, with financial interests in Europe and South Africa.

Delaney walked over to the desk and picked up the phone. He put his hand over the receiver, and said to Pallisder. 'It's Charles.'

Pallisder nodded, got up and wandered over to the decanter to top up his glass.

Delaney turned back to the phone. 'I trust it went

well?' He fell silent and listened to Charles's report, then hissed as he leaned against the desk. 'I want it sorted now. Call me when it's done, not before. I have to present at the conference next week and I want this sorted out by the time I leave.'

As he slammed the phone down, Delaney looked around the office at the framed photographs with himself, prime ministers, international dignitaries, soccer players and rock stars. No way was he letting anyone take this away from him. Not now.

'Problem?' asked Pallisder, as he eased himself back into his armchair.

Delaney sat on the edge of his desk. 'No, not really. Just protecting your investment.'

Pallisder chuckled. 'Good man.'

FIVE

Oxford, England

Aaron Hughes was already in trouble. An hour late, with his mobile phone battery dead, he cycled back home as fast as he could. His mum would kill him. An hour ago, she'd have received the message from the school to say he'd dodged the extra classes she insisted on sending him to during the holidays while she worked. Now the weak winter sun was already beginning to set.

He couldn't help it – the new computer game had been released on Monday and Jack Mills had managed to persuade his parents to buy him a copy straight away as an early birthday present. Within four hours, the two boys had reached level six before Aaron had realised what the time was and left his friend's house.

He turned onto Saint Cross Road, cycled past the college buildings and debated the shortcut through the fields and over the River Cherwell. Already in trouble, it wouldn't matter if his clothes got dirty and mud spattered, but the river bank with its tree-covered weed-strewn tributaries was a bit creepy at the best of times, he'd be the first to admit.

Yet, it was a shortcut to Old Marston and at the moment, he needed all the help he could get. He turned right on to the dirt track behind the college playing fields and changed down a gear.

Aaron slowed his bike and looked over his shoulder. From past experience, he knew he'd be through the fields and back in suburbia within fifteen minutes – if he could only stop his imagination from working overtime.

Aaron sighed. He had to do it. He began pedalling again and made his way along the pathway. Panting slightly, although not sure whether it was through fear or exertion, he cycled across the first narrow bridge over the river, conscious of the traffic noise from the city fading into the distance behind him.

Halfway over the bridge, he stopped and looked down the narrow stream of water which led through the fields to the main river. It turned left before disappearing round a bend, while in front of him the track narrowed to little more than a horse trail. Aaron took one more look at the river and then pedalled as fast as he dared along the loose surface of the track, careful not to skid.

As he drew closer to the next bridge, the track narrowed and he could smell the early evening scent of damp undergrowth, pine sap and horse droppings while snowdrops tentatively poked through the grass verges on each side.

Aaron jumped as a pheasant flew out in front of him, squawking and flapping its wings. He laughed to himself nervously then jumped again as something else screeched nearby.

The narrow path ran between two tributaries of the river before it swept across them and out through the fields to Old Marston. Aaron slowed as he recalled the horror stories of people falling in the water and not being able to survive the icy temperatures at this time of year. He steered the bike to the middle of the pathway, away from the edges of the water, determined not to slip and fall in.

As he neared the bend in the track to take him home, he saw a shape at the water's edge, draped between the shallow grass verge near the water and the gravel track. He slowed, heart racing. It looked like an old bundle of clothes dumped on the side of the path.

Aaron looked around him and suddenly wished he hadn't come this way. He couldn't bring himself to turn back though – it was too far now – so instead, he got off the bike and began to wheel it towards the bundle of clothing. As he drew closer, he could make out the shape of a person. 'Hello?'

He stopped. He'd heard enough stories about 'stranger

danger' when he was younger and despite what his parents thought, he'd listened to their warnings about wandering off with people he didn't know. But this was different. It felt wrong.

'Are you alright?' he called.

Perhaps it was a drunk. It was no good, he thought, he'd have to get closer. He breathed out, and pushed the bike nearer and made sure he kept it between him and the figure as if to add some extra protection. As he drew closer, he could see it was a man, dressed in a suit, his face turned away from Aaron.

He stepped around the figure and screamed. The bike dropped to the ground as the boy turned and ran to the other side of the gravel track and vomited into the long grass.

It seemed like an age before he could muster the courage to run back, grab his bike and cycle as fast as he could down the remainder of the track and home, where his mother tried to calm her hysterical son before calling the police.

It would be even longer before the memory of the dead man's face would begin to fade from his nightmares.

The alarm screeched loudly, twice, before a hand shot out from under a blanket and punched it into submission.

Dan sat up and swung his legs over the side of the bed.

Christ, it was freezing. He stood up, pulled on a thick dressing gown and padded over to the bedroom door. Running his hand through his hair, he wandered downstairs and stared blearily at the timer on the central heating system. He hit it hard with the palm of his hand and instantly heard the soft roar of the heating system starting up.

Yawning, he switched on the kettle and began to make coffee. He turned, and picked up the mobile phone from the kitchen bench. No messages. He frowned – he'd tried to phone Peter back after returning from the pub three nights ago but the voicemail service kept kicking in. He was wondering who he could contact at the university to track down Peter when a footfall at the front of the house caught his attention.

He glanced up as he heard the letterbox squeak on its hinges. He padded out through the hallway, picked up the copy of the *Oxford Times* lying on the mat, then wandered back to the relative warmth of the kitchen. While he waited for the water to boil, he sat at the breakfast bar and flicked through the newspaper until his eyes rested on a report on page five.

He felt his jaw go slack with shock. The headline read: 'Prominent Lecturer Killed in Vicious Attack'.

'Police have confirmed the body found near the River Cherwell in Old Marston twenty-four hours ago was that

of Doctor Peter Edgewater, lecturer in geology at the Department of Earth Sciences, Oxford University. Police are describing the attack as vicious in nature. Doctor Edgewater's colleagues raised the alarm when he failed to turn up for the first faculty meeting of the new academic term yesterday morning.

Doctor Edgewater, best known for his activism for more research into alternative energy, was apparently walking behind the College grounds when he was assaulted. Doctor Edgewater had just completed a successful lecture tour in Europe championing his paper on the theory of a white powder gold extract being used as an alternative to coal for the electricity industry. Doctor Edgewater used his lectures to regularly criticise gas and coal companies for allegedly delaying vital research into alternative energies. At the present time, the murder weapon has not been found and police are appealing for witnesses.'

What a way to start the New Year, thought Dan. He read through the report again, his heart beating hard as he searched for answers which wouldn't come. He pushed the article to one side and slid his mobile phone towards him. Dialling up his voicemail, he listened to Peter's message once more.

It had been strange to hear Peter's voice after so many years. On the same rowing team at university, they'd drifted apart after Dan had chosen to join the army. Dan scratched at the stubble forming on his chin and stared into space. He remembered Peter as a big man who knew how to fight if he had to. It just didn't seem right he'd be so easy to attack.

Dan couldn't remember ever hearing Peter sound so scared before though and as he listened to the message again, he wondered what Peter had uncovered through his latest research to warrant such a reaction.

He stood up, made the coffee, then sipped it slowly, pacing the kitchen. He couldn't ignore his friend's last request. He'd have to check that Peter's ex-wife, Sarah, was okay – if he could find her. He'd heard from a mutual acquaintance that Peter and Sarah had split up a while ago. His put his coffee mug down and slid a notebook and pen towards him. He picked up his mobile again. He vaguely remembered Peter saying his ex-wife was now a reporter for one of the national newspapers. He yawned as he scrolled through the phone numbers listed in the online telephone directory. Perhaps her editor would be able to tell him where to find her.

Dialling the newspaper's office, he was put through to the editor, Gus Saunders who, after giving Dan a grilling the local constabulary would be proud of, reluctantly passed on Sarah's current address and telephone number.

Dan dialled and flicked through the newspaper while he waited for an answer. There was none. He hung up and looked around the kitchen. He sighed. Maybe he should pay a visit to the ex-Mrs Edgewater. At least it would give him something to do, rather than stare at the walls waiting for the next mining job to find him.

Half an hour later, Dan was making his way down the main road towards Sutton Courtenay. After he turned off at the junction, he drove along the ring road until he reached a roundabout and turned left. According to her editor, Sarah's house was located in a small lane about a mile into the village.

He spotted number thirty-seven straight away, a pretty three-bedroom cottage set back from the road. On the end of a row, it had a small neat garden sheltering behind a low white fence, a public footpath to the right of the property leading back to the main road.

He steered the car into a parking bay outside, switched off the engine and got out of the car. He had no idea what he was going to say but Peter had asked him to do this and, in the circumstances, it was the least he could do.

'Here goes,' mumbled Dan to himself as he walked up the path and rang the doorbell.

As he waited for the door to be opened, Dan self-consciously tried to smooth down his wild hair and tugged at his jacket. He glanced down at his boots. He noticed how scuffed they were. Then tried to remember when he'd last polished them. It seemed a lifetime ago when polishing boots had been second nature. He sniffed, forced the memory from his thoughts and glanced up at the front door. The cold air clung to his ears and fingers, a biting bitter breeze whipping at his hair. He willed the door to open – soon, before he froze.

A light was switched on – the pale glow shining through the four panes of glass embedded in the top of the wooden door. Dan's face glowed in the reflection. The grey afternoon daylight was quickly fading; another snow storm threatened. Dan stepped back from the shelter of the front porch and glanced upwards, willing the storm clouds away. He didn't want to get stuck here. Just do the dutiful thing, find out what Peter had been up to, then get out fast.

The silhouette of a figure bobbed in front of the door. Hesitated.

'Who is it?' A muffled question, loaded with intent. Give the wrong answer, the door would never open.

Dan thought about first impressions. And automatically reached up to smooth his hair down again. He took a deep breath. 'My name's Dan. I'm a friend of Pete's.' He paused. 'A real friend.' He peered through the fuzz of the pock-marked glass.

A tall, slender woman, with pale brown hair peered back through. Hesitated.

Then Dan heard the sound of a security chain as it rattled against the wooden surface. The woman hesitated again, then the bolt slid back and the door opened.

Dan looked. The woman was pale, wrapped in a sweater three times too big for her body, thrown over skinny jeans. She wore thick socks. Dan blinked as the warmth from the house enveloped him.

'What do you want?' whispered the woman.

'I want to help,' he said.

The woman nodded. 'He wrote and said you might come.' She held out her hand. 'I'm Sarah,' she said.

Dan took it with a small smile. 'I hoped you would be,' he said. 'Can I come in? It's bloody freezing out here.'

SIX

Dan sat on the sofa opposite Sarah. As he set his coffee mug down on the table between them, he noticed a thin layer of dust had gathered through mournful neglect. A log fire burned in a fireplace, throwing out warmth around the small living area and casting shadows on the walls.

He looked up, caught Sarah watching him and smiled nervously. She looked worn down, her light brown hair tied back in a ponytail and her face devoid of any make-up. Tall and naturally slim, she appeared to have lost a lot of weight in a short space of time.

Leaning forward on his elbows, Dan took a breath and began.

'Sarah, I know we've never met before, and you have no reason to trust me, but I was a friend of Peter's. I don't know what you've discussed with the police but I don't believe the story they're giving the newspapers. There's just too much that doesn't make sense to me and I've got to find out for myself what really happened.'

He stopped and looked up. Sarah continued to watch him silently for what seemed an age. When she spoke, her words were quiet and Dan had to lean forward to hear.

'I'm so glad someone else thinks the same as me – they think I'm being paranoid but I just know something isn't right...,' she drifted off and gazed out the patio windows before turning to him again.

'Peter knew that short-cut behind the college inside out – he used to walk there after lectures to unwind – there's no way... ' she said fiercely. 'They say it was a mugger – an unprovoked attack.'

Dan picked up his coffee mug and studied the surface of the liquid. 'Sarah, I know this may sound a bit weird in the circumstances but was Peter working longer hours or perhaps on days when he was usually at home?' he asked, taking a tentative sip of the hot drink.

'Not that I know of – we only talked occasionally. He used to get so wrapped up in his research and lectures, it was just impossible sometimes.' She folded her hands under her chin, leaning her elbows on her knees, lost in thought. After a while, she looked straight at Dan. 'Why should I trust you?'

'Because I'm a friend of Peter's – we went to university together but lost touch for a few years until he phoned me from Berlin last week. He sounded really excited, something about a discovery. Then, a few days ago, he phoned again – from Paris. I wasn't in, so he left a message on my phone. He seemed in a hurry, the message was really garbled – something about a package he was sending you and wanted to make sure it arrived safely. He sounded afraid – he even said that he thought his life was in danger.'

Dan jumped as a log on the fire popped loudly in the heat. He swallowed and waited for his heart rate to calm down. He glanced into the flames, then back at Sarah. 'He wanted me to make sure you were okay. I tried to phone him back the day after he left the message but I couldn't get through. I left messages for him but he never returned my calls. Then I read in the local newspaper this morning he's been killed. I'd like to know why. I don't know what he was up to but I think it got him in to a hell of a lot of trouble.'

He broke off and looked down at his hands.

'And now you're here,' said Sarah.

'Yes.'

She reached out for her coffee mug, raised it to her lips, then seemed to change her mind. She placed it back on the low table and looked at him.

'Stay here.'

Dan watched her leave the room. He could hear her walking down the hallway towards the rear of the house. He stood up and wandered over to a desk in the corner. The computer screen was blank, the machine switched off. He glanced up to check Sarah was still out of the room and then lifted up some of the documents on her desk. All the paperwork related to her work at the newspaper – nothing that appeared to have been sent by Peter. Moving over to the patio windows, Dan gazed out at the small garden. He wondered what Peter could have known that would threaten his life. He turned as Sarah came back into the room.

'I think you should have this,' she said as she handed him a large padded envelope.

'What's inside?'

'Take a look. It's addressed to you.' She sat back down on the sofa and took a gulp of her coffee before staring at Dan. 'Well, what are you waiting for? Open it.'

Dan sat on the sofa and inspected the package. It was a white A4-sized padded envelope with Sarah's address scrawled across the front in a hasty script. He turned the package over in his hands and raised an eyebrow, looking at Sarah.

'It's already been opened,' he said, pointing to the tape stuck to the back of the envelope.

Sarah smiled faintly. 'I'm a journalist – what did you expect? How was I to know you'd actually turn up?'

Dan shrugged, conceding the point. He tore open the package, noticing the airmail label and foreign stamps. He reached inside and pulled out the contents – a bundle of documents, and Peter's handwritten notes. He flicked through the loose research papers, turning photographs over, reading the transcriptions on the back and inspected the newspaper cuttings and hastily-drawn diagrams.

'How come you haven't done anything with this stuff?'

Sarah shrugged. 'To be honest, I didn't know what to

make of half of it.' She gestured to the laptop set up in the corner. 'I'd made a start, but there was part of me that wanted to know if you'd actually turn up.' She sighed. 'I know me and Peter didn't always see eye to eye, but I remembered him saying a couple of years ago he wondered if he could count on you in an emergency. After you came back from the Middle East, he was really worried about you but you never returned his calls.' She smiled. 'I figured I'd give you a couple of days and if you didn't turn up, I'd take some time off work and find out for myself what was going on.'

Dan turned the document he was holding towards Sarah. 'Well, if I'm going to be able to find out what's going on, I'm going to need someone who can help me translate this god-awful handwriting of his.'

Sarah smiled. 'It didn't improve with age then?'

'You've got to be joking. This just reminds me why I could never rely on stealing Peter's notes for assignments at university.'

He looked across the coffee table at Sarah. 'What are you thinking?'

She held his gaze, and smiled. 'That we should find out what's going on. I'll phone Gus, my editor, and get that time off. Then tomorrow, I'll go over to Peter's house and see what else I can find there.'

Oxford, England

. . .

Sarah vigorously attacked the layer of ice on her car windscreen with her credit card. Every winter she swore she'd buy a proper ice scraper, and every winter she managed to forget.

She cursed as her thumbnail tore, then wiped the plastic card free of ice and began on the side windows. She stamped her feet while she worked, trying to get some warmth into her toes as she methodically worked round the car.

Finally, it was done and she jumped into the driver's seat. As she pulled the door shut, she turned up the heating, relishing the warm, cocooned space. She turned up the radio while she waited for the circulation to return to her numb fingers.

The radio news spat out the usual coverage – petrol prices up, energy companies struggling with the winter demand on gas, and electricity supplies threatened. Sarah shook her head as she listened – the politicians never seemed to get themselves sorted out.

She pulled out of her driveway and was on the main road into Oxford within fifteen minutes, heading towards her destination. She hummed along to the radio as she drove and drummed her fingers on the steering wheel, impatient to reach the house. After a while, she pulled off the main road and began to weave through the suburban streets until she found the road she was looking for.

Sarah pulled the car up to the kerb on a tree-lined

avenue. An affluent area, large houses hid behind well-pruned privet hedgerows or fenced-off gardens. Turning off the engine, she looked at the house a few metres down the road to her right and sighed. They'd been so happy here, once. It felt like a lifetime ago.

The early morning sunlight glinted through the mature trees, early signs of new shoots beginning to show already. In a couple of months or so, the wide street would be framed with pale pink and white flowers, alternating down the avenue. The road was quiet, the commuter rush and school run over with an hour ago. The occasional car passed her where she'd parked, and rocked her vehicle gently as she sat and gathered her thoughts.

A man walked towards her car, away from the houses in front of her, and polished his glasses before replacing them on his nose. Sarah glanced in her rear view mirror as he went by. He appeared to slow as he passed her car, then changed his mind and continued along the road before he disappeared down a side street.

She reached down for the package which lay on the passenger seat. She'd have recognised Peter's handwriting anywhere – four years of marriage and six years of typing up his hastily scribbled lecture notes put paid to any doubt as to who had scrawled her address across the padded envelope. Fondly, she ran her hand over the writing and then pulled out the contents. She'd organised them a bit better after Dan had left – a full set of Peter's most recent lecture notes, clipped together with newspaper cuttings, photographs and a list of bibliographical references in date order.

'Who were you after, Pete?' Sarah whispered softly to herself.

Unfastening her seatbelt, she reached for the door handle and pushed the car door open. Stepping out onto the road, she leaned into the car to get her bag.

The explosion caused her to instinctively duck behind the car door, using it as a shield. A gust of warm, debris-filled air fled past her as she tucked her feet back up into the car, trying to get out of the way. Closing her eyes tightly, she gasped as the air from her lungs was forced out.

Sarah felt the whole vehicle shift backwards with the blast, dragging her with it, the tyres squealing in protest as the force of the explosion fought the parking brake, while Sarah fought to keep her balance.

As the roar of the explosion died away, Sarah climbed out of the car and lifted her head above the car door, surveying the scene in disbelief. Paper and other debris, still burning, fluttered through the air. A car alarm shrieked further along the street. Sarah pushed her hair out of her eyes, blinking. Her ears were ringing, a high-pitched whistle that reverberated in her skull.

The right-hand side of the house had disappeared. Glass from the windows had peppered the street, shrapnel sticking out of the telephone pole that now arched precariously into the road. The force of the blast had destroyed the front wall, flattening it onto the pavement.

Behind it a scorched lawn smouldered, debris strewn over the garden. Flames and black smoke billowed from the front of the house where the study had once been, while hot ash fell through the air. A siren sounded in the distance. Sarah started at the sound of it, and glanced around her.

Then she saw him.

The man with the glasses stood watching her from the side street. Suddenly, he began to walk towards her, never taking his eyes off her. Sarah's heart began to race. Instinct took over. She climbed into her car and turned the key in the ignition. The car turned over once, and then stalled. Sarah glanced in the rear view mirror – the man was beginning to run towards her car. Heart pounding, Sarah turned the key again.

'*Come on*!' she urged the car, hands shaking.

With a choke, the car started, blue smoke belching from the exhaust. Sarah turned the vehicle around in the street, glass and debris tumbling from its roof and bonnet as she fought to keep the vehicle under control. She swerved to avoid the man who had now stepped out onto the road. Sarah screamed, pushing her foot down hard on the accelerator as he tried to grab hold of the car as it drove by. The sound of his fingers scratching against the paintwork, scrabbling for a hand-hold made Sarah's skin crawl before she shot past him.

At the end of the avenue, she turned left, forcing herself to slow down so any police cars didn't stop her. Somehow, she didn't think they'd be able to protect her from the stranger in the street. Catching a flash in the mirror, she looked up to see a fire engine and police car entering the road – both too late to save the house, while the stranger stood on the pavement and watched her, polishing his glasses, before he turned and ran back to a parked car.

Slamming her foot on the accelerator, she drove a weaving course through the suburb and, when she could no longer hear the sirens, she pulled over and took out her phone.

SEVEN

Bright shafts of sunlight broke through the window blinds as a crow cawed noisily from the tree outside. A van drove past, the tyres splashing through puddles of water from the melting ice. A car engine was being choked to death in the background, the sound of kids playing in a school yard carrying a mile down the road. The phone rang, loudly, coarsely.

Dan moved slightly and groaned, buried under a blanket thrown messily across the bed. The pub was always a bad idea. It was just so hard to leave.

'Whoever it is, go away.'

The phone ignored him, persistent in its attempt to gain his attention.

'For fuck's sake!' He threw back the covers and swung his legs onto the floor. He stood up, slowly, carefully, staggered over to the desk in the corner and reached over for the telephone. 'What?'

'Dan, it's Sarah – I need your help.' She sounded like she was out of breath, traffic going past in the background. Dan grabbed hold of the receiver tight, sobering up in an instant.

'Slow down. Where are you? What happened? Are you alright?'

'The man who killed Peter – Dan, I know it was him! The house exploded – there's nothing left!' Sarah broke off, choking back a sob. 'He saw me – he tried to stop me!' she broke off. 'I think he's looking for me.'

Dan thought quickly. 'Sarah, listen to me. Listen to me! Twenty-seven Coltsfoot Street – got that? Right – I'm here. You can park on the driveway – it's sheltered from the street and the car won't be seen.'

'I can't!'

'You can Sarah. You have to. You've got to get out of there. He's got a car too and he's going to be looking for you. He must've realised you have a connection with that house.'

'I know, I know. Okay Dan. I'll leave now. Please don't go anywhere – wait for me!'

'I will. Now, get going.' Dan replaced the receiver.

After a thirty-second shower, he dressed in faded jeans, black t-shirt, black sweater and his favourite boots. He walked down the hallway and into the spare bedroom. Opening a walk-in wardrobe, he groped around on the top shelf until his fingers found what they were looking for. Pulling the box closer, he reached up and pulled it towards him, lowering it to the ground. Lifting the lid, he pulled out his passport and looked at the fading immigration stamps on the yellowed pages. He put it back, lifted up a bundle of papers and checked – the gun was still there, unloaded, oiled and ready, the bullets wrapped in cotton wool at the bottom of the box.

The sound of a car pulling into the gravel driveway interrupted his thoughts. He put the gun back in the box, closed the wardrobe door, then hurried downstairs to open the front door.

Sarah stopped the engine and got out. She closed her car door, ran across the driveway and into the house in one fluid movement. She was shaking. Dan wasn't sure whether she was frightened or angry.

'He nearly got me, Dan! Oh my god, the bastard nearly got me too!'

He squeezed her arm. 'It's okay, you're alive, you're safe here,' he said.

He looked over her head at the car. The bonnet and front panels were peppered with shrapnel from the blast – pieces of red brick, glass, wooden splinters from a telegraph pole. The driver's side window was completely shattered, shards of glass hanging loosely in the frame. A headlamp hung from its fitting, the clear plastic casing torn from its setting from the force of the explosion.

He let go of Sarah and stood back from her, looking. 'Are you hurt anywhere? Any blood?'

Sarah looked down at herself. 'No – no, I think I'm alright. A few scratches on my leg.'

Dan moved closer. Taking her face in his hands, he

looked down at her. 'It's alright. Come on, let's get some antiseptic and clean you up,' he added, leading her into the house and closing the door.

Sarah followed him through to the kitchen. Dan gestured to the breakfast bar. 'Grab one of those chairs and sit down. I'll make something strong for you to drink.' He slid a box of tissues across to her. 'And you look like you could use those.'

Sarah managed a small smile. 'I can only imagine what I look like,' she mumbled, blowing her nose.

'Not too bad for someone who just avoided getting herself blown up.' Dan grinned. 'Have something strong to drink, and then you can freshen up.'

Sarah nodded. 'That sounds good.'

Dan stood up. 'Hang on – I'll stick the news on, find out what they're reporting.' He flicked on an old battered radio perched on a shelf and turned up the volume. The station was playing a series of commercials. He wandered over to the sink and began to fill the kettle with water. Switching it on, he turned back to Sarah. 'The news should come on after those commercials. I'm going to get that antiseptic. Yell if they report anything.'

Sarah nodded and watched him as he left the room. He walked through the hallway and ran up the stairs to the bathroom. As he pulled out cotton wool and antiseptic lotion from his first aid kit, his mind wandered. First, Peter is mugged – almost certainly murdered. Then, his study is blown up, nearly taking down the whole house and destroying any documents that might have been lying around.

He tugged at the cotton wool, pulling it apart. 'What the hell did you find out Peter?' he muttered, 'and what am I getting myself into?'

A shout from downstairs made him jump.

'Dan, the news – it's on!'

Dan picked up the antiseptic and ran back down to the kitchen. The sonorous tones of a radio announcer, placid in the line of duty, finished reading from a mediocre script. '...and now we cross to our reporter, Jan Newbury, who's at the scene.'

'Thank you John. The street here is a scene of complete devastation. Fire crews arrived at the house soon after the blast and had the blaze under control very quickly. Police have joined them here and a forensic team is currently searching the premises for the cause of the fire. They have confirmed no-one was in the property when the explosion occurred and no injuries are reported.'

The radio announcer interrupted. 'Jan, are the police giving any indication as to what may have caused the explosion?'

'John, at the moment the police say it's very early on in their investigation but so far, the evidence leads to a gas leak.'

'Bullshit!' exclaimed Dan. 'That wasn't a gas explosion!' He turned down the radio and handed the cotton wool and lotion to Sarah.

'What makes you say that?' she asked.

'It was too controlled.'

She held his gaze steadily. 'Go on.'

'If it was a gas explosion, the whole front of the house would have blown outwards. From how you described the scene, if it was caused by gas, the upstairs would have collapsed – there would have been more debris, more damage. What you saw points to a controlled explosion, although I'd put money on our bomb-maker turning the gas on to give the impression that's the cause.'

He sat down opposite Sarah and watched as she dabbed at the scratches on her legs, wincing as the antiseptic touched the raw skin.

Sarah glanced at him. 'When you went away, Peter would read the newspapers every day to make sure your name never appeared. He was worried sick about you when you signed up and then joined the bomb disposal team.' She sighed, put the cap back on the antiseptic and stood up carefully. Gathering up the cotton wool, she wandered over to the kitchen waste bin.

'Do you think the police actually believe it's a gas explosion?' she asked, as she sat back down.

Dan stood up and began to make the coffee. 'I'm sure that's what they're going to tell everyone it was, even if they think otherwise. After all, they don't want the residents of Oxford starting to panic thinking there's a madman going around planting bombs.'

He reached up into a cupboard and brought out a bottle. 'Right,' he said, and turned to Sarah, waving the bottle at her, 'I know it's early but I think this is justified in the circumstances.'

Sarah smiled. 'You won't hear any complaints from me.'

Dan splashed a generous measure of the brandy into each coffee and wandered back to the table.

'Here you go. Now, if you start feeling cold or begin to shake, you tell me straight away. You seem like you're doing okay to me but I've seen delayed shock before – it's not pretty.'

Sarah took a sip of her coffee and then choked as the brandy hit the back of her throat. 'I don't think there's any chance of that – my god, how much did you put in this?' she spluttered.

Dan grinned. 'Just enough.'

EIGHT

London, England

The Minister paced his room, nervous. The phone call was late. The Minister always insisted on promptness. He straightened his tie, looked at his worn fingernails. The sooner the next two months were over, the better. His doctor had already warned him about his high blood pressure and his wife had commented on how much shorter his temper was these days. Dark shadows were forming under his eyes and he was noticeably thinner.

The phone rang and the Minister jumped involuntarily. Part of him still believed they'd be found out before the project was finished. He picked up the phone.

'Yes?' He sounded more confident than he felt. His press officer's careful training kept his voice steady, even if he did notice a slight shaking in his hand as he pressed the receiver closer to his ear.

'It's all going according to schedule.'

The caller didn't identify himself – there was no need.

'Where is it at the moment?'

A chuckle at the other end of the line. 'Never mind. The less you know, the more protected I feel.'

The Minister was relieved. He didn't really want to know. The project scared the shit out of him. 'W-what do you need me to do?'

A pause, then –

'Nervous Minister?'

Fuck you, thought the Minister. 'No, just concerned. I want to make sure this will all go to plan,' he lied.

The caller chuckled. 'I'm sure you are. Don't be concerned – it's coming together nicely. Not only will this thing blow the European Union emissions trading legislation clean out of the water, it'll probably take the Australian and the United States' emissions trading schemes with it too. How's it going with the alternative energy lobby?'

The Minister sighed. 'They're a stubborn bunch of bastards.'

The caller laughed. 'Watch them change their minds when your coal-fired power stations close down under European Union climate change legislation and you haven't got enough gas to last the United Kingdom over winter. Ask them where their wind farms are then.'

The Minister grunted. 'We'll be back in the middle

ages before you know it. Do you know we have enough coal in this country to last three hundred years but the European Union won't let us burn it, so it just sits there while we buy gas from the Russians?'

Another laugh, twelve thousand miles away. 'That's why I'm going to sell my coal to your government when you're all freezing your nuts off and come begging.'

The Minister chuckled. 'Yes, well thanks to your kind donations, I'll be sure to winter in the Caribbean when that time comes.'

He looked at his watch. Time to end the call. 'Keep me posted on developments. I don't want any surprises.'

'Neither do I Minister, so you make sure you keep your eyes and ears open.'

The Minister put down the phone as a knock at his office door pre-empted his personal attaché entering the room. 'Thirty minutes until your meeting with the Prime Minister, sir. I've ordered the car – traffic's horrendous this morning.'

The Minister nodded, took his thick winter coat from the attaché and threw it around his shoulders.

Stepping out of the ugly building into a rain-ravaged morning, he walked quickly to a waiting car where the driver was holding the back door open ready for him. He climbed inside and spent the journey daydreaming about a holiday home in the Caribbean.

Brisbane, Australia

Uli Petrov tapped on the privacy glass between him and his driver with a fat forefinger.

The glass lowered slowly. 'Sir?'

'Stop here, by the traffic lights,' Uli instructed and leaned back in his seat.

'Yes sir.' The glass raised once more.

Uli loosened his tie. The car was air-conditioned but his Siberian bulk wasn't designed for the short walk from the vehicle to the building, his ultimate destination.

The car swung into a drop-off zone below a towering skyscraper. Uli waited while his driver got out, walked around the vehicle and opened the rear door. Uli forced his huge bulk off the rear seat and stood up. He almost gasped from the humid air. He swore he could feel it sucking the oxygen out of his lungs.

'Wait here,' he said to the driver and limped towards the revolving doors at the base of the office block.

Uli glared at the people milling around the reception area and stalked towards the elevators. He stepped into the next available elevator car and held his hand up to a hopeful young secretary who tried to enter the elevator at the same time.

'Room for one only,' he intoned. 'The sign says this has a maximum weight capacity.' He chuckled to himself as the elevator doors closed and began to rise through the bowels of the building. *No such thing as a skinny rich Russian.*

The elevator stopped and Uli stepped out into a sumptuous reception area. A woman behind a granite-effect desk looked up, smiled at him as he approached, then stood up.

'Mr Petrov?'

He nodded.

'We've been expecting you,' she said. 'I trust you had a good flight yesterday?'

'Yes,' said Uli, not wanting to waste time talking to his business partner's minions.

The receptionist interpreted his curtness correctly and beckoned him to take a seat. 'One moment please, Mr Petrov,' she said, 'Mr Delaney is waiting for you.'

She dialled a number and announced his arrival, then turned back to her work.

Uli looked up as a door opened down the corridor next to him and Delaney appeared. Petrov stood up and walked over to him, his hand outstretched. Delaney laughed loudly as he walked down the corridor towards the reception area, shook Uli's hand and held the door open to the boardroom for the other man.

'Uli, it's good to see you.' Slapping the man on the shoulder as he walked past, Delaney followed him into the room and closed the door behind him. 'Have a seat.'

Uli ran his hand through his hair, looking around. 'Is this room clean?'

Delaney nodded. 'I had my security experts sweep it

half an hour before you arrived – they check it every morning but we delayed it today so we could seal the room off once they'd finished until you got here.'

Uli nodded, visibly relaxing. 'I got your message. Exactly how is this idea of yours going to help us?'

Delaney walked round the board table, stopping to look down through the floor-to-ceiling windows at the river traffic passing below. 'I'll keep it simple – and only because I don't have time to run through the science of the stuff today, okay?'

The other man nodded. Delaney outlined his plan while the Russian stared at him, open mouthed.

Delaney finished, pulled out a chair and sat down. 'That should protect your gas interests and my coal business for the next thirty years at least.'

Uli held up his hand. 'Okay. You've convinced me. Now – what do you need?'

Delaney grinned. 'I was hoping you'd ask. I need one of your Russian ice-breakers. The fastest ship you can get.'

Uli raised an eyebrow. 'An ice-breaker?'

Delaney nodded. It needs to be in the East Siberian Sea by the beginning of February. Without fail. Think you can do it?'

Uli scratched his chin. 'Let me make some phone calls. I'm sure I can come up with something.'

Delaney grinned maliciously. 'You'd better. All or nothing, remember? I expect all the stakeholders in this joint venture to deliver on time. That's what you agreed to.'

Uli smiled and held up his hands. 'Morris, I'm sure you're a Russian at heart,' he chuckled. 'There's no need for threats. You can count on me.' He stretched back in his seat.

Delaney stood up, striding across to a small cabinet on the far side of his office. 'Drink?'

Uli nodded. 'Of course, if you are.'

Delaney poured two glasses of brandy and handed one to Uli.

Uli sat down on the leather sofa. 'So what are your plans?'

Delaney grinned. 'Well I never divulge all my aces, as you know.'

The other man inclined his head slightly, in agreement. 'And what are you going to do to make sure this can't be pinned on us?'

'Hit a big enough target so everyone will automatically assume it's another extremist terrorism group. They'll never pin it on us – they'd never believe this industry would do anything so extreme to protect its assets.'

Uli blew the air out of his cheeks. 'You're a genius. Who else is on board with this?'

Delaney grinned. 'You know I give every stakeholder the same protection as you. No-one, apart from me, knows who else is an investor in this project. Let's just say one or two like-minded individuals who are concerned about their businesses.'

Uli nodded. 'Fair enough. Can you tell me what the target is going to be?'

'Not yet.'

Uli stood up, drained his drink and stretched. 'Alright. How many casualties?'

Delaney shrugged. 'A few. Think of it as collateral damage, as the military like to say.'

Uli laughed out loud. 'Perfect.' He turned towards the door. 'What happened about that English academic causing all the trouble in Europe?'

Delaney laughed. 'Oh, it's all gone quiet on that front. I don't think he'll be causing us any problems in future.'

NINE

Sutton Courtenay, Oxfordshire

Dan steered the car down the narrow lane. As they neared Sarah's cottage, he pulled out to drive around a parked car and jumped when she gasped and clutched his arm.

'Dan, stop!'

'What is it?' he asked, slowing.

'It's him! Oh my god – he's at my house!' Sarah pointed. A man stood outside the cottage, staring up at the building.

Dan turned the car in the opposite direction, executed a smooth turn and began to drive back down the lane.

'Are you sure it's him?'

'Yes! Yes – I'd recognise him anywhere!' Sarah turned and looked over her shoulder as they drove away.

'No, don't! Look the other way – I don't want him to

spot you.' Dan risked a glance at the house. Sure enough, the man now stood in the parking bay outside the property, polishing his glasses as he watched the car pull away.

'Shit!'

He floored the accelerator. Sarah held onto her seat to steady herself as Dan shot out of the lane onto the road which led through the village and gunned the car forward. He looked in the rear view mirror.

'I don't think he'll find us – with any luck, he didn't have time to get back to his car.' He turned left onto a lane which wound its way out of the village and towards a main road. 'We'll put a bit of distance between us and the house before we stop.'

Sarah chewed on her nails.

'Do I phone the insurance company now and tell them I'll be making a claim after my house blows up from a gas explosion?'

Dan leaned over and squeezed her arm.

'Try not to think about it. Let's just concentrate on getting away from here for the moment.'

Sarah nodded. 'God knows when I'll be going home now. How did he find me Dan?'

He shrugged. 'People like him will have access to all sorts of information. We were right to hide your car from view. He's obviously got your address from the licensing records – he tracked Peter down, remember? I'll bet he's working for someone too.'

'What do you mean?'

'It's just too clinical, the way everything's happening.

First, Peter is killed – probably because of the content of his lectures – then his house is destroyed to make sure any research he may have had there couldn't fall into anyone's hands.' He punched the steering wheel in frustration. 'And now this.'

He slowed as they approached a junction and took a right turn back in the direction of Oxford.

'Dan? Why don't you contact that old university lecturer of yours and Peter's, see what he can work out?' asked Sarah.

'Who? Harry? Bloody hell, Sarah. I don't know.'

'Well, Peter always spoke highly of him. I met him once – he seemed very knowledgeable.'

Dan exhaled loudly. 'Do you want to get him involved?'

Sarah drummed her fingers on the door frame. 'I'm just thinking he might point us in the right direction – we can take it from there. I mean, what other choice do we have?'

Dan grunted. Glancing at his watch, he did a quick calculation. 'Look, I'll drop you off at my place.'

'What will you do?' asked Sarah.

'I'll speak to Harry.' He grimaced. 'Given the way our last conversation ended, I should probably go alone. Do you know where he lives these days?'

'Somewhere near Uffington,' said Sarah. She rummaged in her bag and pulled out a battered address book. 'Here, I'll write down the address for you. I still think I should go with you though.'

'When did you last see him?'

She frowned. 'A couple of years ago, I think. Peter and I took him out to lunch over at the White Horse pub.'

'Is he still pissed off at me?'

Sarah grinned. 'He'll always be pissed off with you – he said you were his star student. Peter reckons Harry was truly upset when you quit the field.'

'I'll bet.' Dan changed up a gear as they reached the ring road and filtered into the busy traffic. 'Look, I really need to speak to him alone. I'm going to drop you off at the house, no hanging around. I'll go over and talk to Harry. Lock the doors and don't switch on any lights – I'll be back before it gets dark anyway. Don't open the door to anyone. I'll phone the house before I knock on the door. Understand?'

Sarah nodded.

Dan glanced at her, then back at the road. 'I mean it Sarah. No deviations from the plan. I don't care how important you think it is. Don't phone anyone either – we don't know if outgoing calls on your mobile are being monitored.'

Sarah paled. 'Y-you think they could?'

'I don't know what to think any more Sarah. I'm just going into survival mode.'

London, England

. . .

David Ludlow slammed the phone down and turned to his aide.

'Bring me the files on a guy called Delaney – immediately. I want photos, shareholder reports, satellite maps of his mines and refineries, especially Australian ones, everything. And keep it classified. No-one outside these four walls is to know.'

As the aide scuttled out of the office, David stood up and looked out the window at the dreary cityscape below him. Jesus, of all the times for this to happen – the Olympic Games only months away, the Prime Minister struggling to maintain any sort of lead in the opinion polls, then this.

'Shit!' David kicked the corner of the filing cabinet, and then jumped as his office door swung open.

'David – glad you're here. What's going on?'

David pulled his jacket straight and forced his shoulders to relax.

Stephen Lowe strolled across the office and sat in David's chair, swinging it round to face him. 'Well? Unusual to see you so worked up about something.'

David walked over and leaned against the window sill. 'Yeah, I know.'

He glanced down at the cold winter morning. Rain lashed against the window, the cold air spilling around the frame, while outside it tried to turn to snow. Commuters dashed backwards and forwards under umbrellas while cars splashed by, headlights blazing.

Lowe coughed politely and David turned his attention back to his boss.

'Sorry sir,' he said. 'Just the thought processes ticking over.' He forced a smile and wandered back to the desk, pulled out a chair opposite Lowe and sat down.

'Come on then, out with it,' said Lowe. 'What's the problem?'

David sighed. 'An organisation we've had our eye on for some time,' he said. 'At first glance, it looks like a legitimate business but I've had a small core team working on it, looking into some of its acquisitions over the past five years or so.'

Lowe leaned back and folded his hands in his lap. 'Nothing wrong with mergers and acquisitions, David. What raised the flag?'

'The death of Peter Edgewater,' said David.

Lowe sniffed. 'Name rings a bell. Remind me?'

'Oxford lecturer. Earth sciences and the like. Completed a very successful lecture tour over the past month or so. He presented a lecture at his college in Oxford on his return to the country, then two days later turned up dead in a nearby nature reserve. Police reckon it was a mugging.'

'And you don't?'

'It's a bit too convenient, isn't it?' said David. 'His lecture tour was causing quite a stir amongst the oil, gas and coal sector. Rumour has it he'd just entered into negotiations with a publisher and one of the national newspapers to do a serialised version of his lecture.

Nothing libellous, but enough for people to work out who he was pointing the finger at.'

'So you think he was murdered?' Lowe asked.

'I'm sure he was,' said David. 'I think someone was following the progress of his lecture tour very closely. I'm sure he was threatened at least once. I certainly got that impression when I spoke with him.'

'You contacted him?' Lowe sat upright. 'When?'

'In Paris, just after the New Year,' said David. He looked away and shrugged. 'I could be wrong, but he seemed on edge. Scared. He certainly didn't appreciate me being there.'

'I'm sure,' said Lowe. 'Did I authorise that trip?'

David glanced at him. 'No need. It's part of an ongoing investigation your predecessor sanctioned. Sir.'

Lowe shrugged his shoulders. 'Well, I'm sure it's just a coincidence,' he said, getting up and looking out the window. 'Oxford has its crime problems, same as anywhere else.'

David stood up and stretched, then joined him.

'So, what's the rest of the investigation about?' asked Lowe.

David shrugged. 'Your predecessor was worried about the lobbying problems in the United States spreading here. Particularly in relation to viable means of alternative energy.'

'Go on.'

'There's a lot of scare tactics used there – as well as misinformation, scientists are being paid off by the coal and oil sectors to sell their side of the story.' David paused and turned to look at Lowe. 'And he was very concerned that members of our Parliament here might be receiving bribes to hold up the research into alternative energy.'

Lowe blinked. 'What have you found so far?'

David shrugged. 'Nothing – yet. But one or two energy organisations based overseas with vested interests in the United Kingdom energy supply keep cropping up. Both were targeted by Peter Edgewater in the lecture series he presented and was about to publish. Both are privately owned but by millionaires who, quite honestly, are megalomaniacs.'

David walked over to his desk and sat down. He picked up his coffee mug, realised it was empty and put it down again in disgust.

Lowe turned from the window. 'So, what are your plans?'

David shrugged. 'I had wanted to speak with Doctor Edgewater's ex-wife to see if she could shed any light but she seems to have disappeared – hasn't been seen at her house near Abingdon for a few days.'

'Perhaps visiting relatives in the circumstances?' suggested Lowe.

'Perhaps. I hope so. I'd hate to think she was in danger.'

'Any grounds for that assumption?'

'Well, Doctor Edgewater's house was partially destroyed by an explosion yesterday.'

'*What*?'

'Yes, I know. We've told the local police to treat it as a gas explosion – no need to alarm the local community. It destroyed his study though, so it was a very targeted attack. Specialised too – the only damage was to that building.'

Lowe stuck his hands in his pockets and paced the room.

'I presume the lecture notes were destroyed then?'

David nodded. Then smiled. 'Apart from the set we think he posted to his ex-wife.'

Lowe stopped pacing. 'Really?'

'Yes.'

'And you can't find her?'

David held up his hand. 'Relax. As you say, she's probably just staying with relatives. Let's face it, she's had a tough week.' He stood up. 'If it makes you feel better, we are watching all the airports for her.'

Lowe visibly relaxed. 'Good. Make sure you do. Wouldn't want any harm coming to her, eh?' He brushed an imaginary speck of dust off his jacket. 'Well you seem to have it under control, David. Just keep me informed about any developments.'

David stood and walked across the room to open the door. 'I will Minister. Thank you for dropping by.'

TEN

Uffington, Oxfordshire

As he drove the car out through the village and down winding country lanes, Dan thought about what he'd learned so far. Sarah was right – Peter must have stumbled across something during his research that he hadn't yet published but which had endangered his life.

Hopefully there would be a clue amongst all the papers he'd sent – if Dan could work out what they meant. Whoever was trying to stop his discovery getting out into the public domain was deadly serious about it too, first killing Peter then destroying his house to ensure any incriminating evidence wasn't discovered. Dan still doubted the police explanation the explosion was caused by a gas leak; in fact he doubted whether the police believed it themselves.

A lacklustre sky flicked through the tree-lined lane and Dan lifted his foot off the accelerator as he passed over wet leaves. Not far to go now, if his memory served him correctly.

The road turned sharply and began to rise up a slight incline. Dan changed the gears down and the car surged forward. He winced as the wheels clipped a pothole, the winter frosts carving out more and more of the fragile bitumen with each snowstorm.

As the road levelled out, he could see for miles over the Oxfordshire landscape, the outline of a white horse carved into a chalk hillside, and the bare trees flickering past as he picked up speed. Wind turbines turned lazily on another hill in the distance. He saw a signpost for the next village and slowed down. Harry's cottage soon appeared on the right-hand side of the road.

Dan pulled the car up to the kerb a few hundred metres from the house and stepped out. The cottage sat on a narrow lane, with a low hedge on the opposite side of the road leading to a barren field tapering down to a river. He walked over to a wooden gate leading into the field and peered over, shivering, an icy wind biting at his ears. Pulling up the collar of his jacket, he squinted at the forlorn landscape through the light rain, the grey sky sucking the colour out of the day.

He sniffed in the cold air and glanced down the lane towards the house. A two-storey cottage with white walls, it had a thatched roof and two tall chimneys, smoke appearing from one of them. He wondered how this was going to turn out. He hadn't seen Harry in over six years now. He felt awkward about turning up out of the blue, but Sarah was right – who better to ask for help?

Harry Kent, scientist, ex-college lecturer and fellow adventurer. He smiled. He had grown up listening to his father and Harry recounting their exploits around the world – travelling to far-flung places for the university, mining companies and private investors. He smiled at the memories and wondered why he hadn't returned for so long. He hadn't seen Harry since they'd crossed paths at Dan's father's funeral. Both Harry and Dan's father had still been angry at Dan for what they felt was throwing his education and future away by joining the army. Dan could never explain to them he just wanted an adventure he could call his own.

I got that all right, he thought.

He turned and walked up the lane towards the house. The cottage hid behind a low stone wall, which itself was beginning to disappear under overgrown ivy. A wooden gate hung precariously on one rusty hinge. Glancing up, he spotted movement in the garden.

'Harry?'

A head, obscured by a Panama-style hat, bobbed up above a ragged rhododendron bush at the sound of his voice. Its owner glanced briefly over the shrub, ducked down again and quickly scurried to the side of the cottage. Dan heard a door slam shut.

'Damn.'

He wandered over to the garden gate. Opening it

carefully in case it disintegrated, he walked up the garden path. He stepped around the uneven pavers that threatened to trip him, and made his way to the front door, then grasped the ornate door knocker. He knocked once, hoping for a response. He knocked again, a little harder, and then stepped back, catching a glimpse of movement in the window to the right of the door.

An enormous ginger cat had leapt up to investigate the visitor and now sat on the window sill, yellow eyes glaring at him while it occasionally contemplated a front paw with disdain. Dan stepped over and tapped on the glass in front of the cat, which took a swipe at his fingers, banging the window pane as it did so.

'Hello tiger – do you think you could let me in?'

Suddenly an arm swept the cat off its perch and a face glared through the window at him. Dan grinned and the face disappeared. Seconds later, the front door swept open.

A tall man, with thinning white hair and bushy eyebrows above piercing green eyes, stood on the threshold glaring at him.

'Leave the bloody cat alone, you're a bad enough influence as it is with everyone else you meet for goodness sake!'

'Hi Harry – does that mean I can come in?'

The stocky figure turned without answering.

Dan closed the door behind him. 'I need your help Harry.'

Harry glared at him. 'You always did.' He stomped off

along the hallway, Dan following until they reached a large kitchen.

'I suppose you'll want a drink' – it was a statement, not a question.

Dan shrugged. 'Only if you are.'

'Hmm. I'll bet.'

Dan looked around the cluttered kitchen. The Panama hat sat discarded on a hook on the back door. Geranium cuttings in small pots covered the surfaces, in varying forms of growth while dishes remained stacked in the kitchen sink. A couple of empty beer cans hung precariously close to the edge of a pine table. The cat prowled around the floor, weaving in between his legs.

Harry opened a cupboard, reached up and closed the door, placing a large bottle of gin on the counter. 'I reckon if you need help, then we'd better start off with something strong – knowing you, I'll probably need it.'

Dan stood out of the way while Harry organised glasses, ice and tonic water. 'Right,' he said, handing Dan a glass, 'Let's sit in the front room and you can explain yourself. How the hell did you find me anyway?'

'Sarah told me.' Dan followed Harry out of the kitchen, the cat following them.

Harry led the way down the hallway into a small lounge area where a fire burned in a small grate. The cat trotted into the room ahead of them and made her way over to a large cushion next to the fireplace, glared at Dan then turned around three times before curling up on her bed.

Harry motioned Dan to a chair and picked up a poker iron to stoke the fire. As the flames roared into life, he picked out a small log from the wood pile and stacked it gently in the grate. He turned back to Dan.

'How is she holding up since Peter's body was found?'

'Not too good after someone successfully blew up Peter's house right in front of her.'

Harry paused halfway to his chair. 'What?'

'Yeah, I know. God knows what he got himself involved with this time.' Dan took a sip of the drink. 'She's upset, obviously – and angry. I don't think the police are taking her seriously.' Dan sat down with a grunt and looked at Harry. 'How are you keeping?'

The older man sighed, shifting in his chair. 'Oh, you know, the garden keeps me busy. The grandchildren visit occasionally, although less now they're growing up and creating lives of their own.'

'Do you miss the teaching?'

'Not to reprobates like you, no,' Harry chuckled. 'Of course I do – that, and being out in the field.' He paused, contemplating his drink. 'How long is it since you left the army?'

'Just under three years.'

'Done anything with yourself since?'

Dan glared at Harry, then softened his gaze. 'No, not really. I don't really know what to do. I've done a couple of feasibility studies overseas, travelled a bit in between jobs. It took me a while to get over, well, you know.'

Harry nodded, contemplating his drink. 'I can only

imagine. What on earth made you decide to join up and go into bomb disposal anyway? You had a promising career ahead of you in geology.'

Dan shrugged. 'I don't know – I guess since I was a teenager I'd just been on this pre-ordained track. You know, follow Dad's footsteps – get a geology degree then get out in the field working in mineral exploration. After graduation, I just felt there would be more exciting things to do while I was still young.' He took a sip of his drink.

Harry looked over at him. 'Most people at that age would have thought a round-the-world trip and a spot of bungee jumping would suffice.'

'Yeah, well in hindsight that probably wouldn't have been a bad idea either. But at the time, I wanted to get involved and help.'

Harry shuffled in his seat. 'I have a sneaking suspicion you didn't come here today to talk about old times. What's on your mind?'

'I've been looking through Peter's research notes and something keeps cropping up in them. What can you tell me about white gold powder?'

Harry contemplated his drink, turning the glass in his hand. 'Why?'

'Because I think that's why Peter's been killed.'

ELEVEN

Harry took a swig of his drink, swallowed and put the glass down on the table. 'What do you know about super-conducted precious metals?'

Dan shrugged. 'Not being a chemistry expert, very little. From what I can work out from Peter's notes, super-conducted metals are already used in car manufacturing but from a commercial perspective, that's about it. Any search on the internet seems to point towards health tonics and strange spiritual claims rather than anything industrial.'

Harry nodded. 'Several interested parties have already lodged claims with patent offices around the world. That includes government agencies. Covertly, everyone's trying to come up with a way of being able to commercially produce white gold powder – or any other super-conducted precious metal – at a viable cost.'

'What are they planning on using it for?' Dan pulled

out a piece of crumpled paper and a pen, and began to write notes.

'That depends on who you ask. Some say aerospace companies, especially those which have big defence contracts with governments, are trying to produce the next super-jet – this stuff has enormous potential for travelling faster than anything we've seen so far because somehow, once produced, it supposedly defies gravity,' Harry paused. 'I see your method of taking notes hasn't improved since I taught you.'

Dan scowled. 'Is there going to be an exam on this?' He paused. 'No? Okay – carry on.'

Harry chuckled. 'Imagine what you could do with this knowledge in the public sector. No-one's done anything about the future of air travel since Concorde was grounded.'

Dan reached over and flicked through Peter's notes. 'He says here some people believe it has spiritual powers and there are companies selling this stuff already though.'

'Well, I don't know about the spiritual claims – I'm only a scientist. And they're only producing it in small quantities.' Harry considered the contents of his glass. 'No – you need to be looking for someone who's already mining gold and has easy access to this stuff – not to mention a lot of money to throw at such a project. It would have to be in a remote location as well, to be able to keep it secret. That has to narrow the search down.'

Dan paused from his note-taking. 'Is it just the expense that's holding people back?'

Harry shook his head. 'Not always. They're dealing with a very unstable substance. I've heard of at least one big accident in the United States which has put production back by years. Then you've got governments trying to claim the technology for themselves. What else have you found in those notes?'

Dan passed the bundle over to Harry. 'I'm still learning at the moment – why don't you take a look and see what you think?'

Harry picked up some of Peter's notes and began to flick through them. 'The other thing of course is, this stuff has the potential to solve the world's fuel problems. Once created, it's clean, doesn't pollute and after the technology is perfected, you've got another potential supply through volcanic ash, not just precious metals. You're going to have to consider the possibility of coal, oil and gas companies trying to block the research. Look at what they did to the electric car.'

Dan chewed the end of his pen. 'How serious do you think those guys could get?'

Harry picked up his glass and peered over it at Dan, then took a sip before speaking. 'Well, I'm sure Peter would tell you, if he could, they can be extremely serious.'

Dan looked at Harry carefully. 'You mean, one of those organisations might've had something to do with Peter's death?'

Harry paused to put his glass on the table, the soft clink of ice cubes breaking the short silence. 'I believe you have to consider that, yes. I think you're going to have to go through those notes very carefully. And be very wary who knows you've got them. Who does know about them anyway?'

Dan picked up the bundle. 'Only myself and Sarah. I think her journalistic instincts have kicked back in and she wants to do some of her own research to try to make some sense of Peter's death.'

Harry grunted. 'Then I would strongly suggest you tell her from me to watch her step. Both of you need to watch your backs if you're going to investigate this.'

Dan nodded. 'We will.' He peered into his drink as if it would provide the answers. He gave up and took a sip instead. He glanced up at a low cry from Harry. 'What?'

'Look at this!' Harry held up a sheet of paper, several diagrams haphazardly scribbled across the page.

'Sorry, I don't get it,' said Dan. 'You wouldn't believe how long I've looked at that.'

Harry grinned. 'It's not what you're looking at,' he said. 'It's *how* you're looking at it. Come over here.'

Dan stood up and crossed the room.

'Here,' instructed Harry.

Dan crouched down next to Harry's armchair and stared at the familiar notebook page in Harry's hand. 'What am I looking for?' he frowned.

'This,' said Harry. He tilted the page until the glow from the fireplace illuminated it from behind.

Dan grabbed the page and held it still. 'You're a genius, Harry.'

In the light of the fire, the imprint of another note

could be seen. Invisible to the eye when the page was held flat, it jumped out once silhouetted from behind.

'Can you read it?' asked Harry.

'Looks something like the letter D. Maybe an E. Is that a C? Christ, his writing's bad. Then there's some numbers. Six. One. Seven. Three?'

Dan sat back on his heels. 'What the hell does that mean?'

Harry glanced down at the page and tilted it towards the firelight. 'There's a plus sign in front of the six.'

They looked at each other. Then spoke simultaneously.

'It's a phone number!'

'Where's your phone book?' asked Dan.

'Hallway.'

Dan jumped up and ran from the room. He saw a small table next to the front door and pulled the phone book out from one of the shelves. He walked quickly back to the room, desperately flicking the pages.

'Found it?' asked Harry.

Dan shook his head and kept turning the pages. He growled in frustration.

'Dan – slow down,' said Harry. 'Just start at the beginning and work methodically.'

Dan perched on the arm of his chair. He turned one page at a time, running his finger down the country listings. He flipped the next page – and there it was.

He walked over to Harry and showed him.

Harry looked at the number, then up at Dan.

'Looks like you're going to Brisbane.'

TWELVE

London, England

David sifted through the documents strewn across the walnut-coloured boardroom table. He chewed on a ragged thumbnail thoughtfully as he turned over pages. He rubbed his hand over his forehead wearily. He felt tired and was becoming increasingly aware that a permanent frown line was developing from the sheer concentration of the past few months.

He picked up a document, caught his finger on a staple, and swore. He flicked through the pages, which contained copies of mining leases, exploration permits and equipment leasing contracts.

'Exactly how many gold mines has Delaney purchased?' he asked his assistant.

Philippa looked up from the document she was reading

and pushed her glasses up onto her head as a hair band. She brushed a stray flame-red strand of hair out of her eyes and looked at her boss.

'Twelve in the past four years,' she said. 'He started off slow – bought one out in Queensland then seems to have become a bit obsessed with it. Five out of the twelve were purchased last year – all under different company names of course and a bitch to trace according to our mergers and acquisitions expert.'

David swore under his breath. 'How many has he purchased in Australia?'

Philippa dropped her glasses back onto the bridge of her nose and consulted her notes. 'Nine. The others are in South Africa and Eastern Europe purchased through his UK subsidiary.'

'Any in the United States?'

Philippa shook her head. 'He's never bothered with the US – he probably thought that if he started purchasing companies there now, it'd raise a bloody big flag for us to see.'

David grunted and put down the document. He sank into one of the faux leather chairs and pulled a manila-coloured folder towards him. Flipping it open, he started to empty the contents onto the table.

Philippa looked up at the sound of him tipping out the papers and frowned at him. It had taken her two days to organise everything into a coherent library of information. David ignored her and sifted through the new documents strewn across the table in front of him.

He pushed the paperwork to one side and collected all the photographic evidence together. Then he slouched back in his chair, and worked his way methodically through the pictures.

Some were aerial photographs, obtained from US spy satellites. David inwardly groaned. He could only imagine the sort of favours his contact at the National Security Agency would call in over the ensuing years for capturing the images. He glanced up at Philippa.

'How on earth did you convince the NSA to get photos of Australia?' he wondered.

She didn't look up from her work. Just smiled. 'I told them we'd heard a rumour terrorist cells were possibly using the outback as a training ground in some places.'

David rolled his eyes. Philippa had a nerve, but she always got results fast. He'd worry about telling the Americans it was a false alarm once he worked out what the hell was *really* going on in Australia.

He reached across, switched on a small desk lamp and angled the beam of light onto an aerial photograph of a patch of scrubland. The scaling printed on the photo told him he was looking at an area approximately two hundred kilometres square. He frowned, then peered closer.

'Philippa?'

'Hmm?'

'Anyone in the photo laboratory working late tonight?'

'Probably. They increased the shift cover with the Olympics coming up. Guess they reckoned on a few more nutters being around.'

David held up the photograph. 'Can you get some copies of this done straight away?' He picked up a permanent marker and circled an area in the top right-hand corner of the picture. 'Get a couple of close-ups of this area.'

Philippa stood up, stretched her tall frame and wandered over to the table. She held out a hand for the photograph. 'Do you want a coffee when I come back?'

'Yeah, thanks. I've got a feeling it's going to be a long night.'

He watched as Philippa left the room then looked down at the remaining photographs in the folder.

As well as aerial reconnaissance pictures, the folder also contained photographs of various people, captured as they left buildings or sat in restaurants. He gathered the photographs together, stood up and walked over to a large whiteboard which covered the length of one wall at the end of the room. Methodically, he stuck each photograph to the whiteboard, then stood back with his arms crossed and stared at the pictures.

Delaney was easily recognisable. The man was over six feet tall, broad shouldered with a mass of thick white hair combed back away from his face. He looked tanned, rich, and completely at ease with his guest at a restaurant.

David's focus shifted to the next photograph. A shorter, broader man was emerging from a chauffeur-driven car. The man was thick-set and appeared to be unused to the hot Australian summer, tugging at his tie as he clambered out of the vehicle. Uli Petrov, Russian entrepreneur –

rumoured to be buying up gas commodities with a view to breaking into the lucrative European market at a rate which even alarmed the Kremlin, according to David's sources.

He glanced briefly at the next picture. Steven Pallisder, Delaney's joint venture partner. David frowned. What the hell was going on?

He turned around as the door opened and Philippa walked in, the photographs tucked under her arm and a coffee cup in each hand. David gratefully took one of the coffees and the photographs from her.

'Let's see what we've got here,' he said and put the coffee cup down on the table. He strode back to the whiteboard and pinned up the enlarged photographs. He stepped back and tilted his head, taking in the increased level of detail.

Philippa pulled out a chair, sat down and began scanning through a series of financial reports.

David stepped closer over to the enlarged satellite photograph pinned to the whiteboard. The photographic team had enhanced the image and had highlighted the area of David's interest.

An angry red felt tip pen mark circled an area of the surface, which seemed to be erupting.

David cocked his head to one side as he looked at it. 'Philippa?'

'Hmm?' Philippa looked up from the report she held in her hand.

David turned to her. 'Do me a favour. See if we've got

any satellite images in the library that show the effects of underground atomic testing.'

He turned back to the photograph.

'I have a bad feeling I might know what this guy is up to.'

THIRTEEN

Dan raced through the dark country lanes, braking hard when he saw headlights travelling from the opposite direction, then accelerating the car around the tight, narrow bends.

His mind raced. They finally had a breakthrough, thanks to Harry.

He risked a glance at the bundle of notes lying on the passenger seat and wondered what other secrets they would reveal in time. He and Harry had spent another hour carefully poring over the other documents, holding them up to the light in case more imprints could be found. In the end, Harry had shaken his head and started to gather up the papers.

'It's no good,' he said. 'That was our lucky break. You're just going to have to find out what D.E.C. means – otherwise you risk a wasted journey.'

Dan nodded then, glancing at his watch, realised how

late it was. 'Christ, Sarah's going to be worrying where I am.' He'd taken the documents from Harry and had given the older man a brief hug. 'Thanks for everything Harry. I don't think I ever said that enough in the past.'

Harry nodded, patted his arm, and then walked with him to the front door. 'You're always welcome, Dan. You should know that.' He opened the door and a gust of cold air rushed into the narrow hallway. 'Come back and tell me how you both get on in Australia.'

Dan had insisted Harry return to the warmth of the house while he hurried to the car, hugging himself against the chill of the night air.

Now, he braked as he entered a small, dimly lit village. He leaned forward and turned down the heater a little. He drummed his fingers impatiently as he drove down the main street of the village, the street lights casting orange pools of light in between the shadows. As he passed the speed limit signs on the boundary of the village, he floored the accelerator once more.

After a while, the country lane spat him out onto the main dual carriageway into Oxford. Within half an hour, he'd reached the outer limits of the city and followed the ring road back to his house. As the car pulled up in the driveway, he saw a curtain twitch open, the light from the living room illuminating the gravel surface. He took out his phone and dialled.

'It's okay, it's me,' he said as he cut the engine and climbed out. He hung up, locked the car and crunched over the gravel to the front door. An automated security light snapped on above his head, just as the front door swung open and Sarah burst out from behind it and across the driveway.

'Where the hell have you been?' she demanded. 'I was worried sick!'

'I'm sorry,' he said, and squeezed her arm. 'Come on, let's get inside.'

She shrugged, nodded and followed him. 'Sorry – I've just been so worried.'

Dan closed the door behind him. 'Well, Harry's got us onto something,' he smiled. 'Let's open a bottle of wine and I'll show you what we've been up to.'

Sarah held the page up to the light, the lettering silhouetted in front of her. 'Do you think D.E.C. is a person?' she asked.

'Or a month,' suggested Dan. 'No idea. But that's definitely the dialling code for Brisbane and the beginning of a phone number. So, we need to find something which connects those letters to Brisbane.'

Sarah leaned across the kitchen table and pulled her laptop towards her. 'Luckily, I had this in my car, not at home,' she said. She tapped her fingers on the surface of the table as she waited for the computer to complete its start-up routine.

As soon as it was ready, she clicked onto a search

engine. 'Might as well start with the obvious,' she said, and typed in D.E.C., Brisbane. Then hit the search key.

Nothing happened for a few seconds. It felt like an age. A list of potential combinations then appeared on the screen. Sarah's eyes scanned down the list, her fingers hovering over the computer mouse.

Dan stirred the pasta and added seasoning to the sauce, reached up and pulled two wine glasses out of a cupboard. He had just set them down on the worktop when he heard an exclamation from Sarah.

'I don't believe it.'

He heard the sound of the mouse as Sarah clicked frantically through internet pages and turned to see what she was doing. 'What have you got?'

She looked up, smiled, then turned the laptop so the screen faced his way. It displayed the home page for Delaney Energy Corporation.

'Bingo,' she said.

Dan turned around, put the red wine back on the rack and opened the refrigerator. He pulled out a bottle of champagne and held it up to Sarah.

'I think we've earned it today,' he grinned.

FOURTEEN

FEBRUARY 2012

Brisbane, Australia

Dan followed Sarah away from the baggage carousel and headed towards the customs queue. Twenty minutes later, they stepped out of the cool airport into what seemed like a hot shower – the humidity was intense.

As they climbed into a taxi, Dan gave the driver their destination, sat back and felt his shirt sticking to him. Once the car started moving, the air blew through the open windows, carrying the scent of the eucalyptus trees along Kingsford Smith Drive.

Dan pulled his sunglasses down over his eyes as the taxi edged through the traffic heading into the city. To his left, the river wound its way past restaurants, ferry terminals and offices as it headed out to the bay, while cruise ships docked at the Hamilton terminal, spitting out their passengers before sending them on to the boutiques of the Queen Street Mall via ferries and taxis.

Sarah sat next to him, turning her head in all directions, trying to take in everything she saw. As they progressed along the river, she realised it twisted and turned, so she soon lost her sense of direction as they headed into the city.

Half an hour later, the taxi pulled up to the hotel. Dan climbed out, picked up their bags and paid the driver. Walking towards the entrance, his clothes quickly began to stick to his skin – the humidity would take some getting used to after the cold British winter.

They stood in the cool reception area, filling out forms. Once checked in, Sarah handed him her room key.

'If you dump our bags, I'll go and grab us a coffee,' she said.

Dan nodded and, taking the keys, took the elevator up to the fourteenth floor. He waited until the elevator ground to a halt. He walked along the hallway until he found Sarah's room, put her bag inside the door, then continued to the next room. Opening the door, he put the 'do not disturb' sign on the handle and dropped his bag on the floor. He bent down to pick up the complimentary copy of the *Courier Mail* and sat on the bed to read it.

As he swung his legs up, he saw an article on the front page promoting Delaney's latest project. Although

Delaney had offices near Eagle Street Pier, he didn't appear to spend a lot of time in town and seemed to be treated as a minor celebrity when he did choose to arrive.

Dan threw the newspaper onto the small coffee table and turned at the sound of a knock on the door. He strode across the room and yanked the door open.

Sarah stood in the hallway, two Styrofoam cups of takeaway coffee in her hands. 'Come on. No rest for the wicked. Here,' she said, thrusting one of the cups at Dan. 'Might as well brainstorm to fight off the jetlag.'

She brushed past him. Dan closed the door and followed Sarah into the room, sipping his coffee. He winced. It was still hot.

Sarah stood at the window, happily drinking her coffee, taking in the view. She turned and gestured at a large skyscraper towering over its neighbours. 'That's Delaney's place,' she said.

Dan wandered over to join her and peered through the glass. 'How do you know?'

'I got talking to someone in the coffee shop downstairs. Told them I was killing time before a job interview at Delaney Energy Corporation and they pointed it out to me. Friendly place this.' She turned and sat on the edge of the bed. 'I was thinking on the way back here – we need to find out more about Delaney. From a local perspective, I mean. Find out if he has any business problems – you know, investment troubles or something. Maybe that will help shed some light on what Peter thought he was up to.'

Dan nodded. 'It sounds as good a plan as any. Got any ideas how we're going to do that?'

'We need access to a fast computer system – and somewhere that's not going to attract attention to what we're going to be looking for.' Sarah stood up, paced the room, then suddenly stopped, and looked out the hotel window over the river.

'I know what we can do.' She spun round, turning to Dan. 'I know someone at ABC Radio here in Brisbane. Let's see if she can get us in there. No-one is going to think twice about a reporter digging around, are they?'

A figure at the far end of the park stood up and waved as Dan and Sarah approached.

Sarah grinned as the lanky woman walked over to them. Dressed in a pale green skirt, white top and wearing flat shoes, she hurried over the plaza to hug Sarah.

'It's so good to see you! You should've told me last week you were heading out here – I could've taken some time off to show you around.'

Sarah stepped back. 'I know. I'm sorry. It was just so last-minute. It's a bit of a whistle-stop trip anyway.' She turned to Dan.

'Dan, this is Hayley Miller, assistant editor at ABC Radio – Hayley, this is Dan, a...'

'...friend of Peter's,' he finished helpfully, shaking Hayley's hand.

Hayley reached out and gently squeezed Sarah's arm. 'Oh, Sarah – I was so sad to hear about Peter. Are they any closer to catching the guy who did it?'

Sarah and Dan glanced at each other, before Sarah spoke. 'No, the police haven't got a clue...'

'...which is why we need your help,' added Dan.

'Me?' Hayley asked. 'Okay – now I'm really interested.' She turned to Sarah. 'What are you up to?'

Sarah shrugged. 'I'm trying to find out the truth about Peter's death. I'm – I mean, we're – not convinced it was a random attack.'

'And you've come all the way to Brisbane?' Hayley glanced around the park. 'Tell you what – I'm just on my way back to the office. Why don't you both come back with me, then we can talk properly?'

***

Hayley pushed a door open for Dan and Sarah. Closing it, she surveyed the small office then strode over to a side table and began to sweep paperwork and reference books to one side.

'Okay Sarah,' she said, handing over a folder of documents, 'Here's what I've got on Delaney so far. Help yourself to the photocopier over there. Sorry it's a bit cramped – I'm lucky to have an office at all.'

'This is fine, don't worry,' said Sarah as she pulled over a chair and began to sift through the paperwork.

Dan wandered over to the window and looked out. The

air-conditioning belied the fact the outside temperature was hitting the mid-thirties. He turned and leaned against the window sill. 'What do you know about Delaney Energy?' he asked Hayley. 'Does it have much of an influence around here?'

Hayley nodded. 'Absolutely. It's owned outright by a guy called Morris Delaney. He likes to give the impression he's a bit of a philanthropist. You know, hands out money to various arts events, a couple of high profile charities. Of course, it's all about marketing his brand.' She stepped round her desk, sat in a chair and indicated to Dan to take the seat opposite before she continued. 'His father owned mining interests in South Australia. When he died about forty years ago, Morris Delaney inherited the business and just kept acquiring more and more assets. He's a shrewd businessman, but there are rumours surrounding him that he's very violent. No-one will say anything to the media though – they're too frightened.'

Sarah walked over to Hayley's desk and began to unravel the bundle containing Peter's lecture notes. 'This is what Peter sent to me, just before he was murdered,' she said. 'We're still trying to fathom exactly what he was investigating but there is a phrase that keeps cropping up – white gold. Especially as a powder. Have you ever heard it mentioned in connection with Delaney?'

Hayley shook her head. 'No – can't say that I have. What's it supposed to do?'

Dan shrugged. 'We're not too sure. We spoke to a friend of ours back in England and he reckons it's to do with alternative energy.' He stretched out his legs. 'Not like wind farms though – apparently, this stuff packs a punch if it can be manufactured on a large scale.'

Hayley turned in her chair and began sifting through a pile of loose papers, then dragged out a white card from beneath a file. 'This might help shed some light – at least where Delaney's concerned,' she said, and slid it across the desk to Dan.

He picked it up and read the ornate writing. It was an invitation to a press conference – to be given that evening, by Morris Delaney. Dan held it up to Hayley. 'Aren't you going?'

'Hell, yes,' she grinned. 'That one was for a colleague of mine but something kicked off in far north Queensland yesterday and he's gone up there to file a report for our six o'clock bulletin tonight.' She turned to Sarah. 'I'm sorry – there's only one. Are you going to fight over it?'

Dan smiled. 'No – because I'm going.'

Sarah looked up sharply and glared at him. 'I'm the journalist around here.'

Dan shrugged. 'And that's precisely why you're not going – I want to gauge what this Delaney character is like, not tip him off to the fact we're onto him. And I know you won't be able to stop yourself asking some rather pointed questions.'

Sarah shrugged. 'Okay, you go. I'll spend the time finding out if there's any connection between Peter's notes and what information Hayley's given me.' She put all the documentation into her bag. 'I'm fascinated by this guy –

he's manipulated laws and everything to get his own way over the years. There must be something here to give us an idea of what he's really up to.'

Hayley nodded, then looked at her watch. 'What I've managed to uncover is more information than what you'll pick up on the internet articles, so at least you'll get a head start,' she said. 'I'm really sorry but I'll have to kick you out so I can get ready for our six o'clock bulletin and get a team prepared for the press conference – is there somewhere at the hotel you can get your head down?'

Dan nodded. 'They have a business centre there we can use.' He stood up as Hayley got up to leave the room. 'Thanks for your help.'

Hayley smiled at him and Sarah as she held the door open for them. 'Hey, it's the least I could do for you – and Peter. Good luck.'

'Did it help?'

They were walking along Southbank, a ferry sauntering past them on the mud-coloured river. Dan walked a little ahead of Sarah, then stopped to look at her.

She caught up and shrugged. 'A little bit. I've managed to get Pete's notes into some sort of coherent order but I feel like I've still got a lot of catching up to do. The sequence jumps around a bit.'

She stood to one side to let a cyclist pass. She shrugged her bag further up on to her shoulder. 'I thought I might go back to the hotel and see if I can reorganise it all. Follow a timeline or something to try to make more sense of what we've got here.'

Dan nodded. 'Okay, well I'm going to go over to this press conference of Delaney's – I want to know what he looks like in person, rather than us relying on photographs all the time.'

Sarah glanced back towards the river, then turned to Dan. 'Just behave yourself,' she said, as she swung her bag over her shoulder and headed back to the hotel. 'And remember to bring me back some canapés!'

FIFTEEN

Dan turned right and began to walk up the street, his jacket slung over his arm. He figured there was no sense in rushing in the summer evening heat.

He noticed how quickly darkness fell over the city. As he walked through the botanical gardens, he heard the chatter of possums and flying foxes interspersed with the steady flow of traffic beside him. Cicadas chanted noisily – a natural white noise that was constant in the humid air.

As he approached the university and government building complex, he reached into his jacket and plucked out the press invitation Hayley had procured for him. According to her, very few invites had been given to those outside Delaney's inner circle.

He slowed as he turned left into the pedestrian-friendly university complex and stood outside the state government building. There was no queue to enter – invitees were being processed thoroughly and efficiently. Invites checked, invitees shepherded through a metal detector, then two sniffer dogs and their handlers present on the other side, just in case.

Dan held the invite between his teeth and shrugged his jacket over his shoulders. He'd have to be careful. The last thing he wanted was to alert Delaney to his presence. He planned to stay in the background, away from the limelight. Merely a casual observer. He cricked his head from side to side, took the invite out of his mouth and strolled across the concourse to the entranceway.

He nodded to the doorman and handed him his invitation. The doorman smiled politely and turned away from him before facing Dan, holding out a small plastic basket in front of him.

'If sir has any jewellery, coins or other metal objects on his person, perhaps he could place them in the basket before passing through the metal detector?'

Dan grimaced, slipped his watch off his wrist and emptied the change from his pockets. The doorman glanced down, saw nothing of interest in the basket and passed it to his colleague on the other side of the security barrier. He turned back to Dan and then frowned.

Dan stared at him. 'What?'

The doorman smiled, embarrassed. He reached into his trouser pocket and withdrew a paper handkerchief. He held it out to Dan. 'Perhaps sir would like to lose the chewing gum as well?'

Dan raised his eyebrow at the doorman, shrugged, spat

the chewing gum into the handkerchief and handed it back to the doorman.

'Don't use it all at once,' he said and strolled through the metal detector.

The security guard on the other side handed the small basket back to Dan and gestured he should move to one side to refill his pockets, to get him out of the way of other arriving guests.

Dan looked around the entrance hallway as he re-fastened his watch. He turned as a member of staff approached him, his arm out wide, sweeping him towards the reception room.

'We'll be starting the press conference in half an hour if you'd like to get a drink, sir,' he said. 'The waiting staff will take care of you.'

Dan walked through a wide doorway and into a large ornate room, lit by chandeliers from a cathedral-height ceiling and, towards the front of the room, large bright television lights. A single hardwood lectern stood in front of a series of camera and microphone stands. A deep blue backdrop, onto which Delaney's corporate logo had been embossed in silver stitching, glinted in the glare of the lights.

A passing waiter carrying a tray of drinks paused next to Dan and gestured to the array of glasses he was balancing. Dan nodded and helped himself to a tall glass of ice-cold beer. He took a mouthful, relishing the cool liquid, then loosened his tie a little. He glanced around the room and noticed people were beginning to take their seats.

He smiled and winked as he spotted Hayley with a work colleague as they walked past him. Hayley smiled but was caught up in another conversation and was swept past him to a front row seat.

Dan looked around and decided if he was merely attending as a casual observer, he may as well sit in the back row. He sat down, smiled briefly at the couple next to him and let his eyes wander round the room.

A hush fell over the crowd as a tall, thin man in a suit approached the lectern. Dan watched as the man fussed over some wires on the floor, then adjusted the height of the main microphone. Finally, once happy with the arrangements, he gave the audience his full attention and held up his hands for silence.

'Please, ladies and gentlemen, please.' He turned to the press, the murmurs of conversation around the room falling away to silence. 'Mr Delaney will be joining us shortly. He will give a ten minute presentation before we open the floor for a brief question and answer session,' the thin man explained. He looked around the room. 'Questions will be limited to the new joint venture and to next month's coal conference in Sydney.'

A collective groan rumbled round the room from some members of the press who were present. The tall thin man looked down his nose at them.

'We are not in the habit of entertaining questions of a spurious nature ladies and gentlemen, so please do not waste our time, nor that of your colleagues.' He ducked his head slightly. 'Thank you,' he concluded and with a small bow, left the lectern.

Dan shifted uncomfortably in his seat. The conversation in the room began to rise in volume again as people grew impatient. After a couple of minutes, a man walked past the front row of reporters and took his place behind the lectern. Dan watched as he observed the crowd.

He looked like a king appraising his subjects. Tall – a broad powerful man with a mane of thick white hair. His face was lined and tanned. Dan guessed he was in his sixties but couldn't be sure – if the guy spent a lot of time out in the sun on his yacht, he may have been younger, it was hard to tell. He walked like he owned the room. Dan figured he probably did, given the number of non-press attendees, all lending their support, all probably indebted to the hulk of a man who now stood at the lectern, preening. A smattering of applause welcomed him before a hush fell over the room.

'Ladies and gentlemen, thank you,' said the man. His voice was smooth, reassuring and powerful all at once, a deep baritone that resonated through the air.

'For those of you who don't know me, I'm Morris Delaney and I am the proud owner of Delaney Energy Corporation – among other businesses of course,' he chuckled. A brief patter of sympathetic laughter sporadically filled the room then died away.

Delaney held up his hand, acknowledging the support.

'We're here today to celebrate the new joint venture between myself and my good friend and business colleague, Stephen Pallisder. Together, we are now capable of bringing an estimated additional seven hundred and fifty million dollars' worth of business to this State over the next two years through our combined coal and rail consortium.'

Camera flashes permeated the room as Delaney's supporters lent a thunderous applause to the moment.

Dan leaned forward and cast his eyes across the attendees. Most were held in rapture by Delaney. He concluded most of them would have a vested interest in Delaney's success in the project, as well as other ventures he might have up his sleeve. He couldn't help wonder who in the room would also resort to murder alongside Delaney to ensure their investments remained successful.

'The joint venture will help cement clean coal technology in this state,' continued Delaney. 'Not only does this keep jobs safe in Australia, it provides us with enormous export opportunities which would be lost forever if we listened to the environmental scaremongers touting solar and wind power as the future for our country.' He paused, soaking up the applause.

Dan tuned out as Delaney continued to sell the joint venture to the press then gestured to his press liaison officer to field any questions.

The tall thin man returned to the lectern and looked down his nose at the assembled guests. 'Ladies and gentlemen, raise your hands please if you have any questions on the joint venture and we'll address as many of them as we can in the short time we have available.'

Dan's mind began to wander. It seemed most of the media representatives were toeing the line when it came to Delaney's rules of engagement and were concentrating on the benefits of his project to the job market and state revenue.

Dan's attention was drawn back to the room as Delaney held up his hands, grinned at the crowd and walked away from the lectern. He disappeared through a panelled door, closely followed by his entourage.

Dan waited until the audience began to stand and file out of the room back towards the reception area. A string quartet struck up a melody and as he glanced through the door, he spotted the same waiters working the small crowd, ensuring everyone had a drink. He followed the other guests through the doorway, and decided to call it a night. He nodded to the security guard at the main entrance and stepped through into the hot humid night air.

A sudden movement on the opposite end of the public concourse caught his attention. He glanced over, then did a double-take. It was a ghost, surely. He stared at the man in the t-shirt and board shorts leaning against the wrought-iron railings opposite the government building.

The man signalled to Dan not to react, his eyes twitching briefly to the doorway behind him. Dan glanced back. A security guard was sweeping his eyes over the small crowd of people which had spilled out of the press conference and were now milling about, exchanging business cards and saying their goodbyes. Dan looked back but the man had disappeared. Dan's head was spinning.

That was Mitch!

He hadn't seen him for three years – and he looked like he had borne a lot more knocks than the ones they'd suffered in Iraq together, but Dan was sure. He turned his head to the left, back towards the main road. The man reappeared and beckoned to Dan that he should follow.

What the hell was going on?

SIXTEEN

Dan rounded the corner. He saw the man walking down the street ahead of him. He quickened his pace. The man side-stepped into a concealed entrance to the park. One minute he was walking along the street, the next minute he was gone.

Dan broke into a run, his jacket flapping open. He reached the park entrance and stepped through the unlit gate. He slipped off his tie and put it in his jacket pocket. No sense in providing a free weapon to a potential attacker. He blinked, waiting for his eyes to adjust to the darkness after the brightly lit street.

'Here,' said a voice to his right.

Dan's head spun round. He looked closer and saw a shadowy figure step out from another narrow path. 'Mitch?'

A tall, lanky man stepped towards him, a broad grin

across his face. 'Good to see you Dan. What the bloody hell are you doing in Brisbane?'

Dan smiled and the two men shook hands.

'Long story – you?'

Mitch shrugged. 'This and that. Basically, trying to keep out of trouble.'

'Doesn't sound like you,' said Dan.

'Yeah, well. Times change, you know.'

Mitch stepped away from Dan and looked over his shoulder back towards the gate.

Dan followed his gaze. 'What?'

'Nothing,' said Mitch. 'Just checking you weren't followed.'

Dan looked at Mitch. 'How've you been Mitch? Haven't seen you since they medi-vac'd us out.'

Mitch shrugged. 'Not too bad, considering. Got a limp and I lost my sight in one eye. I've probably got the mirror image of your scars, given I was standing right next to you.'

Dan looked down at his feet and wondered how long after sleep the nightmares would return that night.

'What about you Dan? You okay?'

Dan shook his head. 'Not really mate, no.' He shrugged. 'You know how it can be.'

Mitch nodded. 'What are you doing this side of the world?'

Dan grinned. 'Learning to surf.'

Mitch snorted. 'Bollocks.' He looked around them, then back at Dan. 'Got time for a drink?'

'Always,' said Dan. 'Somewhere quiet though, okay? I feel like I'm too old for most of the bars around here.'

Mitch grinned. 'I know what you mean. Come on – there's a hotel further down by the river. It's got a courtyard bar tucked away from everyone except paying guests.'

'You going up in the world?' asked Dan as he followed Mitch down a winding path which seemed to follow the direction of the main street.

'Hell no,' grinned Mitch. 'I just know I have to look like I belong there. Don't worry – they're more laid back in most places around here compared with back home.'

'Just as well,' said Dan, as he glanced down at Mitch's apparel of shirt, board shorts and sandals.

Five minutes later, Mitch had ducked down a small alley behind a row of shops. The pathway opened out into a paved courtyard with a fountain and a bronze statue in the middle of it. A doorway to the left led to a small bar. Dan looked up at the sign above the door.

Patrons only.

Mitch followed his gaze and shrugged. 'Well, we're patrons now,' he grinned and walked up to the bar. He ordered two bottles of premium lager, having decided the draught beer would be an insult to his taste buds, and handed one to Dan.

'To better times,' he said, and held his beer up to Dan in a toast.

Dan mirrored the gesture but said nothing.

'Let's sit over in the corner out of the way,' said Mitch, who led the way.

He chose two armchairs which faced the three available entrances to the bar – one from the courtyard, one from the road and another from within the hotel – and gestured to Dan to take a seat. Dan grunted with approval. Old habits died hard. Backs to the wall, facing any potential threat.

Dan took a gulp of the ice-cold beer and set the bottle down on the small table in front of them. 'So,' he said. 'You didn't say what you were doing over here. How come you're taking an interest in tonight's press conference?'

'I could ask you the same thing,' said Mitch, watching the other people in the bar.

'I asked first.'

Mitch smiled. 'After I was shipped home, there wasn't much I was good for so the army pensioned me out. I just couldn't face doing a desk job for the rest of my life with them. Not to mention not wanting to have to be the one sending out people like you and me to do my old job.' He paused. 'We were bloody good you know.'

Dan scowled. 'Not good enough.'

Mitch shrugged. 'Anyway, like I said, I'm no good at sitting on my arse so I applied for a couple of jobs over here. Security and the like.'

Dan stared at him. 'Security? Like what? Guarding Delaney?'

Mitch shook his head and put his hand up to placate Dan.

'Keep your voice down, will you? Christ, you wouldn't believe who that man has in his back pocket.' He took a gulp of his beer and began to pick the label off the side.

Dan watched him. 'You know, one of my old army shrinks would point out that's a clear indication of someone evading the truth or stalling for time.'

Mitch stopped what he was doing and rolled his eyes. 'So speaks the expert.'

Dan shrugged. 'I'm just saying. I've hung out with enough of them over the last couple of years.' He picked up his beer and rubbed his thumb through the condensation collecting on the glass. 'Get on with the story Mitch.'

Mitch looked around the room, then leaned forward, his elbows on his knees. He lowered his voice. 'Secret Service,' he muttered. 'I help them with surveillance and stuff.'

Dan raised an eyebrow. 'Really?'

Mitch nodded.

'What's it like?' asked Dan.

Mitch pointed down to his clothes. 'Beats a proper job,' he grinned.

Dan burst out laughing. Standing up, he pointed at Mitch's beer bottle. 'Another of those?'

Mitch nodded. 'Go on. Then we can compare notes.'

Dan walked over to the bar, handed over one of the red coloured dollar bills and took the beers back to the table in the corner. He handed one to Mitch and looked ruefully at the change in his hand.

'I thought beer was meant to be cheaper over here?' he said.

Mitch grinned and held up his bottle. 'Not if you drink these. And not if you drink here.'

Dan pocketed the loose coins and sat down. 'Okay. What have you found out about Delaney so far?'

'I'll keep it brief – most of it you probably know.' Mitch shuffled, trying to get comfortable in the armchair.

'Delaney owns several large-scale mining operations in Australia. The government here isn't allowing anyone to build any new coal-powered generators, however they are allowing organisations to build clean-coal power stations – the ones that store excess carbon dioxide underground. It's a bit of a balancing act – it keeps the mining companies happy – someone's still burning their coal – and it helps fend off the environmentalists by touting it as "green energy". At the end of the day though, it's just a case of politicians sticking their heads in the sand – coal, oil, whatever, is going to run out and from here on in, it's going to become expensive. You can only open-cut so much coal before you have to go underground to get more – which costs more money.'

'So, you have mining operators like Delaney pushing through their clean-coal projects as fast as they can while no-one has a better alternative on the table – sort of a last hurrah and bank the billions – before it all disappears.' Mitch paused and took a gulp of beer before continuing. 'Add to the fact that all over the world, people are experimenting with the properties of super-conducted precious metals. Of course, the oil and mining companies let them – until it threatens their own existence. Then they'll destroy whoever gets in their way, whether it's by discrediting the research or something more sinister.'

Dan put his beer bottle on the table and sat back in his armchair.

'That's pretty much what I thought,' he said. He told Mitch about what he and Sarah had managed to uncover to date.

Mitch nodded. 'I could use some help if you're interested,' he said.

'What's in it for you?' asked Dan.

'Share what you know with me and I'll watch your back,' suggested Mitch. 'Plus I could probably get my hands on the sort of information you're going to need without putting up a flag.'

Dan sipped his beer and thought hard. It made sense – he and Sarah would only get so far before hitting a dead end, that much was clear. And to have access to the sort of secure information Mitch could lay his hands on would certainly be useful.

'We'll have to talk to Sarah, explain what we're doing,' said Dan. 'Only fair, given it's her ex-husband who got us into this in the first place.'

'Makes sense,' Mitch nodded. 'I wouldn't mind seeing those notes of his.'

Dan put down his empty bottle on the table. 'Well,

she's probably got her nose stuck to the computer screen as we speak, so you may as well come back to the hotel with me,' he said, standing up.

Mitch drained his beer, stood up and stretched.

'Let's do it.'

SEVENTEEN

Dan stepped through the automatic glass doors into the hotel reception area and walked across the polished wooden floor.

Mitch followed, glancing around at his surroundings. 'You're doing all right if you can set up camp here,' he said.

Dan glanced over his shoulder, smiled and shook his head. 'Not me. Sarah's planning on running a story on our findings so she reckons her editor will cover the expenses.'

Mitch caught up with Dan, grabbed hold of his arm and pulled him to a stop. 'No-one said anything about her printing this Dan.' He looked around to make sure no-one could hear them. 'Some of this stuff you say Peter's notes include could be highly classified, you do realise that, don't you?'

Dan shrugged. 'Well, we haven't got anywhere with it

yet, have we? Let's just see what we find out first, yeah? Then let's talk about what does and doesn't get published.'

He began to walk away from Mitch but then turned back. 'And Mitch? Friendly word of advice – don't go saying things like that to Ms Edgewater. There's a very real chance that if you do, you and I will never see those notes again.'

Mitch nodded. 'Fair enough. Just be very careful who knows the content of them – no flashing them around, okay?'

Dan nodded. 'Come on. I'm betting she's still working away on one of the computers in the business centre down here.'

Mitch followed him to the end of the corridor. A frosted glass double door blocked their way. The outline of a figure could be seen, sitting at a low desk.

'Stay here,' murmured Dan, and pushed the door open.

'Hey,' he said, taking off his jacket and strolling over to where Sarah sat, her face illuminated by the light of the computer screen. 'They ran out of canapés.'

Sarah glanced up and smiled. 'If I relied on you to feed me, I'd be ten kilos lighter by now.' She held up an empty plate. 'Luckily, they make half decent sandwiches here.' She put the plate back down on the desk and went back to work.

Dan pulled out a chair next to her and watched. 'Are you having any luck?'

Sarah scrolled through the latest search string she'd

entered, hit a key and sighed. 'I just wish I knew what half this stuff meant – I feel like we're going round in circles.'

'Maybe not,' said a voice behind them.

Sarah turned and saw a thin, wiry sun-tanned man with a gold stud in his left ear, wearing board shorts and a surf t-shirt. He leaned against the door frame, looking fed up.

Sarah looked at Dan. 'Does he belong to you?'

Dan shrugged. 'I've been known to feed him occasionally. Mitch – I thought I told you to wait outside?'

The tall man wandered over. 'I know – I got bored.' He stuck his hand out to Sarah. 'Mitch Frazer.'

Sarah glared at Dan, and then shook Mitch's outstretched hand. 'And you're here because...?'

Dan interrupted. 'He's our secret weapon. There are only so many websites you can access before a flag's going to go up with Delaney's security. You should've seen them crawling over that press conference – god knows who he's got on his payroll. Mitch here is what we call, shall we say, a back-door man.'

Sarah smiled at Mitch, who grinned and sat down at her computer, and then she turned to Dan and pulled him over to a corner of the room.

'Where exactly do you know Mitch from?' she asked in a low voice.

'Army days,' he said, not wanting to elaborate and not sure why. 'I bumped into him outside Delaney's press gig. Turns out he's working here for some people who want Delaney monitored very closely. I figured we might as well use him.'

138

Sarah folded her arms and stared at Dan. 'What's the trade-off though? We tell him everything we know so far?'

Dan nodded. 'We have to stop Delaney, Sarah – no matter what it takes. We've been looking at this for over a week now and we're no closer to working out what he's really up to, are we?'

Sarah's shoulders slumped. 'I know... really, I do. It's just, well, I was sort of looking forward to breaking the story myself.'

'Sarah, this isn't just about a news story, you know better than that. Delaney's dangerous. We have to try to stop him.'

'Anyone fancy going to a party?'

Dan and Sarah turned around to look at Mitch.

Dan frowned. 'What?'

Mitch grinned and inclined his head towards the computer screen. 'Party. At Delaney's. Tomorrow night.'

Sarah glanced sideways at Dan. 'Shall we?'

Dan shrugged. 'Probably – but how the hell are we going to get in?' He looked at Mitch. 'What's the occasion?'

Mitch looked at the computer screen. 'It says here he's celebrating the launch of the new joint venture. It's probably just another way of persuading the right people to provide financial backing after they've consumed copious amounts of free alcohol.'

Dan walked over to the screen and looked at the news report. 'Where did you find this?'

'More to the point,' said Sarah, 'I thought you were

supposed to be helping us with our research, not bumming around on the news sites?'

Mitch grinned and turned to the computer. He scrolled up the web page until Dan saw a familiar banner across the top of the screen.

'ABC website,' he murmured, and looked more closely. He glanced up at Sarah. 'It says Hayley filed this story half an hour ago.'

Sarah smiled. 'And you want me to find out if she can get us in there, right?' She had already pulled out her mobile phone from her bag. 'I just hope she doesn't think we're after invites to every event in town.'

Dan grinned and slapped Mitch on the back. He lowered his voice, aware that Sarah was chattering away in the background on her phone. 'It'd be a perfect opportunity to have a look around.'

Mitch nodded. He glanced out the corner of his eye at Sarah. 'It's going to be heavily guarded, you realise that?'

Dan smiled. 'I always did like a challenge.'

EIGHTEEN

'Good grief Mitch – where'd you get the suit?' laughed Dan.

Mitch looked hurt and pointed at Sarah. 'She made me do it.' He looked down at his outfit. 'I can't remember the last time I couldn't see my legs.'

Sarah rolled her eyes and grabbed his arm, propelling him towards the elevator. 'There's no way I'm letting you walk in there wearing board shorts. We're trying to blend in, remember?' She waited until they were all in the elevator car then pressed the button for the underground car park.

Mitch looked at Dan, who just shrugged.

'She's the boss. Better do as you're told,' he said and stepped out into the basement parking area.

'Help me,' pleaded Mitch as Sarah dragged him out of the elevator and towards the car.

Dan drove the car north, and within half an hour they

had left the bright lights of the city. The dual highway narrowed and Dan checked the GPS – they were now heading westwards, away from suburban civilisation. Large properties lined the roads, mailboxes at the end of long hidden driveways providing the only indication anyone lived in the area. He took a left fork in the road and slowed down, wondering what sort of damage a wallaby would do to a car out here. He didn't talk, just drove and listened to the banter between Sarah and Mitch go quiet as they settled in for the ride. The adrenaline was beginning to kick in. Dan had no idea how Delaney would react if he found out they were at his house.

Mitch began to snore contentedly on the back seat. Dan smiled. *Sleep whenever you get a chance.* It appeared Mitch hadn't forgotten the old rules either.

Dan spotted the house from several miles away. It was huge, even at a distance. It sat perched on a promontory carved out of the volcanic landscape, overlooking the valley and its distant neighbours. He wondered what the views were like and tried to guess how far up the coast he'd be able to see from there.

He slowed, turned on to a minor road and spotted the gates to Delaney's property after a couple of kilometres. Tall granite pillars supported a wrought-iron security gate, guarded by two hired hands. Ornate lanterns fixed to the pillars bathed the entrance in a warm yellow glow, moths and bugs fighting for position on the light bulbs.

'Wake up Mitch, party time,' he said.

Mitch stirred on the back seat. 'Ready when you are.'

Dan stopped the car, left the engine running and lowered his window. He took the invites from Sarah and handed them to the security guard who approached the car.

The man used his torch to read the invites, then shone the light into the car, careful not to shine it right in Dan's face and blind him. He nodded, handed the invites back to Dan, then turned and walked back towards the gate. He hit a switch and the gates slid open silently. He waved the car through and stood back to let them pass.

Dan steered the car carefully up a paved driveway which had once been an earth path cut between tall eucalypt trees. The driveway continued to wind its way up the hill. It had been widened so cars could pass each other. A procession of sports cars and luxury sedans lined the driveway, their owners parking over to one side so others could pass.

Dan pulled over and switched off the engine, then turned to face Sarah and Mitch. 'Right, there are a few rules tonight,' he said. 'First, no risks. Absolutely none. Second, use your real names – might as well. People can tell when you're lying and if Sarah bumps into someone she knows from the media, she's going to have problems if she's using a false name.'

Mitch and Sarah nodded their assent.

'Lastly,' said Dan. 'I'm going to be the only one searching Delaney's property.'

Sarah opened her mouth to protest and Dan put his hand up to stop her.

'That's the rule. Otherwise we turn around now. If

anything goes wrong and I get caught, I need you two to get back to the car and get out of here. Mitch – try to keep an eye on the security guards for me once we're in. I might need you to distract them while I get away from the party and take a look around.'

Mitch nodded. 'Sure.'

'Okay,' said Dan. 'Let's go party.'

They got out of the car and Dan handed Mitch the keys. 'Look after them.'

They began to walk up the driveway to the house. Ornate pots containing exotic plants lined a gravel path which led to a wide stone staircase that swept upwards towards the double front doors which were open, guarded by two more security men as wide as rugby players.

Dan could see holsters strapped to their waists. They looked capable of using them if they had to. As he glanced behind him, he realised more security guards probably prowled the grounds, watching from a distance, and he wondered if they'd shoot first and ask questions later.

The house was extraordinary. It loomed up over the gardens. Built from sandstone brick, two storeys high, a wide deck began at the top of the front steps and wrapped itself around the whole building. The railings were painted to complement the natural stonework of the house. The front doors were open, so as they walked up the front steps they were confronted with the enormity of the hallway. A polished wooden floor gleamed from the lights which swung from the ceiling. It was stylish, Dan had to admit.

The beat of a sound system greeted them as one of the

security guards at the door held up his hand to stop them and checked the invites, before motioning them towards a reception room. The gorilla of a doorman stood to one side and Dan led Sarah and Mitch through to the crowded room. An eclectic crowd laughed, drank, and swayed to the music. A few people stared as they walked towards them.

Dan smiled, giving the impression that, like them, he belonged there. He nodded to a man as he stepped out of the way to let them pass, then turned to a passing waiter and took drinks from the proffered tray.

'Here,' he said to Sarah under his breath as he handed her a glass of wine, 'this will help steady your nerves.'

He turned to Mitch and they clinked their beer glasses together.

'Well,' said Mitch, 'you're in. Now make it count.'

NINETEEN

Dan left Sarah and Mitch and began to walk a slow circuit of the room. He smiled at people when he passed, and made occasional small talk, while he glanced around and checked his surroundings.

Once all the guests had been accounted for, the two security guards on the front door made sporadic forays into the room, checking on their employer while they tried to maintain a low-key presence.

Dan looked out onto the terrace. A few guests lined the ornate railings, while another security guard appeared to be walking a regular circuit around the enclosed deck and patio area, keeping an eye on the guests. Several couples had taken advantage of the pool facilities – the sound of splashing water and laughter carried through the open windows and cut through the music playing in the background.

He turned back to the room, caught the attention of one

of the waiting staff, and handed his empty glass to her. He smiled his thanks as she walked away, then glanced around the room. He moved his eyes slowly, taking in his surroundings, sweeping the crowd of guests at regular intervals. He stepped out into the hallway. Standing to one side to let a giggling couple run past him, he contemplated his next move.

He thought quickly. Whatever he did here tonight, he'd have to make sure he got out with something. Once Delaney found out who was on his trail, they wouldn't get another chance.

He had seen Delaney at the far end of the reception room, but he hadn't yet been spotted. Glancing down the hallway, he glimpsed a staircase guarded by ostentatious ornaments, both of them in bad taste. He nodded to a couple who would now spend the evening wondering how they'd previously made his acquaintance, before he turned and climbed the stairs.

Pretending to admire the artwork on the walls, he glanced up towards the rooms on the next floor as he climbed – all the doors were shut. His eyes wandered across the landing then back down towards the stairs.

He frowned as a familiar figure came into view, climbing the stairs towards him. He walked over and took Sarah by the arm as she stepped onto the landing.

'What the hell are you doing here?' he snapped. 'I thought I told you to stay with Mitch?'

Sarah shrugged off his grip. 'He's fine,' she hissed. 'I wanted to help you.'

Dan shook his head. 'It wasn't Mitch I was worried about,' he said.

Sarah smirked. 'I know. I told him to create a scene if any of the security guards looked like they were heading this way. What's the plan?'

Dan looked down the hallway. 'Try a door I guess.'

He beckoned to Sarah, and then wandered along the hallway.

He kept close to the wall and tested the door handles as he went. Three of the rooms led to what appeared to be guest bedrooms, the next one a lounge area with floor-to-ceiling windows overlooking the airport and docks in the far distance.

Sarah tapped him on the shoulder. 'What are you looking for?' she whispered.

Dan glanced along the hallway, then turned to her. 'A man like Delaney won't keep all his secrets at the office. He must have a study or something at home. And I'll bet it's locked.'

Sarah nodded and gestured for him to continue, looking behind her as they carried on. They passed a large media room, the surfaces of various appliances glinting in the reflection of the light from the hallway, then stopped at the next door. Dan twisted the handle. It held fast. He turned and nodded at Sarah.

Taking a small multi-tool from his pocket, he pushed a sliver of steel into the lock and moved it from side to side. He figured it worked in the movies, so it was worth a try.

He glanced up at Sarah. The dress suited her, he thought, the peach tones complementing her pale skin.

She stared intently at his hands, holding her breath as he worked the lock, then realised he was watching her. 'What?'

Dan nodded his head towards the empty hallway. 'Keep watch – we can't risk anyone seeing us here.'

She nodded, turning her back to him. He risked another glance at the dress, smiling to himself as he worked.

'Dan – there's someone coming!' Sarah hissed.

He looked up from the door, just as the lock clicked open. A man and woman had just left one of the rooms and were walking towards them along the hallway, talking and laughing. Sarah glanced at Dan, fear in her eyes.

He improvised.

Grabbing Sarah's hand, he laughed and dragged her into the room after him, pulled her into an embrace and planted a lingering kiss on her lips. He looked up and winked at the couple as they passed the room, then slammed the door shut.

As the door closed behind her, Sarah pulled away from Dan, stunned. Then she slapped him across the face, hard.

'Hey!'

'What the hell are you doing?' she hissed, flicking on the light switch.

Dan rubbed his cheek, blinking in the sudden light. 'They would've found it suspicious, us sneaking around like that – now they won't think twice about what they just saw,' he said, glaring at her, then laughed, seeing the confused look on her face. 'Don't tell me you thought I was serious.'

Sarah stared at him. 'S-sorry. I – no,' she stumbled, then pushed past him into the room, trying to look busy.

Dan grinned to himself and shrugged. It was a good kiss. He looked around the room, which appeared to be Delaney's private office.

'Bingo,' he murmured. 'Right,' he said, pulling two sets of gloves out of his pocket and handing a pair to Sarah, 'use these. Move things carefully. Put things back where you found them,' he added.

'What are we looking for?' she asked, slipping the gloves on and wandering over to a bookshelf.

Dan walked over to an ornate hardwood desk and switched on a small lamp, illuminating papers, reports, files. 'Everything and anything. Photos, business cards, the lot. Has your phone got a camera function?'

Sarah nodded, patting her bag.

'OK, get it out and for Christ's sake, make sure you've got it switched to silent and the flash is off. We'll just have to hope the detail shows up without it.'

TWENTY

Dan angled the lamp's beam so it avoided the blinds on the windows. He sat down in the chair behind the desk. The seat swallowed his tall athletic body, creating a sudden awareness of the sheer enormity and power of Delaney.

He glanced across the room at Sarah. She turned documents over, frowning and then photographing the occasional page if it warranted further investigation. He smiled to himself. Sarah hadn't asked him how he'd known how to break into the room, which was just as well – he wasn't sure himself how that had happened so easily – but he was happy to take advantage of a bit of luck every now and then.

He looked back down at the desk surface, reached out and ran his fingers along the dark mahogany wood.

He pushed the chair away from the desk – three drawers were fitted on each side, with ornate metal handles protruding from the wood. He started on the left-hand side.

He held the handle of the top drawer between his finger and thumb and tugged it gently. *Locked.* He repeated the process with the remaining two drawers and then turned to his right and began again. All were locked.

Dan slouched back in the chair, thinking hard. He glared at the desk. Then he saw something. He slid off the chair. A thick rug covered the carpet under the desk and chair to prevent it being worn through. He knelt on it and peered at the desk more closely.

Then he grinned. Poking out between the surface of the desk and the lip of the top drawer was the corner edge of a slip of paper. He raised his head above the surface of the desk and called gently.

'Sarah?'

'Hmmm?'

'How long are your fingernails?'

She stopped, a document turned halfway in her hand, and glanced round to look at him. 'What?'

'Come and see this. I need your help.'

He ducked back behind the desk. He looked up as Sarah joined him, then pointed to the corner of the page protruding from the desk. 'Can you get that?'

Sarah crouched down beside him. 'I can have a go. Move over a bit.'

Dan shuffled out of the way. He watched as Sarah raised her hand and put her finger and thumb on each side of the sliver of paper. She paused. Dan held his breath.

Slowly, Sarah increased the pressure against the page and carefully began to pull it towards her. It stuck, momentarily, until Sarah moved it slowly left and right to free it. With a final tug, she pulled the document loose, sat back on her heels and then looked at Dan.

He breathed a sigh of relief. 'Well done. Let's have a look.'

Sarah turned the page over and showed him. It was off-white in colour with small puncture holes running along both sides. He could make out faint red lines crossing the page. He took it from Sarah and read the entries written on the page. He frowned then glanced up at the company logo and details at the top of the document. He eased himself back into the chair.

'It's a shipping manifest,' he said. 'But what the hell is he shipping?'

Sarah stood up and looked over his shoulder at the document in his hand. She reached out and pointed at it. 'That's where it's going,' she said. 'S.I.N. – isn't that Singapore?'

Dan nodded. 'I reckon so – it's what was on our luggage tags on the way out here.' He held the page up to the light. 'There's a number here – looks like twelve, twelve, twenty, eleven.'

'The date it left,' said Sarah. 'Whatever it was, we've missed it by over a month.'

Dan scratched his chin and thought hard. 'There's another sequence of numbers here – maybe it's a reference number or something Mitch can track for us.'

Sarah nodded. 'Maybe if we can…'

They both looked up at the sound of a crash and a

shout from outside the door. Dan switched off the desk lamp and folded the shipping manifest. Standing, he slipped it into the pocket of his trousers and pushed Sarah round the desk.

'Quickly,' he whispered. 'Put the back documents you were photographing. Grab your things – make sure you've got everything.'

Sarah hurried to the other side of the room and tidied the documents as best she could.

Dan grabbed her by the arm. 'Leave it. We're out of time.'

He walked over to the door and beckoned to Sarah. 'Come over here. I'm going to open the door to see what's going on. Stay close.'

Sarah nodded.

He gently squeezed her hand. 'Do me a favour. For once, do as you're told. Okay?'

She nodded. 'Okay.'

He hit the light switch and the room plunged into darkness. He grabbed the door knob and twisted it slowly, then began to pull the door in towards him. He stood still and listened. He could hear Mitch at the bottom of the staircase. It sounded like an argument with one of the security guards.

Dan craned his neck around the door frame and looked down the hallway. Opening the door wider, he pulled Sarah out into the hallway with him and closed the door. It locked with a dull click. Dan and Sarah stood still, looking at each other, holding their breath.

Dan nodded, and then walked slowly along the hallway. Carefully, he edged closer to the banister at the top of the stairs and peered over. He could see the top of Mitch's head as well as that of two of the security guards. One of the guards was remonstrating with Mitch.

'This is a private residence sir. You can't go upstairs. Guests are restricted to the lower level this evening.'

Mitch held up his hands. 'I'm sorry guys. I saw one of you walking up the stairs and thought it was okay. I just wanted to take a look at Mr Delaney's art collection. He has some fine pieces around here. He obviously knows his stuff.'

Dan watched as Mitch drew the guards' attention away from the staircase and back out towards the reception. Dan turned and pulled Sarah towards him.

'Listen to me. Go downstairs now, get Mitch and you go and start the car. I think we've been found out. If I'm not out of here in five minutes, you leave. You got that?'

Sarah grabbed hold of his arm. 'We can't leave you!'

Dan pulled her fingers away. 'You can. And you will. Do it – I'll be out as soon as I can. Now go!'

He propelled her across the hallway and down the first steps. She glanced back at him, once, then turned and hurried after Mitch.

Dan heard her improvising a minute later.

'Darling, there you are! It's time to go.' There was a pause. 'Yes, I do apologise – he can be a terrible bore after a few drinks…'

The voices faded. Dan waited until he heard the sound

of the front door close over the murmur of voices from the remaining guests, then began to edge steadily down the stairs.

He almost reached the bottom tread when a security guard emerged from a catering kitchen, turned and looked straight at Dan.

'What do you think you're doing?' he demanded.

Dan froze. 'Looking at art work?' he tried.

He glanced to his left, through the reception room. The patio doors through to the terrace and deck were wide open. He glanced back at the security guard. The guard realised a fraction of a second too late what Dan was planning and made a grab for his arm.

Dan quickly took a step backwards, turned, then bolted for the terrace. He wove his way through the guests in the reception area, pushing people to one side. He could sense the security guard in pursuit.

Dan ran out onto the terrace and looked both ways. Security guards emerged from each side of the house, running along the decking towards him. He glanced behind him, just as the first security guard pushed through the crowd.

Dan turned back, and ran.

He vaulted over the ornate stone railing at the edge of the terrace and felt himself falling through thin air.

TWENTY-ONE

Dan tumbled into a shrubbery, and covered his face with his arms to avoid getting his eyes scratched. He rolled, breaking his fall, then grunted as he came to a stop on the edge of a gravel path. He stood up and looked back up at the terrace. He brushed himself off and grinned up at the security guard staring down at him.

He stopped smiling when he saw the guard reach down to his belt and pull out a small walkie-talkie radio.

Dan looked around, realising the guard's call for reinforcements only left him with a few seconds before he was found. He ran along the gravel path in the direction of the driveway. As he turned a corner, he slid to a stop as another guard ambled towards him from behind a tree, his head down as he whistled gently to himself. Dan forced himself to relax and walked nonchalantly towards the guard.

'Evening,' he commented as he got closer.

'Evening sir – leaving so early?' asked the guard.

'Ah, early morning tomorrow,' shrugged Dan.

Suddenly the guard's radio crackled to life. 'Jimmy? Watch out for a bloke, about six feet four, brown hair, black suit and tie. Probably looks like he fell into a hedge. He did. Apprehend him if you see him and bring him back to the house.'

The guard looked up at Dan, stunned. Dan made the most of the split-second delay. He ducked out of reach of the security guard as he made a half-hearted grab for his jacket and then ran down the path. Vaulting over the security rope slung across the end of the path, he ran head-first down the steps of the manicured gardens. Reaching the ornamental lawns, he looked up long enough to check the car was parked on the driveway. Sure enough, it was there. Mitch had parked it right between the pillars at the entrance to the driveway so the security gate couldn't be closed on Dan.

Glancing to his right, Dan spotted two guards energetically running down the length of the driveway between the trees, gaining on him. He ran for the car. He saw another guest's vehicle coming around the bend from the direction of the house. He couldn't risk slowing down, the guards were too close. He lunged forwards and as the car passed him, he slid across the bonnet of the small sedan. As it skidded to a shocked halt, the driver slammed the heel of his hand on the horn.

Dan picked himself up off the grass, stumbled to his feet and began to run across the lawn to the car. He could feel his lungs burning, his legs aching with every last stride. He slid to a halt next to the vehicle. Pulling the door open, he threw himself onto the back seat head-first and pulled the door shut behind him.

'Go, go!' he urged, careering backwards as the car accelerated and lurched into the narrow lane.

He pushed himself up straight and peered between the seats. 'Slow down and turn there – let's not draw any more attention to ourselves than we need to,' he said, rubbing his hand over his eyes. 'Jesus, Mitch, your driving skills haven't changed, have they? I still feel like I'm doing the bloody Paris-Dakar whenever I'm with you.'

'No, you're right,' said Mitch drily as he peered across from the passenger seat. 'I still leave it to others while I do the navigating.'

Dan did a double-take and looked at the driver's seat. 'Sarah? What the hell are you doing?'

She laughed. 'Mitch didn't get a chance to tell you he's not allowed to drive anymore, so it looks like you're stuck with me.'

'Could be worse, I suppose,' mused Dan, then yelped as Sarah accelerated down the mountain. 'Hey, steady!'

Delaney stared at the computer monitors, his eyes searching. 'There. Stop the playback.'

The head of security obeyed.

Delaney jabbed a finger at a frozen image of Sarah. 'Who the hell is she?'

The other man hit some buttons and the image enlarged. 'We'll soon find out.'

Delaney followed as he stood up and walked over to a series of desks, each with its own computer. He ignored the young security guard who was now slumped dejectedly at the row of monitors. Playing games on his mobile phone, he had missed the evening's activities and was now regretting his earlier laziness.

Sitting down, the head of security punched a series of buttons and brought up a copy of the image on his computer screen, then ran a program.

Delaney peered at the screen as images flashed by. 'Where did we get this from?' he asked, indicating the program.

The head of security chuckled. 'Best you don't know, sir.'

Delaney nodded. He didn't really care, as long as it worked.

'Here we go.'

The computer program emitted a soft *ping* as two images appeared side-by-side – the image from Delaney's security cameras and another, taken some years before at an outdoor media function, the woman's hair blowing around her face as she stood laughing next to her colleagues. The head of security typed out a search string and Delaney waited while the computer hunted through its massive database. Suddenly, a text box appeared, and the security guard began to scroll through the words.

'It says here she's a reporter with the *Telegraph* in the UK. Strange – she seems to be a prolific writer but hasn't filed a story for a number of weeks now. Hang on.' The man opened the next page of text. 'It says here her ex-husband was killed last month.'

Delaney stopped pacing the room and turned to stare at the two images on the screen. 'What's her name?'

The head of security hit a key, bringing up a new window with a driver's licence displayed on it. 'Sarah Edgewater.'

Delaney blew the air out of his cheeks. He glanced down at the holster hanging from the other man's belt. He reached down and pulled the gun out of it. 'Are these any good?' he asked, turning the weapon over in his hands.

The man looked at him. 'I wouldn't use anything else.'

Delaney grunted. He released the safety catch and strode over to where the young security guard sat. And then shot him between the eyes. Delaney turned back to the screen showing Sarah's image and pointed at it.

'Call Charles.'

TWENTY-TWO

Hayley walked through the car park, rummaging in her handbag for her keys. The basement echoed with the sound of car doors slamming shut and engines being started as the last of the day's commuters settled themselves in for the journey home.

As she approached her car, Hayley hit the remote, killing the alarm system. Opening the door, she tossed her handbag onto the passenger seat and turned the key in the ignition.

The engine coughed, then stalled.

Cursing, Hayley turned the key again and lightly tapped the accelerator. The car roared into life and Hayley breathed a sigh of relief. It was old and temperamental but she wasn't in a position to buy a new one just yet. Besides, she had a soft spot for it – it was a small two-door four-wheel drive, ideal for getting around town without being a gas-guzzler.

While she waited for the engine to warm up, Hayley pulled off her three-inch heels, slipped on a pair of flat sandals and then released the handbrake.

As she pulled out of the parking space, she hit the brakes hard. A man had walked out in front of her car, obviously lost in thought as he polished his glasses. Hayley gestured at him to hurry up and he raised his hand apologetically before picking up speed and jogging past her through the car park.

Easing the car out of the space and weaving her way out of the basement area, Hayley noticed a stream of traffic queuing to get in – early theatre patrons, eager to find a place before they went for their pre-show evening meal.

Reaching the exit, Hayley leaned out the window and pushed her prepaid ticket into the machine. She tapped her fingers absently on the steering wheel as she waited for the barrier to rise. As she slipped through the exit, a white rental sedan pushed its way into the line of traffic, ignoring the frustrated gestures from other drivers and slipped into the queue behind Hayley, waiting for the traffic lights to turn green.

Hayley turned right, drove over the bridge spanning the river and switched on the radio. Water from a brief summer storm earlier in the afternoon glistened on the bitumen. The white sedan behind her kept a respectable distance, while all the time making sure no other cars could slip in between them. Unaware, Hayley pulled up at the next red light before making her way down Caxton Street and up through Paddington.

The temperature had dropped a little after the rain. Hayley powered down her window and switched off the air-conditioning, enjoying the breeze that blew through the car. Pulling up at a pedestrian crossing, she gazed at the restaurants to her right, already beginning to fill with the evening's patrons. The lights turned green and she accelerated, turning right and headed towards Ashgrove. There would be no restaurant outing for her tonight, she thought sadly – too much work to do. She smiled. At least there was a good bottle of Verdelho waiting in the refrigerator.

Her house on Mount Nebo was a good twenty kilometres out of the city and it never ceased to amaze her that within an hour she could be winding her way up the mountain and into the bush, away from the frantic pace of the city. She passed the last set of traffic lights at The Gap and relaxed, pushing the accelerator a little. As she did so, she checked her rear-view mirror and frowned. The headlights of the car behind her hadn't changed since leaving the city.

As Hayley eased the car round the left-hand bend, she accelerated hard, the small car protesting against the sharp incline at the start of the mountain road. Red dirt lined each side of the narrow bitumen highway before dropping away sharply to dry rainforest and granite rocks.

She reached the top of the first incline and glanced in the rear-view mirror – the other car's headlights were still on her tail. Her heart beat faster as she tried to visualise the upcoming bends in the road. The road was the only direct route along the mountain – any roads leading off it for the next eight kilometres would simply lead to scenic viewpoints and picnic areas.

Properties along the road had long driveways, often sealed with steel gates. She wouldn't be able to simply drive off the road and onto someone's private property for help – if it turned out they weren't home, she'd have nowhere to turn and no way to escape her pursuer.

Hayley forced herself to ease off the accelerator a little as she approached a notorious double-bend – the small memorials on the corner erected by friends and families of previous crash victims served as a reminder of the road's reputation.

As she exited the bend, the car behind her accelerated hard, hitting her small four-wheel drive and throwing her forwards in her seat. Hayley screamed and hit the accelerator, swerving round the next bend and almost hitting a car coming in the opposite direction. She forced herself to slow down again, her hands shaking as she changed gear.

Hayley braked hard, trying to steer the car round another sharp curve in the road. As she did so, the car behind her sped up and slammed into the back of her vehicle, turning it into the granite hillside. Hayley screamed and flicked the steering wheel to the right, desperately trying to avoid an impact but the back of the car began to slide across the wet bitumen. Instinctively, she stepped on the accelerator to try to control the skid but the vehicle swung too far the other way.

Hayley screamed and threw her hands up to protect her face as the car pivoted, smashed into the barrier at the edge of the ravine and crashed down through the trees lining the mountain road.

The car rolled side over side before landing upside down against an old eucalypt, the tyres spinning slowly as the engine spluttered to a stop.

———————

The driver of the sedan pulled over into a small parking area a few metres along the road and switched off his headlights.

Opening the door, Charles got out and slipped on his jacket. He casually shrugged it over his shoulders and fastened the two buttons down the front. Looking both ways, he checked there was no other traffic coming and switched on a small high-beam torch. He slipped on a pair of gloves, then pulled plastic bags over his shoes and walked over to the barrier. Tell-tale skid marks showed where Hayley's car had left the road. Burning rubber from her car tyres filled the air, permeating the sticky-sweet scent of the eucalypts.

Charles stepped over the skid marks and churned up grass verge, being careful not to leave tread marks from his shoes. The plastic bags would only serve to disguise the tread a little. Leaning over the edge of the ravine, he shone the torch down to where the car was lying upside down, the bonnet crumpled against a tree and the side panels dented and scraped apart by its uncontrolled descent. Glass glinted on the ground around the vehicle, while various parts lay strewn down the ravine, showing the car's progress as it rolled.

Charles caught the sound of movement from the vehicle below and strained his ears. It was Hayley, calling for help. He held the torch up as a hand appeared, waving desperately out of the driver's window.

Charles placed the small torch between his teeth, holding it while he reached into his pocket. He pulled out a cigarette lighter and methodically flicked it to life. He held up the flame to his face, mesmerised by the heat and colour. Calmly lowering the lighter, he took the torch from between his teeth and held the beam steady while he tossed the lighter towards Hayley's upturned vehicle, aiming it at the fuel dripping from the rear of the wreckage.

The car lifted off the ground with the force of the explosion before rocking to a halt at the base of the tree, flames beginning to lick at the undergrowth and surrounding bushes.

Charles stood and watched the flames as they engulfed the car. Hayley's screams penetrated the night air. He smiled as they gradually died away. Swinging the torch beam across the grass verge at his feet, he scuffed the faint tread marks from his shoes into the mud, obliterating any chance of a forensic team finding a trace of his existence. Switching off the torch, he hurried back to the car and started the engine, coaxing the vehicle back down the mountain.

By the time he reached the outer suburbs of Brisbane, two fire engines had raced past his car, heading up to the scene of the accident.

TWENTY-THREE

The caller dialled a sixteen digit number then put the mobile to his ear and heard the tell-tale ring tone of a foreign exchange.

He walked briskly through the park as he waited for the call to be answered. He looked up as a fruit bat swooped low over his head then watched as it flew, screeching, into the trees. The lights from the city shone through the trees in places near the boundary of the gardens. He walked deeper into the park, away from the light and disappeared into the shadows near the river, following a concrete bike track which swept around the park and past the university campus.

As he walked, he turned his head and looked around to check if he'd been followed. Finally, the phone connected.

'Philippa Price.'

'Pip, it's me,' the caller said. 'Is this line secure?'

'It is.'

'We've got company.'

Silence at the other end.

The caller waited for Philippa to speak and began to pace along the pathway circling the gardens. He stopped and stepped off the path as a lone cyclist pedalled past him. Looking back to check his progress, the caller continued to walk.

Eventually, Philippa spoke. 'How much does she know?'

'Not she, they,' corrected the caller. 'And they're making good progress.'

'Who's helping her?'

The caller chuckled. 'Tell David it's an old friend of his. He'll work it out if you can't.' He smiled to himself, knowing Philippa would make sure she found out before telling their boss.

The caller could hear Philippa's breathing over the line. Calm, calculating. 'Does she have the lecture notes?'

'Yes. And photos. And stuff her ex-husband didn't want the public eye to see. It's explosive stuff, Pip. I wouldn't want to see her publishing any of it.'

'What are their plans?'

'Right now, they've located a shipping container which left Brisbane for Singapore. I reckon they'll be on a plane there within the next couple of days to try to find out what's in it.'

'A shipping container?'

'Uh-huh. Do you think that's what Delaney's using?'

Silence. Then, 'Maybe. Can you find out anything to confirm that?'

'I can try.'

'Will you follow them to Singapore?'

'Not unless David says so. It might make them suspicious.'

'True.' Silence again.

The caller stopped, glanced around him, then sat on a park bench. His eyes ached. He rubbed them with his free hand and yawned. He slouched, trying to get comfortable against the rough surface of the seat. 'How much closer are you getting?'

He could hear a sigh at the end of the phone line before Philippa spoke. 'It feels like we're getting nowhere fast. At the moment, I'm going through mergers and acquisitions to find out what gold mine interests Delaney has. We can't find out what he's really up to though. We think it's something to do with when the white gold powder is turned back into metallic gold – some sort of atomic reaction.'

'Like a dirty bomb?'

'Yeah, something like that. David's trying to get information from the other agencies here but of course, chances are they're playing around with the stuff themselves so they're not exactly being helpful at the moment.'

'I'll bet.'

'Listen, I'm going to have to go – we've got a briefing

with the Minister in half an hour I'm supposed to be preparing for. Was there anything else you needed?'

'Not at the moment. Look out for them in Singapore in a couple of days. I'll phone you if I find out anything else.'

'Okay, take care Mitch.'

———

The elevator car rose through the building. Dan cast his eyes sideways at the mirrored walls and noticed how tired they both looked. He could feel the adrenaline through his veins, keeping him fired up in spite of the exhaustion. He smiled to himself. He couldn't remember the last time he had felt so energised, so focused. As the elevator ground to a halt, Sarah brought out her swipe card and waved it at him.

'Nightcap at mine?' she asked, raising an eyebrow.

He grinned. 'If your expense account can afford the mini-bar prices here, then you can definitely count me in.'

He followed her down the hallway and waited while she unlocked the door to her room.

She flicked on the light and dumped her bag next to the television. 'I'm too excited to sleep anyway,' she explained. 'I feel like we're finally getting somewhere at last. Get yourself a drink – I want to change out of this dress.' She closed the bathroom door behind her.

Dan walked over to the refrigerator and turned back, holding two beers. Twisting the lids off, he handed one of them to Sarah as she emerged from the bathroom dressed in jeans and t-shirt. They clinked their beer bottles together and grinned at each other.

Sarah turned and picked up her bag. Pulling out her mobile phone, she reached over and picked up her laptop. 'Might as well take a closer look at those documents I photographed,' she said. She sat down on the bed and switched on the laptop.

Dan slumped on the small two-seater sofa, his legs hanging over the end. He swung them lazily while he sipped his beer and held up the manifest to the light to read it again.

Sarah took a swig from her bottle of beer, waiting for the laptop to finish its start-up routine. She reached behind her and pushed the pillow further up her back. Curling her legs under her, she sat back and sighed as she flipped through the pictures as they downloaded from her phone. 'I took some pictures of some invoices,' she explained. 'It looks like they're for small amounts of chemicals. Will that help?'

Dan looked up briefly from the manifest, and then continued reading. 'I'm not sure – Harry reckons you'd need a ton of equipment to manufacture it – I think we're missing something on that one.'

Sarah continued to flick through the images they'd downloaded, carefully looking at each one as it appeared on the screen. 'I might have something here. Letters to government ministers. Here and back in the UK. Looks like Delaney's been a bit busy lobbying them to support mining industries rather than the environmentalists. I wonder if he...'

They both jumped as the phone on the small desk began to ring.

Dan looked at Sarah. 'Did you give anyone this number?'

She shook her head. 'Should we answer it?'

Dan walked over to the phone, his hand hovering above it. He turned to Sarah. 'You answer it.'

He stepped away, waving her over to the phone. 'Quickly.'

Sarah stumbled across the room. 'Why me?'

'Because you're a known entity with friends in this city – I'm not. Whoever is phoning might not know about my existence yet – I'd like to keep it that way as long as possible.'

Sarah nodded. 'Okay – pass me that notepad and a pen would you? If this is anything important, I don't want to forget anything.'

She picked up the receiver. 'H-hello?'

A chuckle permeated the line. 'Well, well. You are there after all. For a minute there, I thought you were going to ignore me.'

Sarah clutched the receiver. 'Who is this?'

'You're not much of a journalist if you can't work that out for yourself.'

Sarah heard a sigh, as if the caller was sitting himself down for a long chat.

He then continued. 'Now, I'm only going to say this

once because you're an intelligent woman and will probably take good advice when it's given.'

'Save the flattery,' Sarah interrupted. 'What the hell do you want?'

Again, the chuckle. 'Okay, if you won't be civil, then I'll get to the point.'

'At last,' said Sarah.

'What are you doing next Wednesday?' The caller paused, waiting for a response.

'Next Wednesday? Why? What's happening next Wednesday?' asked Sarah, snatching the notepad and pen Dan waved at her.

'I presume, as a journalist, you're writing all this down?' asked the caller.

'Yes.'

'Good. I hate repeating myself.'

'Go on,' urged Sarah.

'Write this down – two o'clock, next Wednesday. Place called 'Pinaroo' on Albany Creek Road.'

Sarah did as she was told.

'What's there?' she asked, as she held up the notepad for Dan to read. He shook his head, not knowing the answer.

'It's a crematorium,' said the caller. 'You wouldn't want to be late for Hayley's funeral, would you?'

The phone went dead as Sarah dropped the receiver, covering her mouth with her hands.

'What is it? What did he say?' urged Dan, grabbing hold of Sarah and turning her towards him.

She shook her head in response, unable to answer. She shrugged off his grip from her shoulders and ran to the bathroom. He began to follow her, and then stopped as the sound of her vomiting reached him. He spun round in the room, running his hand through his hair, feeling utterly helpless and unsure what to do. What the hell had just happened?

He waited until the noises from the bathroom ceased, then took one of the water glasses from the small kitchenette and filled it with cold water. Walking through to the bathroom, he tentatively opened the door.

'Hello?'

The door opened, the smell of vomit reeking through the small room. He ignored it, instead taking in the figure hunched over on the downturned toilet seat, her head in her hands.

'Sarah?'

Dan crouched down next to her, setting the water glass on the floor.

'Talk to me Sarah. Who was that? What just happened?'

He reached over and took her head in his hands, raising it until he could look her in the eyes.

'Sarah, talk to me. Who was that? What did he say to you?'

She shook her head, closing her eyes and refusing to look at him.

'Please.'

He let go, gently, willing her to start talking to him.

Sarah took a deep, ragged breath then turned, pulled a wad of toilet tissue off the roller next to her and blew her nose. Holding onto the sodden tissue, she gazed at him, then through him.

'They've killed Hayley.'

Dan sat back on the tiled floor, stunned.

'I don't know who it was on the phone,' continued Sarah. 'But I can hazard a guess, as I'm sure you can.'

Dan ran his hand over his face. 'Jesus, Sarah.'

'Yeah, well he's not much good right now – never was, never will be,' Sarah retorted, standing up and flipping the toilet lid. Throwing the tissue in the bowl, she pressed the flush button.

Dan handed the glass of water up to her. 'Here.'

Sarah took it from him, finishing its contents in two gulps. She handed the glass back to him as he stood up.

'Sarah, I don't think Hayley would have wanted you to quit now – we're too close to finding out what's really going on,' he said, following her into the living area. 'At least we got what we needed. We can follow up those leads up tomorrow, book flights to Singapore and find where that container is.'

Sarah spun round, glaring at him. 'What did you say?'

He shrugged. 'Hayley was a journalist too. She'd want to know why this is all happening. We can't give up now – she wouldn't have wanted us to.'

Sarah put her hands on her hips, glaring at him. 'Oh, is that right? Well, when I see her parents back in the UK, I'll be sure to convey that to them. I'm sure they'll be really fucking chuffed to know that.'

She snatched up her handbag from the table. 'You know what Dan? Sometimes, there's more to life than just finding out the answers. I just lost a really good friend because I agreed to help you work out what Peter's research notes said. The same damn notes that got *him* killed.'

Dan reached out to her and she drew back, snarling.

'Don't you dare. How many people have to die Dan? How many?' she gulped. 'Christ, I wish I'd never met you. I wish I'd never agreed to help you.'

She swept past him.

'Sarah – don't go – it's not safe!' Dan commanded, reaching out to grab her arm.

'Fuck you,' she hissed, shrugging off his grip.

He turned and punched the wall in frustration. He felt the rush of air as Sarah stormed out of the room, and closed his eyes as she slammed the door behind her. He rubbed his hand over his face in disbelief, angry with himself. Closing his eyes, he tilted his head back, blinking hard.

'Dammit,' he breathed. 'Fuck.'

He kicked the end of the hotel bed, sending splinters flying over the cheap carpet, and then slumped down on the soft mattress, running his hand through his hair.

Dan nearly gave himself whiplash as the phone rang, making him jump. He stood up, pulling the mobile out of his pocket.

'Hello?'

The caller sniffed hard.

'Sarah?'

'You bastard. You complete and utter inconsiderate idiot…'

He held the phone away from his ear, letting the tirade finish before taking a deep breath. 'I'm sorry.'

'Sorry?' choked Sarah, 'Do you have any idea?'

He closed his eyes. 'I screwed up.'

'You certainly did.'

Dan began to pace the room. 'Sarah, I need you to come back here. We need to move on – it's getting too dangerous. Delaney has worked out who you are – that has to be why Hayley was killed. It's a warning to us…'

A sharp knock on the motel room door interrupted him. Dan threw the door open. Sarah stood in the hallway, the phone in her hand.

He raised an eyebrow. 'Finished?'

She nodded.

'Feel better?' He stood aside as she stalked past him into the apartment.

'Asshole.'

He smiled. At least they were back on familiar territory.

TWENTY-FOUR

London, England

Dressed in a grey trouser suit, Philippa strode across the open-plan office, the carpet doing little to silence her step as she hurried to one of the glass-panelled rooms at the rear of the large open space, glancing at the documents in her hand.

She stepped sideways to avoid a harried secretary before approaching the office on the right and peering through the glass wall. The room was in darkness, the light from a presentation on the opposite wall illuminating the rapt faces of the occupants. She straightened, knocked once and stepped into the room, flicking on the lights to a chorus of protests.

'Hey!

'Philippa! Turn off the lights!'

Philippa ignored them and strode across to the meeting room table and began to hand out copies of the documents to each delegate.

Closing the presentation, David Ludlow stood and reached over the boardroom-style table for the sheaf of papers Philippa was waving at him. 'What have you got?'

Philippa pulled out a spare chair and sat down, pulling herself closer to the table with her heels and folded her arms. 'An old friend of yours just resurfaced.'

David sat down and began to flick through the documents. Following his cue, the four delegates in the room began to read the papers in front of them while Philippa studied David's face for any trace of emotion.

David threw his copy on the table, clasped his hands behind his head and stared at the ceiling, deep in thought.

One of the delegates, a young man fresh out of university with a teenager's acne problem stopped reading and looked first at Philippa, then David, confused. 'Sorry, sir, but what exactly are we looking at?'

David chuckled, lowering his hands. 'Steve, what we have here is a way to get close to Delaney – without actually getting involved.'

Philippa nodded. 'As well as having military training, this guy also has a geology background so once he realises what white gold powder is capable of, I reckon he'll help us do whatever it takes to stop Delaney.'

David stood up and motioned to the four analysts sitting round the table. 'We'll continue this meeting tomorrow morning. Have your reports updated to include the latest facts, run the scenarios again and give me a one-page summary before you leave tonight.'

He turned to Philippa as he opened the door. 'Find out what Dan Taylor has been up to since leaving the army three years ago. I want everything.'

Philippa knocked on David's office door and walked in. David sat at his desk, his phone to his ear. He motioned to Philippa to sit in the chair opposite him. As she waited for David to finish his call, Philippa cast her eyes around the room. Framed commendations jostled for position with photographs on one wall – pictures of David during his varied military career – in the jungle, in the desert, Belize, Iraq, Cyprus and a few unidentified locations in between.

And then after. The bravery award, the recruitment out of the army and a side-step into the secret services and a reputation built quickly on fast results with minimum fuss.

Philippa wondered how many politicians' careers would be left in shreds if David was ever cornered or compromised by his superiors. She glanced round as David slammed the phone down.

'Problem?'

He shook his head. 'No – he's just further along than I gave him credit for. That reporter friend of his obviously does a good job.'

Philippa frowned, her natural competitiveness surfacing, briefly, before being locked away again. She changed the subject. 'I've found out what your friend has been up to for the past three years.' She tossed a thin manila file onto David's desk.

He picked it up and tested its weight, before looking up at her. 'I presume the answer is 'not much'?'

Philippa rolled her eyes. 'Talk about a lost cause.' She pushed back the chair and stretched out her legs. 'After being discharged from the army, it looks like he went back into mineral exploration. Just as a hired hand, mind – nothing permanent.'

She watched as David flicked through the file contents. She continued to recite the potted history from memory. 'In between geology assignments, he seems to have floated around the globe. Worked in a bar in Marsaxlokk in Malta for four months, then as a cook for a Greek island tour company. Seems to have been fired from most jobs he's had over the past couple of years. I've found evidence of his passport being used in Canada, Brazil, Argentina, New Zealand – pretty much anywhere that has a mining industry...'

David shook his head in wonderment. 'He seems to go off the rails after every geology job,' he said as he flipped through the documents. 'Some things don't change – he's still trying to get out from under his father's shadow,' he murmured.

Philippa frowned. 'What's all that about?'

David shrugged. 'His father was a well-known minerals expert. Spent most of Dan's childhood travelling the world for mining companies. He was responsible for some of the biggest mineral deposit finds in the nineteen seventies and made an absolute fortune. I remember Dan saying once he felt like he could never get out from under his father's shadow. Shame really – reading this, they both seem to have the same sense of adventure.'

He threw the file down on his desk.

'So, what's the next step – follow them?' asked Philippa.

David nodded. 'You and I are going to Singapore – I want to monitor him more closely. Plus, I don't want him pushing Delaney too hard. We need to find out if Delaney has in fact managed to create some sort of weapon from this stuff, before jumping in.'

Philippa watched David closely before speaking, then chose her words carefully. 'We do need to take control of whatever he's created too,' she said. 'There's no point letting it be destroyed for the sake of it. The technology would be... useful.'

'Our priority is to find it and prevent it being used against us,' David corrected her. 'If, and only if, those two factors have been taken care of to my satisfaction, will I start to worry about the technology behind it.'

Philippa shrugged as David stood up and wandered over to the wall of photographs. He pulled one of them off the wall, and stared at the four men grinning, standing next to their Warrior armoured vehicle in the middle of a barren desert landscape, the breeze ruffling their shirt sleeves. David had his arm round the shoulders of another man, the pair of them laughing at the photographer, pointing to something out of the camera's view.

Philippa joined him and stared at the photograph. 'Do you think he'll do it?'

David sighed, then carefully set the frame back on its picture hook. 'I think he will once he realises what the odds are against us. He's incredibly loyal. He's never let his mates down before, despite what he thinks.'

Philippa stepped away and gathered up her notebook from the desk. 'I'd better go and make sure our flights get booked then.'

TWENTY-FIVE

Singapore

The check-in formalities complete, Dan and Sarah put their bags in the hotel room and decided the balcony was the best place to spend the humid evening, with an occasional raid to the room's mini bar facilities.

They sat at a small table, Dan with his chair wedged in a corner between the balcony and the room, and gradually worked through Peter's notes and the prints of the photos Sarah had taken in Delaney's study.

Dan rubbed his hand over his eyes. 'Some of this stuff is incredible. You just don't realise how much influence industry has over politics, do you?'

Sarah nodded. 'I know. I never know whether to be angry or depressed about it. The thing is, Peter was right – it very rarely gets reported. I mean, look at this,' she said, holding up a newspaper clipping. 'Here's a report on how the major oil and gas players have used lobby groups to plan protest marches against US environmental policy changes – by using scare tactics threatening the loss of jobs in the industry if any emissions trading scheme was implemented.' She threw the article down in disgust. 'No wonder the public has lost interest.'

'Yeah, but if these people are willing to kill to prevent people like Peter drawing it to the public interest, maybe they should be taking notice,' added Dan.

'Do you really believe that?' Sarah put down the document she was holding.

Dan shuffled the notes back into place. 'Well, if Peter was going around telling everyone about this wonder-fuel that could effectively put the oil, gas and coal industry out of business, then yes.' He leaned back, propping the chair against the wall. 'Someone out there is extremely serious about preventing that technology being used and it's looking more and more like Delaney.' He shook his head. 'I thought they were all going on about clean-coal technology being the best compromise.'

'That's being pushed through as a quick-fix for climate change,' said Sarah. 'Clean coal technology is expensive – not to mention inefficient. Yes, it'll cut down on carbon emissions but to get the same output as one of the old-style coal power stations, you need to burn up to forty per cent more coal.'

'That kind of defeats the object for being 'clean' then,' said Dan.

'Not to mention why the coal producers are rubbing their hands with glee – imagine what the demand for coal will be once this so-called 'clean' technology is perfected – especially in places like India and China.' Sarah put her notebook down. 'No, the truth is, compared with all the other alternatives, coal is still a cheaper and more reliable fuel to power generation companies.'

'So, where do you think this white gold powder comes in?' mused Dan.

Sarah leafed through the research notes. 'From what I can tell, Peter's just used that as a reference point – it's when gold is put through a piece of equipment called a spectroscope at a high temperature. Apparently it can develop a white gold powder that organisations like the defence industry are interested in but also the energy companies – if they can harness that power, we won't need coal and oil anymore.' She yawned and stretched. 'Remind me again why we've only got one room?'

Dan smiled. 'Because I'd worry about you if you were somewhere else.' He stood up and leaned on the balcony and watched the lights across Boat Quay below. 'You can choose which bed you want though.'

'Ah, the perfect gentleman, right?' laughed Sarah.

Dan winked. 'No, I just knew I was going to lose that argument, so I'll quit while I'm ahead.' He walked back to the mini bar and picked up another beer before heading back out to the balcony. 'Sleep well.'

Dust, blood, screaming, the sheer noise...

Dan woke up with a start, sweat beading on his brow. A light was on. He glanced around the room, trying to get his bearings. His heart was racing and he panted like he'd been running. He blinked, and concentrated on the present. And saw Sarah sitting on the edge of his bed.

'What's wrong?' he asked, blinking in the light of the small bedside lamp.

Sarah smiled, just a little. 'Nothing – I mean, I'm fine.' She looked away. 'You were shouting out in your sleep – it sounded urgent.'

Dan ran his hand over his eyes and sat up. 'Sorry – must've been dreaming.'

Sarah ran her eyes over the scars criss-crossing over his chest and arms before looking away and speaking again. 'It sounded more like a nightmare.'

Dan nodded. 'Same one, at least twice a week.' He sighed. 'That's an improvement though.'

'Would it help to talk about it?'

Dan shook his head. 'Twelve months of army shrinks couldn't fix it so, no, it probably wouldn't.'

He reached up and touched her cheek, warm, soft. Sarah smiled, never taking her eyes off him. He ran his hand down her shoulder, and then rubbed his thumb gently over a bruise on Sarah's arm. She winced.

'Sorry,' he smiled. 'I didn't realise it hurt.'

She shrugged. 'I'm not as tough as you.'

Dan looked at her, keeping his hold on her wrist. 'I don't know – you're doing pretty well, so far.'

Sarah pulled away, then stood up and crossed the room. She browsed the small bottles lined up next to the kettle and selected two. She unscrewed the metal caps and tossed them into the waste basket. One missed, clipped the edge of the basket and bounced onto the cheap carpet. She ignored it. She turned back to Dan and held up the two small bottles. 'Brandy or whiskey?'

'Whiskey.'

She handed him the bottle, then eased herself back onto the end of his bed. Taking a sip of the brandy, almost as if to steady herself, she looked at Dan. 'I know absolutely nothing about you, do I?'

Dan smiled gently. 'Just as well. You wouldn't want dreams like these.'

'Do you trust anyone?'

He shook his head. 'Not really. I've given up, to be honest. From my experience, it just leads to disappointment.'

Sarah looked away again.

Dan kicked her gently through the sheets. 'Don't take it personally. It's just the way it is.'

She nodded, and watched Dan take a swig of the whiskey. He grimaced, and then glared at the label.

'Rough?' Sarah asked.

'Bloody awful,' he grinned. 'Which probably means it'll work.'

TWENTY-SIX

The Singapore skyline shimmered in the early morning haze. Sarah turned up the air conditioning in the car, then glanced up and looked out the windscreen as Dan steered the car along the busy highway. She checked the map laid out open on her lap and pointed left.

'Here,' she said. 'This is Keppel Harbour. The entrance to the docks should be about a mile down here on the left.'

Sarah studied the map. 'Look out for a sign to Pasir Panjang. I spoke to a guy at the freight company before we left Brisbane – he said it would have probably been unloaded there.'

Dan slowed the car and made the turn. 'Have you thought about how we're going to get through the gates?' he asked. 'I'm presuming it's going to be guarded.'

Sarah rummaged in her bag and held up an identity card.

'Press identification. I'll tell them I'm running a story

on the shipping port for a travel magazine or something. Hopefully they won't ask too many questions.'

Dan slowed as the entrance to the docks came into view.

'There's the sign for the terminal,' said Sarah, pointing to her left.

A small, stocky man leaned out of a small cinderblock guard house, saw the car approaching and stepped out next to the horizontal red and white striped barrier blocking their way. He motioned to Dan to stop.

Dan wound the window down and slowed the car to a halt, leaned his elbow on the window frame and tried his best to look nonchalant.

'Help you?' asked the guard. Not friendly. Not helpful. Just doing the same job, day after day.

Sarah leaned over Dan and smiled up at the guard as she flashed her press identity card at him. 'Hi! I'm from the UK. I'm writing an article about the shipping port for a magazine for cruise passengers. My editor should've phoned ahead.'

The guard inclined his head and grunted. Thought about it. 'And him?' he asked, pointing at Dan.

'I'm the photographer,' grinned Dan. 'We should get some great shots this evening with that sunset.'

The guard nodded. 'Wait here.' He returned to the guard house. The barrier stayed down.

'What's he doing?' whispered Sarah.

'Probably looking for a record of when your 'editor' phoned.'

They could see the guard through the window of his concrete and corrugated iron roof hut. His head was down. The tops of pages could be seen as they flickered in and out of view as he went through a register. Eventually he glanced up. He looked out the window straight at Dan and Sarah as they sat in the car, hopeful expressions on their faces. Dan smiled and raised his hand at the guard.

'What's going on?' said Sarah. 'Is he going to let us in do you think?'

'No idea,' murmured Dan as the guard came back out of the guard house and began walking back towards the car.

He frowned, carrying a clipboard. 'When did you say your editor called?' he asked.

'I didn't,' said Sarah, still smiling, 'but I think it was last week some time. I really don't know – I was too busy trying to book a last-minute flight.'

The guard straightened up and looked beyond the barrier to the docks ahead. Dan and Sarah followed his gaze. They were tantalisingly close.

The guard seemed to make a decision. Perhaps he didn't want to be mentioned in the article as being an example of over-zealous bureaucrats; perhaps it was just the end of his shift. He bent down to Dan's open window again and thrust the clipboard at him.

'Okay. You both sign here.'

Dan took the register and wrote his name as illegibly as he could before passing it across to Sarah. He motioned to her to do the same. She took the hint, scrawled across the next space on the register and handed it back. Dan passed it through the window to the guard.

The ceremony complete, the guard took the clipboard and frowned momentarily at the two entries. He paused, thought about asking the two people to re-sign, then changed his mind. The shift change was in less than an hour and he really didn't care – he didn't get paid enough to make sure visitors' calligraphy skills were above average.

'Go through when I raise the barrier,' he instructed and walked away.

Dan breathed out while he wound the car window up. Sarah could hardly contain her excitement.

'We did it – we're in!' she exclaimed.

'Yeah, well, calm down otherwise he's going to wonder why on earth you're so excited about your magazine assignment and we'll end up getting pulled over.' Dan watched as the barrier was raised and drove slowly through. No point in rushing.

Sarah bit her lip and held her breath until they were past the guard house and under the barrier, then began to punch the air. 'Yes! Now let's find that container!'

Dan steered the car carefully over the pock-marked bitumen. The sun was beginning to set and it was becoming difficult to see in the fading light. He found the unfamiliar switch for the headlights. The beam caught signs for various docks, pointing in different directions. He risked a glance to his right at a huge freighter being unloaded under floodlights. An enormous crane picked up each container as if it was a matchbox then set it on a flat-bed truck waiting patiently below. Dan slowed and turned his head to see a procession of trucks lined up along the length of the dock, all waiting their turn.

'How big is this place?' exclaimed Sarah.

'It's huge,' said Dan. 'Well over half the world's shipping comes through here.'

Sarah pointed to a sign displayed on a post at a junction in the road. 'There – follow that road.'

Dan drove slowly down a wide concrete path and pulled the car up behind a container. 'Here goes,' he said, and climbed out.

They walked slowly round the towering stacks of containers. Neither spoke – they were too over-awed by the sheer enormity of the port operations and the task they had set themselves.

'It seemed so simple when we were talking about it in Brisbane,' said Sarah. 'I had no idea this place would be so big.'

'I know. It just makes me more thankful the guy at the freighter company told you it was this terminal on the manifest.' Dan looked around them, at the stacks of containers disappearing from view whichever way he looked. 'We could've been here forever otherwise.'

'Let's have a look at that manifest again. I'm sure there was a note of an identifying stamp or something on it. Maybe that will help.'

Dan felt in his shirt pocket and pulled out the well-thumbed document. He unfolded it and stared helplessly at it. A noise behind him made him look around.

Two dock workers chattered away in Malay, laughing.

'Stay here,' Dan said to Sarah and turned to the two men.

'Hey!' he said, raising his hand and smiling. The two men glanced up at him a little sheepishly, their smoking break forgotten.

'Sorry guys,' said Dan. 'Could you tell me which of these stacks might have got delivered since the New Year?'

The men eyed him suspiciously.

'Why do you want to know?' asked the shorter of the two, shading his eyes from the glare of the setting sun behind Dan.

Dan shrugged. Stayed relaxed. He nodded back at Sarah.

'Me and the missus just moved here from the UK.' He lowered his voice conspiratorially. 'I'm going to be in big trouble if our furniture hasn't got here in one piece.' He winked.

The two men laughed, nodding. The taller man of the two took a long drag on his cigarette and looked down the long line of containers.

'Have you got the container number?'

Dan showed him the number on the manifest. The man nodded. He put his hand on Dan's shoulder and turned him back towards the harbour.

'The ones that didn't get put on trucks when they arrived – the last three columns down there.'

Dan thanked the two men and walked back to Sarah, grinning.

'Bingo,' he said. 'Follow me.'

TWENTY-SEVEN

Dan began to walk towards the columns of containers the dock workers had pointed out.

'Hope you enjoy your stay here!' the shorter man called out.

Sarah turned to Dan. 'What did he say?'

'Doesn't matter. Keep walking,' he said and turned and waved back at the dock workers.

They reached the last few columns of stacked containers.

'Okay,' said Dan. 'According to our friends back there, these containers are the most recent arrivals. So let's start looking. Got a pen?'

Sarah reached into her bag and dug around. She handed him a pen and watched as he wrote the manifest reference number on the palm of his hand before handing the document back to her. He glanced up, noticing her watching him.

'No, I *don't* have a photographic memory,' he explained. 'I'm just an ordinary bloke.' He grinned and handed back the pen.

They split up. Dan indicated to Sarah to take the right-hand stack while he searched the left.

He began to walk around the coloured containers. There seemed to be six colours available – red, green, blue, white, rust and more rust. He craned his neck upwards, reading the serial numbers on the side. Every now and again, he looked down, just to counteract the ache developing in his neck. A sudden shout made him spin round.

'Dan! Look at this!'

He turned, searching out the sound of Sarah's voice. 'Where are you?' he shouted.

'Go back to the main corridor between the containers – I'll look out for you.'

He jogged back the way he came. As he turned a corner, he almost ran into Sarah. He grabbed hold of her shoulders. 'Are you okay?'

'Yeah, yeah,' she nodded. 'Come and see this.'

She took hold of his hand and led him through the container stacks on the other side until she came to a rusting light blue one. The door was wide open. Sarah handed Dan the manifest.

'This is the one.' He stared at the manifest, then at the number stamped on the door of the container. 'Shit. We're too late.' Dan punched the side of the container in frustration. They'd been so close.

Sarah looked at Dan. 'Now what do we do?'

He shrugged, handed the manifest to Sarah, put his hands in his pockets then stepped into the open container. He stood in the middle of it, just outside of the shadows and turned around. He looked down. Frowned. Then crouched, looking at the floor. A wide grin spread across his face.

'Look at this,' he called, turning back to the open door.

Sarah frowned. She stepped into the container and looked at where Dan was pointing.

'Looks like… like engine oil,' she said, confused.

Dan was still smiling. 'So, he's got a car, right?'

Sarah looked at him. 'So, where is it?'

Dan brushed past her and jogged back down between the containers looking left and right until he saw a tell-tale puff of smoke. He ran up to it.

'Hi!' he said.

The two dock workers jumped. Kicked a deck of cards under a nearby container and turned to Dan in unison.

'Yes?' asked the shorter one.

Dan held up his hands. 'It's okay – no problem.'

The two men relaxed and smiled.

Dan looked behind him at the row of containers, then back at the two men. 'Have you seen a car being driven around here over the past few weeks – out of one of the containers?' he asked.

The taller of the two men grinned. 'Ah! Nice car!' he exclaimed.

Dan smiled and nodded, trying to keep his excitement

in check. 'Listen,' he said, lowering his voice, 'the missus says it's meant to be a surprise for my birthday next week, but,' he added, turning as if to make sure Sarah wasn't within ear shot, 'any idea what sort of car it is?'

The man giggled, pleased to share the secret. 'Yes, yes! Black sedan – four doors. German make. Latest model.' He grinned. 'You are a very lucky man!'

Dan punched the air. 'Where did it go?' he asked.

The dock worker pulled Dan with him and walked between two columns of containers. As they broke through the boundary, the man pointed in front of them.

'They drove it in there.'

Dan followed where the man was pointing and found himself staring at a row of warehouses. He thanked the dock worker and ran back to where Sarah was standing.

'Come and see this – we might be in luck yet.'

They hurried to the line of warehouses, now silhouetted in the fading light. Dan glanced round as, one by one, automatic timers switched on floodlights around the terminal and the docks were bathed in orange and white lights. Even at night, it appeared the dock activity continued, with container ships and freighters being pulled towards the terminals by tugboats, while cranes swayed backwards and forwards.

Dan and Sarah slowed as they approached the warehouses. After the disappointment of the empty container, Dan couldn't help the excitement he felt as he stopped in front of the first set of doors.

'Did he say which one the car went in?' asked Sarah.

'Third from the end. Apparently, these have double doors on the other side which face the docks but that dock worker said he definitely saw a car being driven out from that container and into that warehouse through those doors down there.'

Dan began to walk towards it.

'Wait.' Sarah grabbed his arm. 'Won't it be guarded?'

Dan stopped. 'You know, I don't think so. I reckon Delaney's so arrogant, he won't think it's necessary.' He paused. 'I reckon we should keep our eyes open though.'

Sarah nodded in agreement. 'Okay. Works for me.'

They kept close to the front of the warehouses in an attempt to blend in with the shadows caused by the roof overhang and crept closer to the third building. When they got nearer, Dan pushed Sarah behind him and held up his hand. *Wait.*

He continued towards the third warehouse without her until he was outside the huge double doors. They were simple, made of corrugated iron with a chain wrapped through the handles which was secured with a padlock.

Sarah crept closer to him. 'Do that trick with the lock, like you did at Delaney's place in Brisbane,' she whispered.

Dan rolled his eyes. He had known he was going to pay for that piece of luck. Shrugging, he reached into his jeans pocket for the small multi-tool and flipped it open at random.

'Watch my back,' he said to Sarah, 'Because this is going to look really suspicious.'

She nodded and turned away from him.

Dan closed his eyes, offered a prayer to a god he didn't believe in and set to work. Twisting the small metal implement left and right in the padlock, he raised his eyebrows in surprise as he felt the mechanism give, then watched as the padlock slipped open. He glanced at the heavens in a silent salute and turned to Sarah.

'We're in.'

He pushed the switch for the warehouse door and it groaned open. As the beams from the dockside floodlights filtered through the dark interior, Sarah gasped. The warehouse was full of cars – hundreds of them. They walked into the entrance of the warehouse.

Sarah put her hands on her hips and turned to Dan. 'Okay, now what?'

He ran his hand through his hair, exasperated. 'Shit! It's got to be here somewhere!' He narrowed his eyes, squinting in the dim light. 'Okay, first let's find some lights.'

Sarah ran back to the warehouse door and scanned the bank of switches. 'Here goes – try this.'

A bank of fluorescent lights began to flicker on in sequence along the ceiling of the warehouse. It seemed to take forever.

Sarah gaped up at the ceiling as the lights went on. 'Jesus – how big is this place, Dan? This is going to take forever!'

'The only way we're going to find it is to split up,' he said. 'Dial my mobile and keep your phone connected – if there's any problem or you find something, you can say so straight away.'

Sarah nodded, turned towards the left-hand side of the warehouse and walked away, checking the cars parked either side of her.

Dan turned and began walking along the right-hand side of the warehouse. As he walked, he looked left and right – it had to be here, had to be. He glanced up and saw Sarah walking alongside the opposite wall. He assumed she had the same stunned expression on her face. There were just so many vehicles. All different makes, models, configurations, colours. Parked end to end in row upon row, all the way through the building.

Sarah's voice crackled over his mobile. Dan held it up to his ear. 'Say again?'

'I said – are all of these privately owned?' Sarah asked.

He looked around. 'Yes. The ones going to dealerships are parked on the dockside by the stevedores as soon as they arrive so the car transporters can be loaded up.'

He dropped the phone back into his shirt pocket and glanced up. Sarah was making good progress, gradually disappearing into the shadowed bowels of the far end of the warehouse. Dan sighed, looked at the cars surrounding him and dreamed about test driving just one of them.

He scuffed along the narrow path between vehicles, careful not to brush against any in case he set off an alarm. He frowned as he approached a low-slung silver sports sedan. It seemed to have more space around it than the others.

As he got closer, he saw the sports car straddled two parking bays. He walked past it, checked the angle and walked back. He crouched down and peered underneath.

A dark pool of liquid behind the front wheel to his right caught his attention as it captured the reflection of the warehouse lights. Crouching down on his hands and knees, Dan stretched his left hand under the car and dabbed his finger in the viscous liquid. He drew his hand back and stared at his finger.

Engine oil.

He looked underneath the silver sedan again. The oil was in the wrong place. It wasn't aligned with the engine block of the vehicle above it.

'Which means this car's been moved to hide the fact the black sedan's already gone,' he murmured.

'Great powers of deduction, as always Dan,' said a voice from behind him, a fraction of a second before he felt the cold steel of the barrel of a gun against the back of his neck and then heard the safety catch as it was released.

TWENTY-EIGHT

South of the Sea of Japan

Miles Brogan took his hands off the controls and checked the readings printed out in front of him. A storm warning for the waters beyond Socotra Rock heading towards the Sea of Japan remained current and Brogan had ordered his men to ensure the cargo was lashed down to prevent the ship from rolling in high seas.

At fifty-six, Brogan had more than thirty years' experience at sea. His brown hair, bleached by the sun, showed only a little grey whilst his skin had the deep-set tan of someone who had spent most of his life outdoors.

Unknown to his crew, he planned this to be his last voyage with the freighter named *World's End*. A customer, booking at the last minute, had insisted his luxury sedan be included with the cargo and had paid highly for the two berths the car now occupied. It wasn't unusual for people to ask for this service and Brogan had gone out of his way to accommodate the customer's request. The client had been impressed and Brogan appreciated the bonus the customer had insisted on paying him for the effort. Brogan had no intention of telling his employer but the payment was going to fund his retirement plan of sailing around the world with his wife for the next few years before settling down for good.

The owner had been most insistent on keeping the extra space to either side of the vehicle, paying to have two bays in which to keep the extra distance. The owner had even insisted on sending an employee to drive the sedan onto the freighter himself, presumably not trusting the highly qualified stevedore staff at the port in Singapore.

Brogan shrugged to himself. The client was paying a premium price for the car to be transported to South Korea, so he could do what he liked as far as the captain was concerned. After the vehicle had been loaded, Brogan had leaned down and attempted to look through the tinted windows but couldn't see anything. He knew there was no point trying the door handles – the employee had locked the doors and pocketed the keys while smiling at Brogan.

'You won't need these,' the man had said to him as he polished his glasses, 'I'll meet you when you reach your destination.'

Brogan had taken the money and not asked any questions. All he had to do was sail towards the port of

Busan in South Korea as originally planned. Just with an extra car on board. Easy.

He shifted in his seat at the controls, settling down for the next leg of the journey. The *World's End* operated with a crew of nine, including Brogan. It was a lean operation, with most crew members being engineers to ensure the freighter's engines ran smoothly over the course of its journey.

Brogan yawned. It would soon be time to swap shifts with the first mate. Brogan contemplated Chris Weston's reaction when he found out about the extra cargo. Brogan hadn't offered an explanation and Chris hadn't asked for one. He'd just shrugged his shoulders when Brogan had told him to mind his own business when he'd found the sedan parked in the hold and the captain staring at it.

Brogan picked up the microphone for the tannoy system which linked to speakers around the ship.

'Hey Chris? Bring us back a mug of coffee on your way up, thanks.'

Brogan settled back into his chair and raised his feet up to rest on the controls. Not in the manual, obviously, but comfortable, he mused.

His eyes automatically scanned the horizon. The sun was beginning to set to his port side, pulling clouds and aircraft vapour trails over the edge with it. Brogan let his eyes drift over the horizon, the pinks and yellows of the sunset casting shadows over the ship's deck. He daydreamed about what sort of yacht he'd buy on his return. Home. Retirement.

He heard the door open behind him and a gust of wind rustled the charts. Brogan knew he could rely on the GPS and radar but he liked the old-fashioned charts – they seemed to hold a lot more history than the computer did, evident in the tell-tale folds of the maps from years of use. He dropped his feet down from the controls with a sigh and inched himself up into the chair.

Brogan jumped as Weston tapped him on the shoulder, pulled a gun from his waistband and pointed it at him.

'Change of plans, captain,' said the first mate.

Brogan slowly sat up straight. 'What the hell do you think you're doing, Weston?' he demanded.

Weston shrugged. 'I got paid more than you. And they decided they couldn't trust you to keep the car a secret.'

He reached into his pocket and pulled out his mobile phone. Scrolling down through the text messages, he waited until he found the right one.

'Change our course to bear north-north-east forty-five degrees,' he said.

Brogan frowned. 'There's nothing there but bare coastline.'

'Just do it.'

'Where's the rest of the crew?'

Weston smirked. 'In the safe room. I expect they'll start to smell after a couple of days.'

Brogan felt a chill down his spine. *What the hell was going on*?

His hand automatically covered the controls for the transponder – the system that tracked the ship's progress and sent out a beacon at all times to other ships in the area.

'Move away,' said Weston. He aimed the gun at the console and fired.

Brogan reared back from the blast, his ears ringing from the noise in the confined space.

Weston grinned. 'Now no-one knows where you are. Change course.'

Brogan's hand hovered over the navigation system. As he plotted the course Weston had set, he noticed his hands were shaking. He trembled as he realised he was on his own, on a large ship in the middle of nowhere, with a psychopath for a crew member.

Suddenly retirement seemed a long way away.

TWENTY-NINE

Singapore

'Put your hands in the air – slowly,' said the voice.

Dan did as he was told.

'Now stand up.'

Dan stood and turned, then his arms lowered slightly and snorted in surprise.

'Pleased to see me?' asked David.

'I'll let you know,' said Dan. 'What are you doing here?'

David backed away, keeping the gun trained on Dan.

'Probably best I ask the questions,' he said then turned slightly and called over his shoulder. 'Philippa?'

A figure appeared from the side of another car – Sarah, followed by another woman who was holding a gun at Sarah's back.

Dan turned to David. 'Let her go.'

David shook his head. 'Sorry – no can do.'

'What do you want?'

David smiled. 'Well, for starters you can tell me what you're doing breaking into private property with a journalist.'

'Why – are you working in private security now?'

David scowled. 'Very funny. Answer the question. I've got enough authority to make the pair of you disappear for a very long time. Don't push your luck.'

Sarah glanced at Dan, fear in her eyes. 'Dan? Do you know this guy? Just tell him, yeah?'

Dan ignored her and looked at the other man. 'How long have you been following us David?'

David shrugged. 'A while. You saved us some legwork. Let's say we don't want to show our hand to Delaney just yet so it's time to get you two out of circulation.'

He turned to Philippa. 'Stay here with our friend the journalist – I'm going to take Mr Taylor for a walk.'

Philippa nodded, leaned against one of the cars and folded her arms, keeping her gun pointed at Sarah.

David took Dan by the arm and shoved him further down the pathway formed by the lines of vehicles. Dan glanced ahead of him and saw a steel staircase leading up to a solitary office. David indicated to Dan to climb the stairs ahead of him. Dan grunted. He would have done the same if their roles had been reversed.

When he reached the top of the stairs, he turned and opened the door to the office. David followed him in and switched on the lights. Dim fluorescent tubes flickered to life. Dan cast his eyes around the room. The office was a mess. Four filing cabinets to the left of the door had their drawers open, the contents strewn over the floor. He looked around the room – a desk stood in the middle of the office, facing the door. It too had been trashed, the contents of its drawers littering the desk surface and the floor.

'Been busy?' asked Dan as he turned to face David.

'Like you wouldn't believe,' said David. He sat down in a chair behind the desk, put the safety catch back on the gun and laid the weapon on the desk.

'Close the door,' said David, and motioned Dan to the seat opposite him.

Dan closed the door and then slumped into the chair. He looked at David and noticed how weary he looked. 'You're trying to stop him too.'

David nodded and said nothing.

'So, what have you got?'

'We know Peter sent some notes to Sarah before he died. And we know you've used them to get this far. Impressive,' said David. 'I wonder what else is in those notes?'

Dan shrugged. 'Not as much as you'd like to think. I presume Mitch works for you?'

David nodded.

Dan grunted. 'Figures. There's no way you'd have

worked out we were here on your own.' He leaned back in the seat. 'Forget the notes. If we hadn't broken into Delaney's house and found the shipping manifest, we wouldn't have got this far. And now we know he's using a car for some reason. But we don't know where it's gone.'

He looked over at the other man. 'What's going on, Dave? What's so important about this white gold powder? Why are you all chasing it?'

David sighed and leaned forward. 'Academics in the UK have already pointed out to our government there that existing green energy technology is still decades behind demand, and as the old coal-burning power stations are decommissioned, wind and solar power won't be ready to take its place. We're talking nation-wide blackouts before 2020,' he explained.

'The coal mining and oil production companies are lapping this up – they know they've got at least another thirty years or more where despite protests from the green lobbyists, they're still set to make billions – and they're not letting that chance go without a fight. Delaney is just one of them – a particularly nasty one. There's plenty who would take his place, given the chance. All these organisations are distorting the truth for their own means, so the general public doesn't know who to believe – and, frankly, they're starting not to care either. Think of it as apathy caused by information overload.'

Dan nodded and motioned to David to continue. 'Where does white gold powder come in to all of this?'

David smiled and stood up. He paced the room. 'White gold's the answer to buying us some time – a lot of time – without having to consider nuclear energy; something that will give us the extra thirty years we need to develop sustainable, alternative energy.'

'Which the coal mining and oil companies don't want.'

'Exactly. To the point where some of them are paying substantial amounts of money to some very questionable characters to keep the whole concept quiet.'

Dan leaned forward. 'So where does your lot come into this?'

David shrugged. 'We're just making sure it doesn't fall into the wrong hands. Or gets used for the wrong reasons. White gold has to be produced in a safe, controlled environment.'

Dan laughed. 'By 'controlled' you mean *you* want control of it – government, not private enterprise, right?'

David looked at him. 'It's the safest way, believe me. There are other things about this white gold powder you have absolutely no comprehension of Dan. And I'm not at liberty to tell you.' He stood up. 'But you will help me find Delaney's car.'

'I'll have to think about it. I'm not even sure I want to help you.'

'There's nothing to think about,' said David. 'You're going to help me whether you like it or not.'

Dan stared at him. 'What do you mean?'

David brushed some papers off a table. They fluttered

to the floor as he leaned back and folded his arms. 'I don't care whether you use the journalist to help you, but you're going to help me stop Delaney. You've got the skills, the knowledge – and you owe me.'

'I owe you?' asked Dan. 'What on earth for?'

'Because you've given up on yourself,' said David. 'I'm doing you a favour. Giving you a sense of purpose.'

'I don't need a sense of purpose.'

'Really? What have you been doing for the past few years?' asked David.

Dan scowled. He stood up and wandered over to the large office window which overlooked the warehouse. He could see Philippa and Sarah, deliberately ignoring each other, leaning against opposite cars.

'It's not healthy, Dan,' continued David. 'I've seen too many just bury their head in a bottle every night.'

'Have you been spying on me?' asked Dan, as he turned to face the other man.

'Looking out for you,' said David. 'Like any mate would.'

'Bullshit. You just want me to solve this so you can take all the credit and add another award to your office wall.'

David shrugged and stepped closer to Dan. And then punched him in the stomach, hard.

Dan collapsed to the floor, taken by surprise. He grasped the edge of the table, wheezing, a fire burning in his abdomen.

David bent down and sneered in his face. 'I'll give you

a week. You either help me or I'll start investigating Hayley's death a little more closely. You never know where your name might turn up.' He stalked past Dan and walked down the stairs.

Dan watched him go, his eyes watering. He rubbed his stomach, thinking hard.

THIRTY

Orono-Shima, Japan

Brogan peered out the window of the freighter as the landmass drew closer. An occasional light blinked out of the darkness but otherwise, the coastline was pitch black.

'Slow here,' instructed Weston. 'Keep her level so the coast is on our port side.'

Brogan obeyed and hoped to hell someone didn't run into them. Weston had switched off all the ship's running lights, all the lights in the cabins below and the control room. Brogan's face glowed green from the reflection of the radar and GPS systems.

'Okay. Now stop,' Weston said and stepped away from Brogan. He looked at his watch and nodded to himself.

Brogan shook his head in disbelief. Weston would know as well as he did that stopping a ship quickly when it was the size of the freighter they were on wouldn't be easy. Brogan reached out and pulled back the throttle levers for each of the engines. He did it in stages, mindful of the irreparable damage he'd cause the enormous engines if he tried to stop too fast. As the ship began to slow, he steered hard to port to add more braking power, and then straightened the ship out before the engines went completely silent.

Weston walked over to the door and opened it. Cold air filtered through the room. Brogan shivered. Not from the cold. His mind was racing. It had to be something to do with the mysterious black sedan in the cargo hold, it had to be. Weston had more or less confirmed it. But what the hell had he been paid to do?

Brogan risked a glance over his shoulder. Weston was staring out at the coastline, as if he was searching for something. Brogan followed his gaze. No beacon shone, no signal was being emitted from the coast.

Brogan knew they must have already taken a kilometre or so to stop. The ship would now be drifting, wallowing in the tidal flow.

Brogan turned sideways in his chair and strained his ears. He could hear an engine, something heading out of the darkness, aiming for the freighter. He stood up.

Weston glanced at him and grinned. 'Reinforcements,' he explained.

Brogan's heart was racing. He glanced around the control room, looking for something, anything he could use as a weapon.

Weston watched him and laughed. 'Don't bother,' he said. 'I was busy cleaning up this afternoon. You won't find anything here you can use on me.' He turned back to watch the sea.

Brogan walked over to the door and stared out. As the clouds parted, he glimpsed a dinghy with a powerful outboard engine approaching the freighter. As it drew closer, Weston reached around outside the door and threw down a coiled rope. It fell down the side of the ship, pulling taut when it had reached its length.

Brogan stared in amazement as he heard the dinghy's engine die then, one by one, five figures ascended the rope and boarded the ship. He backed into the control room, holding up his palms in surrender.

He looked on helplessly as the hijackers crawled over his ship. They were experienced at sea, he could tell. Orders were being carried out efficiently, deftly. *Special Forces*, he thought. *Mercenaries*.

He watched as one of the men fitted a silencer to a gun then fired over the edge of the ship. The man turned to face Weston with a grin on his face. 'Won't need the dinghy any more I guess,' he said.

Weston didn't smile back. Brogan noticed that since the boarding, he had ceased to look like he commanded the group any more. Instead, he deferred to another man who had his back to Brogan and issued instructions to the four other invaders. He turned to Weston.

'Where's the safe room?'

Weston nodded in the direction of the stairwell. 'They're all down there.'

The man nodded and dismissed the four men in front of him. Brogan's heart sank as he watched their progress along the side of the ship, then saw them disappear through another door. In a matter of seconds, he heard shouting, gunfire. Then silence.

His attention snapped back to the man listening to Weston, stooping to hear him. Brogan watched as the man nodded to Weston and barked an order.

'Start her up. We need to be out of here before sunrise.'

Brogan was shoved out of the way by Weston as he stepped back into the control room and flicked a switch. Brogan felt the rumble of the enormous engines as they roared into life. He took a deep breath and looked out at the coastline, its dark outline silhouetted by clouds. He shuddered. Somehow, he didn't think he'd get the chance to pay it another visit.

He jumped as a door further along the ship crashed open. A man backed out of the doorway, stooped over as he dragged a heavy load after him.

Brogan broke out in a cold sweat as he realised what was happening. He leaned against the railing enclosing the deck. The hijacker caught the movement from the corner of his eye. He turned and grinned maliciously at Brogan. A shout from behind the door made him look back and continue to drag the body out. A second man came through the door after it. Once the hijackers had dragged the body across the deck, they kicked at it until it rolled over the side.

'Six to go,' said one, then they disappeared back through the door, closing it behind them.

Brogan turned away from them and closed his eyes. His hands gripped the rail. He couldn't think straight. A shout from behind him made him open his eyes. Brogan stared at the man walking towards him. The man's face was a mess. One side of it was torn, with blotchy pink new skin poking out from behind old scars. Brogan shivered. A malevolent glint shone in the man's tawny eyes. Like he knew the world owed him.

The man stopped in front of Brogan. He grinned and held up a mobile phone, the screen pointing at Brogan. 'Watch carefully,' he said, then hit a button.

Brogan felt the tears rolling down his cheeks as he watched the recording. It didn't have sound. It didn't need it. His wife, his poor wife.

The man lowered the phone and placed it in his pocket. 'If you refuse to cooperate, we'll pay a visit to your daughter next,' he said. 'Understand?'

Brogan closed his eyes and nodded.

'Good,' said the man. 'Now show me where the car is parked.'

THIRTY-ONE

Singapore

Dan rubbed his abdomen. Nothing broken, just wounded pride. He grunted to himself.

'OK?' asked Sarah.

Dan shrugged. 'I'll live.' He turned and walked along the dock. The noise from the quay had grown quieter in between shifts. A slight breeze ruffled his hair. Further along, bright arc lights enveloped a large container ship being unloaded, the containers being craned onto waiting trucks for their onward journeys. He leaned against the railing, and then turned his back on the activity. He gazed up at the warehouse.

Sarah walked slowly towards him, rubbing her elbow.

Dan glanced at her. 'Did you get hurt?'

She shook her head and smiled sheepishly. 'My own fault. When Philippa pulled a gun on me, I was so scared I literally jumped. I knocked myself on the side of one of the cars. They're surprisingly hard.'

'I should've known we wouldn't be the only ones trying to work out what Delaney's plans are,' said Dan.

Sarah shrugged. 'At least they're on our side. Bit of a coincidence though, them being here at the same time as us...' She trailed off, eyeing him accusingly.

He grimaced. 'Yeah, I know – we were followed. Chances are, they've been watching us for a while to see what we'd do.' Dan rubbed his chin, thinking.

'It does make me think they were struggling to find any information,' Sarah continued. 'I mean, if their only lead was to follow us.'

Dan nodded. 'I got the distinct impression they know, or have a pretty good idea, what Delaney's up to. They just haven't been able to work out *how* he's going to do it.'

'Until now,' added Sarah. She leaned against the railing and looked along the dock. She could just see their car parked in the gloom. 'Come on. Let's get out of here.'

Dan eased himself off the railing and looked at his watch. Almost four o'clock. Dawn. 'Okay. Breakfast on the way back?'

'Sounds good to me.'

They walked back to the car. Dan slid in behind wheel and started the engine. Sarah climbed into the passenger seat. The engine coughed once. Dan felt his heart beat. Hard. Then he pushed Sarah out of the passenger door as he opened his.

'*Run*! Get away from the car – it's wired!'

He leapt out of the car, ran round to the passenger side and took hold of Sarah's hand. She looked stunned. He pulled her with him, away down the dock side as fast as he could.

'Keep up!' he yelled.

They sprinted away from the vehicle. Dan glanced at the buildings to their left until he saw what he was looking for.

'Here!'

He pulled Sarah into a narrow alleyway then leaned against the wall of the warehouse, panting.

Sarah bent over with her hands on her knees, gasping for breath. She slowly raised her head until she was staring at Dan. 'Are you sure?'

He nodded. 'I think...'

His words were lost in the noise of the explosion. Sarah screamed as the impact blast swept by the narrow alleyway. Dan pulled her close to him and turned his back to the dock, trying to shelter them from the debris and shrapnel as it blew past on a hot wind.

As the roar of the explosion died away, Dan heard a ringing in his ears. It took a few seconds for him to realise it wasn't tinnitus but a mobile phone. He looked down at Sarah and raised an eyebrow.

She held up her bag. 'It's mine.'

Dan looked at her incredulously. 'We just out-ran a bomb and you remembered your *handbag*?'

Sarah shrugged. 'I couldn't leave it behind – it's got all Peter's notes in it. Hang on.'

Dan waited while Sarah reached into her bag and brought out her phone. She held it up to Dan.

'Should I?'

It continued to ring. Dan took it from her and answered it. 'Hello?'

'Lucky escape,' the voice said. Then the line went dead.

Dan spun round to face the containers stacked opposite the warehouse as the sound of screeching tyres sounded across the complex. A large sedan powered its way through the arc lights and sped away along an exit road, its tail lights shining in the distance. Dan handed the phone back to Sarah.

'It was the guy with the glasses, wasn't it?' she asked.

He nodded.

Sarah put the phone back in her bag. 'I think I'll skip breakfast.'

'It's okay, we'll get something to eat at the airport,' said Dan.

'Airport?' asked Sarah

He looked down at her and nodded. 'It's time to get you home. This has become too dangerous here. Let David and his team deal with it.'

She shook her head. 'Unbelievable. You really think after all I've been through, I'm just going to walk away?'

Dan pulled her out of the alleyway and pointed at the burning wreck of the car.

'You very nearly didn't get the chance.'

Sarah felt her knees weaken. The car wasn't recognisable. It looked like a wrecking ball had landed on it, sending the doors, windows and wheels in all directions. Debris littered the dockside. She looked behind them – the blast had sent broken pieces of metal and shards of glass several metres down the road past them. Splinters of metal protruded from the front of the warehouse.

Sirens sounded in the distance. Voices could be heard from the dock, figures pointing at the wreckage. Across the harbour, a motor boat was being launched and started to make its way towards them, a blue light flashing on its stern.

Sarah turned to Dan. 'Get me out of here.'

He nodded. 'Let's go.'

They walked for several miles, exhausted, before Dan deemed it safe enough to stop and flag down a taxi without arousing suspicion. When they reached the hotel, Dan paid the driver and then ushered Sarah through the foyer to the elevators, ignoring the receptionist. As they rode up to their room, Dan issued instructions.

'Pack everything. We'll leave immediately. Don't phone anyone. Don't answer the phone. We'll sort out flights at the airport – just tell them there's been a family emergency and we're going back early.'

Sarah nodded, not saying anything.

The elevator doors opened.

'Give me the room key,' said Dan.

Sarah watched as he unlocked the door and checked the room. She stepped in after him. Dan walked into the bathroom then out again. 'Okay. All clear. You pack first.'

Sarah began throwing clothes into her suitcase. She tore shirts off hangars, swept cosmetics off the bathroom shelf and piled them into the suitcase. No time to fold anything. She glanced around the room, checked she hadn't left anything then locked the case.

'Got everything?' asked Dan, leaning against the door.

Sarah nodded. 'Yes.'

Dan straightened up. 'Okay – my turn.'

Same procedure. He threw his clothes into his bag. They checked the room one last time and closed the door behind them. They carried their bags to the elevators and rode a car back down to reception.

Sarah paid the bill while Dan used the receptionist's phone to order a taxi. Ten minutes later, they were on the kerb, a blue taxi pulling up next to them.

Forty minutes later, they walked into the international terminal and arranged flights back to the UK.

Dan rested his elbows on his knees, trying to get comfortable on the hard airport lounge seat. He looked up as Sarah approached and gratefully took one of the takeaway coffee cups from her.

She sat down next to him. 'Only an hour to wait.'

He grunted in reply. He hated being dependent on schedules and timetables and was eager to be in the air as soon as possible.

Sarah shifted in her seat and turned to look at him. 'Dan, was it the right thing to do, to go to Brisbane? I mean, we put Hayley in danger, didn't we?'

Dan eased back in his seat, and stretched his legs before answering. 'We wouldn't have found out half as much as we have if we'd stayed in England. Hayley knew what she was doing, same as you. I'm sorry she's gone, really I am, but without her help, we'd have achieved nothing.' He paused, sipped the coffee and grimaced before he continued. 'Besides, we might not have found Mitch – he was the last person I would have thought to have asked for help – I just wouldn't have known where to start looking for him.'

Sarah didn't say anything. She watched the crowd changing before them, people rushing to last-minute flight calls, pacifying children, checking departure information for boarding gates and times. Dan watched her out of the corner of his eye.

'Don't feel guilty Sarah. Everyone has a choice. You'd have done the same for her. If you want someone to blame, then blame Delaney.'

Sarah stood and dropped her coffee cup into a nearby trash can. Turning back to Dan, she shrugged. 'You're right, I know. I just wish I'd realised sooner how real a threat Delaney is. I mean, until that point, it was still conjecture he'd been responsible for Peter's death. It's a shock to find out there really are people out there who would go to such lengths to protect themselves.'

'Nothing surprises me about anyone any more,' said Dan, draining his coffee.

Sarah smiled. 'Are you really that jaded about the world?'

'Yep.' He stood up, threw his coffee cup away and stretched, looking around the airport crowd, instinctively checking the faces at random, looking for any familiar ones in case they were being followed.

Sarah followed his gaze. 'Do you think they'd follow us?'

Dan shrugged, watching the constant stream of human traffic. 'Honestly? No. No – I think Delaney's running an extremely low-key operation. The less people that know about his plans, the better – it means he has more control over it. As long as our friend in the glasses doesn't appear, I think we can assume that Delaney believes that he's frightened us off.'

Sarah stood up, shouldered her bag and handed the other to Dan. 'Come on – show time. Let's get this flight over and done with.'

They wandered through the vast airport towards their boarding gate, the early morning sun glinting through the windows as it created a haze over the airport and across Singapore city in the background.

As the aircraft eased itself off the runway, Dan peered out the window at the steady stream of freighters lining up to enter and leave the busy port below them.

And wondered how on earth he would find Delaney's car.

THIRTY-TWO

London, England

Dan threw Sarah's suitcase and his battered old kit bag onto the back seat of the taxi next to Sarah then climbed into the passenger seat.

'Where to?' asked the driver.

Good question, thought Dan.

'Willesden Green,' said Sarah.

Dan turned and glanced over his shoulder at her. She smiled. 'Pete and I never sold our apartment in London,' she explained. 'I use it when I know I'm not going to be leaving the office on time or have to work weekends.'

Dan nodded and relaxed. Neither of them felt like filling the silence of the journey with idle chatter for the benefit of the taxi driver.

Sarah spent the journey staring out the window and

Dan closed his eyes. Old habits died hard. *Sleep whenever you get the chance.*

The journey was uneventful. After half an hour of fighting through the north circular's usual traffic queues, the taxi driver turned right off the main road and began to thread his way to the northern suburb of Willesden Green.

Sarah leaned forward, told the taxi driver where to stop and paid the fare while Dan climbed out, stretched and then bent down to lift out the bags. He put them on the pavement next to his feet and looked up at the building.

A five-storey dark brick structure, it had been subdivided into apartments. A single entryway led into the building, with a series of names and doorbells on the left of the wide double doors. Dan looked down the road. About two hundred metres down the street, a service station did a brisk early evening commuter trade while opposite, an open-air tube train line blinked between houses.

He glanced back as the taxi drove away.

Sarah walked over to him. 'Okay?'

He nodded. 'I guess.'

She smiled. 'Come on. It won't take long to warm up the place. You'll feel better after a hot shower.'

Dan picked up the suitcase and kit bag and followed her. He felt completely out of his comfort zone.

'Oh,' said Sarah, as she opened the door for him. 'I forgot to say. There's no elevator and we're on the top floor.'

'No problem,' Dan grunted as he stumbled through the

front door. He grinned, then dropped Sarah's suitcase at her feet. He hoisted his kit bag over his shoulder and began to climb the stairs.

'Bastard,' said Sarah under her breath. She picked up her suitcase and followed him.

Dan reached the top landing several minutes ahead of Sarah. He took in the wide carpeted staircase he'd just climbed, ornate wooden banisters gleaming from a recent polish. He turned and looked out the hallway window over the scene below.

Rain began to lash against the window, the brake lights from cars reflected in the droplets that crawled down the pane. Dan sighed, feeling depressed after spending time under the open blue skies of the southern hemisphere. He wondered if he could move there permanently like Mitch. And then decided he probably could.

His daydream was broken by the sound of Sarah dropping her suitcase on the plush carpet of the landing below him.

'Okay, I give up. Help,' she called up.

Dan grinned and walked down the stairs to meet her. 'You know, you're the only person I know who would have the top floor apartment in an apartment block with no elevator,' he said.

Sarah smiled. 'That's exactly what Peter said when I told him I wanted us to buy it,' she said. 'Come on. I just want to get through the front door and stop travelling for a while.'

When they reached the top floor, Dan picked up his kit

bag and followed Sarah to a nondescript front door with a single deadlock. He waited while she pulled out a set of keys from her bag, then he followed her into the apartment.

'Just put the bags next to the door,' said Sarah. 'Relax. I'll put the kettle on. Make yourself at home.'

Dan watched as she turned right along the narrow corridor and disappeared into a room at the far end which he presumed was the kitchen.

He turned left and found himself in a small living room. It felt bigger due to the floor-to-ceiling windows at the front of the apartment which overlooked the train line below, then out over the cityscape beyond.

Two armchairs faced a small television, a gas fire and a coffee table. Tasteful art prints took up some of the wall space.

Dan wandered back along the hallway, pushing open doors quietly. He found the guest bedroom. It had a single bed, a wardrobe and a small desk with a computer and printer set up on it. He closed the door and made his way along past the bathroom. He hesitated at the next door and checked back along the hallway. He could hear Sarah humming to herself in the kitchen.

He looked at the closed door in front of him, took a deep breath and pushed it open. Obviously Peter hadn't spent any time at the apartment since the split eighteen months previously. The bedroom was feminine in both decoration and assorted items displayed on a low dressing table.

Dan turned and pulled the door closed behind him and padded towards the kitchen, which was small, but bright and functional. A small gas cooker stood in the far corner and an old-fashioned kettle whistled on the hob.

Sarah turned as he entered the room and smiled. 'I sent a text message to my neighbour yesterday to let her know I might call in so there's fresh food,' she explained. 'Are you hungry?'

Dan nodded. 'Absolutely.'

'Okay,' said Sarah. 'Give it half an hour and there'll be hot water too if you want to freshen up.'

Dan nodded and sat down at the small kitchen table. He suddenly felt very weary. How was he ever going to put any of this right? He looked up as Sarah walked around the table, put her hand on his shoulder and squeezed gently.

'It's okay Dan,' she said. 'I mean it. Relax. Give your mind a break. I'll open a bottle of wine if you prefer?'

He smiled, looked up at her and took her hand off his shoulder. He held it for a moment, briefly, then squeezed it and let go. 'That's the best thing you've said to me since we got off the plane.'

Sarah gently slapped his shoulder with the back of her hand and wandered over to a wine rack. She glanced out the window.

'Red wine weather,' she said, and pulled a bottle of Shiraz towards her.

THIRTY-THREE

Arctic Ocean

Chris Weston checked the GPS and slowed the engines. Miles Brogan methodically scanned the dark horizon. Somewhere out there, their ticket through the Arctic ice waited for them and, given what was at stake, it wouldn't be prudent to make a mistake like missing an appointment with a Russian ship flying a flag of convenience.

'There!'

Weston lowered his binoculars and pointed to a break in the darkness of the Arctic winter. 'There she is.'

Brogan took the proffered binoculars and peered through them. As a weak moon shone through the clouds, two piercing searchlights reached out to them. The lights drew closer, and then Brogan gasped. Shark teeth, bright white, with a gaping red mouth between them, jumped out of the darkness at him. He lowered the binoculars in shock.

Weston laughed. 'Nervous Captain? It's only a ship.'

Brogan raised the binoculars to his face again. The effect was staggering. The black hull of an ice-breaker rose through the darkness, a set of teeth painted on the bow like an old warplane.

The hijacker's leader told Weston to slow the freighter, and then picked up his mobile phone. Brogan continued to watch through the binoculars, mesmerised, while the other man placed a call.

The leader walked over to Brogan. 'Okay. Signal them. I've told them we don't expect to have to stop so we want them in front of us as we approach. We'll worry about the pleasantries once we're safely in Severnya Zemlya.'

Brogan looked out the freighter's windscreen at the bleak seascape. He tried to maintain a constant surveillance of the grey, wind-chopped sea, looking for rogue icebergs. Even with the icebreaker as escort, the freighter was vulnerable. As the winter darkness paled to a half-hearted dawn, the light reflected off the grey tones of the water, making it hard to spot icebergs until they were dangerously close. Brogan knew the ice-breaker's crew would be paid to do a good job, but years of experience meant he kept his eyes scanning the horizon, just in case. Better to be prepared than to have to take evasive action, especially with a ship the size of the *World's End*.

He took a sip of coffee and glanced at Weston. 'Have you heard a weather report?'

The former first officer nodded. 'It's not the perfect run we'd hoped for but to be honest, I thought it was going to be much worse than this. That storm should pass over us tomorrow morning so at least we'll be able to see where we're going. It wouldn't be much fun going through that at night around here.'

Brogan gestured with his coffee mug at the icebreaker. 'How did you end up with a Russian-flagged escort?'

Weston shrugged. 'Best not to ask.'

Brogan murmured his agreement. He peered through the ice-covered windows at the grey expanse before him. The enormous freighter bucked gently over the white tipped swell as he followed the ice-breaker's wake. He cast his eyes over the instrument panel below him. Normally, he'd have both GPS and radar monitors to guide him but his new bosses were insistent on not switching these on.

Brogan wondered what the hell they were hiding from the authorities. Somehow, it was connected with the black sedan in the cargo hold, but so far he couldn't figure out what it was. He kept his head down and his ears open, to try and find out more. He was sailing blind – the gunmen wouldn't even let him find out weather reports for their position. Instead, he was going to have to rely on information relayed from the Russian ship in front of him. He wondered what would happen once they reached their destination. Were they planning on sailing further?

Brisbane, Australia

Delaney put the phone down, turned to the other two men in the room and smiled. 'An update from my team leader. We're on schedule.'

The other two men grinned and provided spontaneous applause.

'That is great news my friend,' said Uli Petrov. 'I always had faith in you and my investment.'

Delaney bowed his head, acknowledging the praise.

Pallisder took a swig of the amber liquid in his glass, glanced out the window at the city lights below and turned to Delaney. 'How come you didn't develop this at one of your Eurasian mines, Morris? Surely that's one hell of a risk sending it by ship – we can't risk this freighter being hijacked at sea. Those idiots round the Suez don't care what they take – hell, one Japanese firm lost 4,000 cars six months ago. What makes you think ours is going to be safe?'

Delaney leaned back in the leather chair. 'We're not going to have to worry about Somali pirates.'

Pallisder turned his head to look at him, then looked at Uli. Petrov smiled indulgently and looked to Delaney.

'Don't tell me you're planning on taking on all the pirates along that coastline as well,' Pallisder laughed, looking at each man in turn.

Delaney smiled at him and shook his head. 'We're not going that way.'

Pallisder sat down and leaned forward on the boardroom table. 'Go on.'

Delaney stood up and began pacing the room. 'A couple of years ago, two German-flagged ships went through the Arctic North-West Passage. They left South Korea, travelled north, then headed west through the Arctic ice.'

'That's impossible!'

Delaney smiled. 'It was once.'

'Hang on a minute,' said Pallisder. 'They did that trip in the Arctic summer. There's no way you're getting through there now.'

Delaney folded his arms. 'Thanks to a little-known phenomenon called *global warming*,' he smiled, acknowledging the ripple of laughter round the room, 'it's now possible to navigate the route most of the year.'

He nodded towards Uli. 'We have a Russian icebreaker leading the way and we've ensured the crew are experienced on that route.'

THIRTY-FOUR

Near Uffington, Oxfordshire, England

Dan walked up the ice-covered garden path and banged on the front door. He shoved his hands in his jacket pockets and stamped his feet, then turned round to take in the sprawling view opposite the house while he waited.

He grimaced. A yellowing grey sky hung over the hillside, meaning another imminent snow storm was due for the Thames Valley. He spun round as the door opened, the warmth from inside rushing by his legs.

Harry grinned out at him. 'Acclimatised yet?'

Dan shook his head and smiled. 'No – let me in before I get hypothermia.' He walked up the step and hung his jacket on the stair banister as Harry shut the door behind him.

'What did you find out then?' asked Harry.

Dan explained. 'And we just can't work out what he's trying to do with the stuff – or where it's going,' he concluded.

Harry headed off down the hallway and pushed open a door which led through to a small dining room. Dan stood to one side while Harry cleared the dining table, sweeping crosswords and a half-finished jigsaw puzzle to one side.

'Retirement games,' he shrugged, and held out his hands for the documents in Dan's hand. 'Let's see what you've come up with.'

Dan handed over the updated notes and watched as Harry carefully laid them out on the table, side by side. Once complete, the documents covered the surface. Harry bent over each one, his finger thoughtfully tapping his chin. Dan wandered over to the window and stared down the country lane, letting his mind drift as he looked at the scenery. He heard Harry murmur behind him and turned.

'Sorry, what?'

Harry was grinning at him. 'Fuel cells.'

Dan walked back to the table and stared at the documents. 'Say again?'

'Fuel cells. That's what he's up to.'

Dan glanced at Harry. 'Are you sure? How did you work that out?'

Harry picked up Peter's lecture notes and held them up to Dan.

'Right from the start, Peter has been telling us 'white gold', 'alternative energy', right? We just looked in the wrong place. We've been looking for something big. That's where we went wrong.'

Harry put down the lecture notes and turned to the financial documents. 'Delaney and his group have been buying up gold mines – but if you look closer, they've been buying up interests in all mines which produce *platinum* group metals – gold, platinum and the rest.'

He put the documents down and turned to Dan. 'We've gathered Delaney's a maniac, and will do anything to protect his real interest – coal, of which he has a lot.'

Harry turned Dan towards the window and pointed. On the far horizon, the cooling towers of Didcot power station could be seen through the grey afternoon haze. 'We also know, despite everything that's being said by the politicians, the UK is going to have to start decommissioning its old coal-fired power stations before too long just to keep our masters in Europe happy. We haven't got anything to take their place Dan – none of the so-called 'alternatives' are ready – we haven't got enough wind farms, no solar arrays and nobody wants a nuclear power station in their back yard.'

Harry turned back to the room and began to gather up the notes. 'Do you know how close we've come to having no electricity the past three winters? We've had to buy in gas from Russia just to keep up with demand. And that's when we *do* have the coal-burning power stations on line.'

Dan folded his arms across his chest. 'So what do you think?'

Harry smiled and beckoned Dan to follow him. 'Come

on – living room. Let's have a warming drink. I think I've earned it.'

Dan followed Harry to the next room and slumped into one of the armchairs next to the fire. The cat raised its head off its bed next to the hearth, opened one eye to glare at Dan, then went back to sleep.

Harry picked up a bottle and two crystal glasses from a side table, handed one of the glasses to Dan and filled both. He placed the bottle on the floor next to his own armchair and sat down.

'Cheers,' he said to Dan.

They both took a swallow of the amber liquid and Dan gestured to Harry to continue.

'I think,' said Harry, 'our own government has been a bit sneaky. As usual. In the United States and here, companies have been researching and perfecting fuel cell technology since the nineteen fifties. It's no big secret – the NASA space program has always relied on them, including the space shuttle. It's the only way they could generate the fuel to power the rockets while at the same time producing water for the crew and craft. What if our own government has been doing the same thing, trying to perfect fuel cell technology on a large scale so when the coal stops burning, they can effectively switch over to fuel cells instead?'

'What's that got to do with Delaney though – not to mention this group of his? What's their interest in it?' asked Dan.

Harry smiled. 'A lot of organisations have been

working on making bigger fuel cells – some are already widely used, but it's really starting to take off now. I should've put two and two together at the beginning – I just didn't see it,' he said.

'Harry – we couldn't have got this far without your knowledge, so don't beat yourself up,' said Dan gently. 'Just help me work this out so I can stop them.'

Harry nodded. 'I know. It's bloody frustrating though. I'm out of practice.' He shrugged, took another sip of his drink, and then continued. 'Fuel cells use platinum group metals.'

'The same that Delaney has been buying into?' interrupted Dan.

'The exact same,' Harry nodded. 'In a fuel cell, the platinum group metal, gold we're presuming in this instance, is used to coat the catalyst – the driver of the fuel cell if you like.'

Dan held up his hand. 'Hang on, slow down. I didn't do physics, remember?'

Harry grunted. 'You did. I seem to remember you flunking it though.'

'Thanks for the reminder,' glared Dan. 'Give me an idiot's guide to fuel cells then.'

Harry smiled. 'Easy. You need a reactant fuel – hydrogen for instance. The catalyst separates the protons and electrons within the fuel and the electrons are forced through a circuit – that's what converts them to electrical power. Once the reaction has taken place, the catalyst puts the electrons back into the mix, which creates waste products like water. Very effective.'

He paused. 'There are a few issues that have cropped up over the years though. It's expensive – obviously, when you're using platinum group metals – and you have to make sure the membrane around the fuel cell is kept hydrated so it doesn't dry out. If it does, it'll create too much heat and the fuel cell itself gets damaged. At the same time though, you have to make sure the water evaporates at a specific rate. If it evaporates too slowly, the fuel cell will become flooded which prevents the hydrogen reaching the catalyst.'

Harry took a sip of his drink then watched as he swirled the liquid around in his glass. 'If someone has worked out how to perfect the manufacture of white gold powder on a large scale, they're going to be able to generate a hell of a lot of energy in just one tiny fuel cell for a fraction of the cost it currently takes.'

Dan closed his eyes, lost in thought. Then he opened them. 'David seems to think Delaney has worked out a way to make an atomic-like weapon. What do you think?'

Harry stared at the fire. The cat stood up and stretched lazily, then yawned and settled back onto its bed. Harry looked over at Dan.

'He might have a point. When you try to turn white gold powder back into metallic gold, it can let off a small amount of radiation. If Delaney's perfected that element of the process, he could very well use the hydrogen to propel the white gold reaction and generate an atomic explosion I suppose, especially if he lets the fuel cell dry out so it generates enough heat to start the reaction.'

Dan nodded. 'That's what I think he's done. He's going to take an alternative energy, probably the best one we've got, and scare people out of using it,' he mused. 'Do you think it'll be enough to protect his coal business?'

'Depends how big it is,' said Harry. 'If he's successful and there's an explosion somewhere, the media is only going to have to use the words 'atomic bomb' once and you've got mass hysteria.'

'And in the meantime, we've got a car on a ship going somewhere and we don't know much more,' groaned Dan, slumping back into the armchair. Suddenly he sat up straight. 'How is Delaney going to make sure the bomb will work when it reaches its destination – don't fuel cells go flat?'

'All he'd have to do is keep the fuel cells charged up – probably by wiring them up to the car battery,' said Harry. 'Until he hits the switch or whatever to trigger the reaction between the white gold powder and the hydrogen, it'll be safe enough to transport.'

'That black sedan is the key,' agreed Dan. 'We have to find it.'

THIRTY-FIVE

London

Dan parked the car on the side of the street and got out, hitting the alarm button on the key fob. He pulled his jacket closed and zipped it up against the cold breeze. He shoved the keys in his jeans pocket, checked the road for traffic then jogged over to the entrance of the apartment block.

He took the stairs two at a time. As he neared the fifth-floor landing, he happened to glance up, and then stopped in his tracks. He held onto the banister, and took another step, peering over the balustrade at the top of the stairs and across to the door to Sarah's apartment.

It had been left slightly open.

He slunk closer to the outer wall of the staircase and

crept upwards. He glanced over the staircase, listening for any movement.

Nothing.

He focused on the open door as he reached the top of the stairs. He edged closer, holding his breath. He stepped carefully over the carpet on the landing. The building was old, despite the modern renovation works, and he didn't trust the floorboards. The last thing he wanted was for one of them to creak theatrically and forewarn anyone still in the apartment.

He took a deep, slow breath through his mouth. His heart beat hard, a vein in his neck pulsing from the adrenaline rushing through his system. He stared at the splintered door frame. Whoever had forced their way into Sarah's apartment had considerable strength – and a crowbar.

Dan hugged the wall as he got closer until he was level with the door. The door was open no more than a few centimetres. Dan crouched down. No sense in giving someone the opportunity of a free headshot if the intruder was armed. He held out his hand and gently pushed the door open. It rocked back on its damaged frame and swung inwards.

Dan craned his neck, peered round the edge of the frame and glanced inside. His heart cranked up a notch.

The apartment had been trashed. He stood up and listened carefully. He couldn't hear a sound. He crept into the hallway and pushed the door behind him, to keep away any nosy neighbours.

He turned left towards the living room first, keeping the shortest distance between him and the front door. He peered around the door to the room. The television had been kicked over, glass shards strewn over the fireside rug while the small coffee table lay upside down, one of the art prints stabbed over the table's upturned legs.

He strode over to the coffee table and wrenched off one of the table legs. Testing its weight in his hand, he glared around the room at the damage and sniffed the air. No gas, at least. Perhaps he'd frightened off the intruder.

Dan tightened his grip on the makeshift weapon, then turned and edged his way along the hallway towards the kitchen. He checked the two bedrooms and bathroom as he progressed. All were turned upside down in the intruder's haste.

He shouldered the table leg as he gently pushed the kitchen door open. Cupboards had been emptied, their contents thrown across the floor. The microwave lay in one corner, its door hanging off its hinges while the refrigerator teetered precariously on one side, water dripping out and over the tiled floor.

Dan turned around, surveying the damage, then stopped dead and stared at the wall. Two words, splashed across the wall in a red liquid.

You're next.

Dan's stomach lurched. *Sarah.*

Dan felt his heart accelerate and a cold sweat creep between his shoulder blades. *Please, no!*

He walked the length of the apartment again,

desperately searching for signs of a violent struggle amongst the debris of the break-in. His eyes scanned across each of the rooms as he strode down the hallway, opening doors, lifting broken furniture off the carpet.

There was no sign of Sarah. What about her computer?

Dan ran back to the guest room where, the day before, he'd spotted a small desk and a printer. He burst through the door. Everything had been smashed to pieces.

He tightened his grip on the table leg and stalked back to the kitchen. He stopped and stared at the wall, then closed his eyes, thinking hard.

He jumped as he heard the front door being pushed open. He opened his eyes and tested the weight of the table leg and then raised it to shoulder height. Someone was moving carefully along the hallway towards the kitchen, creeping along the carpeted surface.

As the kitchen door began to open in towards him, Dan raised the weapon.

He dropped it in surprise as Sarah stepped into the room, her face three shades of white as she surveyed the damage.

She stared up at Dan. 'Been busy?'

He stepped over the debris strewn over the floor and pulled her towards him, hugging her tightly.

'I thought they'd taken you,' he whispered.

Sarah held him, and looked around her at the devastation. She stopped and stared at the message on the wall. 'What happened?'

Dan followed her gaze. 'I think they came looking for

us – and the notes.' He began to straighten the furniture, just to give himself something to do.

Then he turned to Sarah, his heart beating fast. 'We need to go and check on Harry. The bastards might've got to him too.'

She nodded. 'Let's go.'

Darkness fell over the countryside as Dan floored the accelerator and the car sped down the motorway. The traffic lessened the further they left the city behind, the headlight beams picking out bare trees and hedgerows. Dan didn't speak. His only thought was to get to Harry. He'd never forgive himself if something happened to his mentor, his friend.

As they approached Oxford, Dan turned left onto the ring road and hit the main road towards Swindon.

Sarah glanced at her watch. 'It's been two hours, Dan,' she said.

'I know, I know,' he muttered, and pressed his foot to the floor.

He slowed to take a left-hand turn and pointed the car towards Uffington. As the road narrowed, it twisted and turned. Dan guided the vehicle along the lanes, switched the headlights to high beam and concentrated on the road. He noticed his knuckles turning white as they gripped the steering wheel and forced his heart rate down.

Dan turned up the lane to Harry's house and slowed the car to a halt.

'Oh no,' said Sarah.

Dan looked to where she pointed. The front door was wide open. No lights shone from the windows.

'Come on,' he said and jumped out of the car.

THIRTY-SIX

Dan walked slowly up the garden path, looked at the open door and frowned. He used his elbows to push the door open and winced as it creaked on its hinges.

'Harry?' Dan stopped on the threshold. He could smell gas – strong, pungent. He heard a movement behind the living room door. Scratching, scraping.

'Harry?'

He heard a groan from behind the door. Dan stepped round the wooden frame.

'Bloody hell Harry – what happened?'

He dropped to the floor, where Harry was lying in a congealed pool of blood. Groggy, but alive.

'Get me out of here – and switch off the gas taps for goodness sake, I'm not insured,' he murmured, then passed out.

Dan looked back to where Sarah was standing near the doorway, leaning on the wall, her hands over her mouth.

'Don't touch any light switches,' he said. 'Go down the road about one hundred metres and use your mobile to call an ambulance.'

She nodded, turned and ran.

Dan pulled Harry up onto his shoulder and, stooping under the weight, carried him out and away from the house. He set him down gently on the grass verge next to the car, leaning him against the vehicle. Turning, Dan ran back into the house and found the gas outlet outside the back door. He walked through the house, opening all the doors and windows, letting the breeze carry the stench and fumes out of the building.

Dan ran back down the garden path and crouched next to Harry. He picked up an arm, held Harry's wrist in the palm of his hand and checked for a pulse. It was weak, but there.

Harry murmured in his comatose state and began to waken. He opened his eyes and looked around wildly.

'It's okay Harry, I'm here,' said Dan, putting his arm around the older man. 'The gas is off. Ambulance is on its way.'

Harry nodded and closed his eyes again. 'Thank you.'

'Can you tell me what happened?' Dan asked.

Harry swallowed. 'Bastard forced his way in. Whacked me over the head and left me for dead. Probably turned the gas on to make it look like an accident.'

Dan nodded. 'Sounds familiar. Can you remember what he looked like?'

'Tall, thin – academic looking, wore glasses,' murmured Harry.

The sound of a siren in the distance broke the silence.

'You were lucky, you know that?' said Dan. 'A cut like that on your head, you're lucky you didn't bleed to death.'

Harry smiled and reached into the pocket of his cardigan. He drew out a small bottle and shook it. 'Heart medicine. Trust me – I wasn't going to bleed to death. This stuff could stop a flood.'

Dan grinned. 'You're still going in the ambulance.'

Harry grimaced. 'Damn,' he said, and then passed out.

Dan squirmed and tried to get comfortable on the hard plastic chair and did his best to ignore the smell of antiseptic in the air. He shivered. He could hear his own cries of pain as he was carried through to an emergency hospital unit, far away. The stench of his own blood and shit. Fiery shrapnel in gaping wounds festering in his limbs. The screams from his friends as the medical staff did their best to save lives, stop the pain.

Dan shook his head, rubbed his eyes and stood up. He wandered over to a notice-board, reading whatever was pinned there to try to keep the memories away. He looked around at the sound of heels on the tiled floor. Sarah was hurrying towards him.

'How is he?' Dan asked, clutching her arm as she reached him.

'He'll be okay. They've got him on a low dose of oxygen to help get the gas out of his bloodstream and they've given him a mild sedative to help him rest.'

Dan hugged her with relief. 'Did you tell them what happened?'

Sarah shook her head. 'Not exactly. I told them he's living on his own, tends to be a bit forgetful about things.' She shrugged. 'I didn't think you or Harry would want to make a big fuss of it, given the circumstances.'

Dan nodded. 'Good thinking.'

Sarah looked around. 'So, the man with the glasses *did* follow us from Singapore.'

'Looks that way. He moves fast too – Delaney must be beginning to worry about us.'

'Do you think Harry will be safe here?'

'Probably,' said Dan. 'They've got security on the main entrances. The nurse's station in the ward won't let anyone visit without an appointment and identification. I'll have a word with someone I know and ask him to look after Harry too.' He looked at his watch, then nodded to himself.

Sarah interrupted his thoughts. 'What is it?'

Dan looked along the hospital corridor, then down at Sarah.

'Come with me,' he said, and hurried out to the visitors' car park.

Near Denchworth, Oxfordshire

Dan swung the car left and slowed to a halt in front of two large gate pillars. A rusting wrought-iron gate blocked their way, a chain and padlock hanging between the bars.

'What is this place?' asked Sarah, sitting up straight in her seat.

'Home,' said Dan, as he opened his door and stepped out into the frosty air.

Sarah frowned and turned to ask him what he meant, but stopped short as he slammed the car door shut. She heard the muffled sound of his boots on the gravel driveway and watched as he walked towards the gates, removing a set of keys from his jeans pocket. He turned slightly back towards the car, holding the keys up in the light. Once satisfied he had the right one selected, he turned back to the gate and inserted the key in the padlock. Removing the chain, he first opened one side of the gates, then the other and walked back to the car.

Dan climbed in, throwing the chain and padlock on the floor by Sarah's feet. Easing off the handbrake, he drove the car slowly through the gates. He stopped, retrieved the padlock and chain and got out, locking the gates behind them. He walked back to the car, pocketed the keys and got in.

'That's bloody freezing out there,' he said, releasing the handbrake and guiding the car up the driveway.

Sarah remained silent, watching the headlight beams as

they shone across trees and overgrown shrubs while the gravel driveway wound its way between them. After a few hundred metres, the shrubs gave way to what had once been a manicured lawn. It was now overgrown, with whole flower beds lost to a jungle of green.

Dan coaxed the vehicle round the driveway as it curved to the right, the headlights illuminating a large house. Built from brick with large bay windows facing the driveway, the house looked forbidding.

Dan glanced over at Sarah. 'It looks better in daylight.'

'Really?' She looked up at the building as Dan brought the car to a halt. 'I hope it's got heating,' she said as she unbuckled her seat belt.

'It will have once I've lit some fires,' he replied and opened his door. 'It'll be ages before the old oil furnace gets up to speed.'

Stepping round to the back of the car, he reached in and pulled their bags off the back seat. Dan's feet crunched across the gravel as he made his way up to the front entrance, a large double door under a covered porch. Dropping the bags at his feet, he retrieved his keys from his pocket and unlocked the door. He hit a switch just inside the doorway and a series of lights lit up through the hallway. He turned to Sarah and executed a mock bow.

'After you.'

Sarah glanced at him briefly and stepped through into the house, intrigued by the thought this really *was* Dan's home. He followed her, took off his jacket, hung it on a coat rack and placed the bags at the bottom of an ornate flight of stairs.

'We'll deal with those later. Let's get a fire going then I'll show you around.'

Sarah hugged her coat around her, wrinkling her nose at the musty smell of neglect. She followed Dan through a doorway to the right of the hallway. He hit another switch and a series of wall lamps flickered to life. A couple of light bulbs had blown, sending pockets of shadows across the room in places. Dan walked into the room and leaned over an armchair, switched on a table lamp and then turned and stepped over to the large bay window and pulled large velvet drapes over the glass.

'That'll help keep the cold out,' he said.

Sarah looked around the room in amazement. It was a living area, that much was evident, but most of the space had been taken up with bookcases. She walked up to one of them and cast her eye over the titles, brushing away dust and cobwebs. *Geology of Scotland*, *The Jurassic Coastline of Dorset*, *Petrified Forests of Papua New Guinea*. Journals and articles filled the spaces in between. She wandered along the display, turning her head left and right to read the spines, faded gold leaf catching the light.

In places, fossils and lumps of rock jostled for space with the books, leaving crumbs of mineral deposits scattered across the shelves and mixing with the dust. Sarah picked up one of the rocks, a large black, shiny lump of stone with small holes like pinpricks dotted over the surface.

'Tektite,' Dan called out from the other side of the room. 'Driest rock on Earth.'

'Hmm,' said Sarah and put it back. She turned to watch Dan as he tore up an old newspaper and stacked it in the grate with kindling wood.

He rolled up his sleeves, reached up to the fireplace and felt around until his fingers found a matchbox, then lit the fire, moving the kindling around until it caught properly. He leaned over and picked up a couple of logs from a basket next to the fireplace and stacked them neatly on top of the flames.

'Right, that should do it,' he said standing up. He turned to Sarah. 'What?'

She was looking at him with her arms folded across her chest. 'You know what. When were you going to tell me about this place?'

He shrugged. 'Probably never. But we needed somewhere safe to stay and I don't think anyone will find us here. I hadn't even really thought of it myself until earlier at the hospital.'

Sarah fell into one of the armchairs next to the fire and looked at the dust cloud that reached into the air. 'When was the last time you were here?'

'I don't know – hang on a minute.' Dan reached down into the fire and pulled out a piece of newspaper, the end smouldering. Squinting in the bad light, he waved it in the air to put the flames out and read the date at the bottom. 'Here you go. January twelfth.'

Sarah looked around. 'Only two months ago – and you didn't clean?'

Dan laughed. 'January twelfth – *last year*.'

Sarah stared at him. 'Is there anyone else here?'

He shook his head. 'No. Not unless next door's cat still hunts in the barn.'

THIRTY-SEVEN

MARCH 2012

London, England

Dan walked out of the underground station and began to walk up the street. The pavements were slick with rain and grease, slippery to the step. Dan grimaced. It was a dirty city, with chewing gum and dog shit vying for position with litter strewn over the path and gutters. Pulling up his jacket collar to shield himself from the fine drizzle being blown horizontally down his neck, he side-stepped an empty fast food container and turned the corner.

The offices of David's team occupied a nondescript nineteen-sixties edifice four doors down, the steps partially hidden behind two vagrants wrapped in blankets sleeping off the depressing morning. Dan caught the eye of one of them as he climbed the step and reached into his pocket for some money, handing it to him as he passed. The man nodded in appreciation and pulled his woolly hat down lower over his ears. Dan bent down to whisper to him.

'Grow a beard or something – you stand out a mile.'

The man's eyes opened wide and he stared after Dan as he opened the entrance door and stepped through. Grinning to himself, Dan walked over to the sleek reception area and waited while the security guard finished a phone call. He looked around at the sand-coloured marble walls and at the installation art gracing the atrium and wondered if he could work in such a place. Probably not.

He turned around as the security guard finished his call. Walking over, he handed him David's business card. 'Hi – can you tell him Dan Taylor is here to see him?'

The security guard glared at him. 'Have you got an appointment?'

Dan glared back. 'No. I don't need one.' He turned and sat down on one of the chairs set back against the front wall of the building. Picking up a six-month-old magazine, he ignored the security guard, who took the hint and picked up the phone.

Minutes later, Dan threw down the magazine and stood up as the elevator doors opened. He waited while David Ludlow strode across the reception area towards him. They appraised each other silently before David held out his hand.

'I'm glad you could make it.'

Dan shook hands, tentatively accepting the peace offering.

David steered him towards the elevator and they stepped in. As David punched a key, the doors swept closed and he turned to Dan.

'What made you change your mind?'

Dan shrugged. 'It got personal when Delaney went after Sarah and Harry.'

David nodded and said nothing. The two men rode up through the rest of the building in silence. When the doors opened, David led the way to his office, closed the door behind Dan and walked over to his desk. Philippa stood in the centre of the room and eyed Dan warily.

'What exactly is your field of expertise?' she asked.

Dan grinned. 'This and that. Yours?'

Philippa arched an eyebrow. 'I'm not sure I should answer that.'

Dan shrugged, smiling. He turned to David. 'Is she always like this?'

David nodded. 'Yes – so watch yourself.'

Dan pulled out a chair and sat down without being asked. 'So, are you going to tell me what you do here? What is it – MI5?'

David sat down and swivelled his chair to face Dan and shook his head. 'Nothing on the radar. Mostly, we protect the UK's energy assets from terrorist organisations. I report directly to the Minister for Energy as well as filing reports and advice to the Ministry of Defence. Sometimes I provide a brief directly to the Prime Minister. A lot of the time we just advise, keep our eyes and ears open and provide support to the other agencies. Every now and again though, we find someone like Delaney and the rule book goes out the window.'

He stood up and paced the room, turning a pen between his fingers. 'MI5 and MI6 are aware of our existence, as are our colleagues in the United States and Australia. We're picky about who we work with. At the end of the day, I'm responsible for safeguarding a future for this country's economy from anyone who might be a threat.'

He stopped pacing and looked at Dan. 'I have to ask. What's Sarah's involvement in this?'

'I guess she's just trying to figure out why Peter had to die,' said Dan.

'And she's probably worked out it will make one hell of a story,' added David. He threw the pen down on the desk. 'Tell her from me that any article she intends to write will be subject to scrutiny by this office first. I won't have this project compromised by anyone – especially a reporter.'

Dan shrugged. 'I'll try.'

David slammed his hand down on the desk. 'You'll do better than that, Dan. You'll make sure she doesn't. There are people higher up than me who will do anything – *anything* to make sure information about this technology doesn't reach the public domain before we're ready. If

Sarah goes to print, I will not vouch for her safety. Or yours.'

Dan nodded. 'I'll speak to her.'

David shook his head, turned and walked over to the office wall which was strewn with notes, photographs, satellite images and maps. He beckoned to Dan and tapped the photo of them and two others next to the Warrior armoured vehicle.

'Remember this?'

Dan stepped closer and looked at the picture. It seemed a lifetime ago. He shivered. 'I wish I'd known that was the last time we'd all be together,' he said. 'After all we'd been through, we still went down like a naive bunch of amateurs.' He looked away. The memories were still too painful.

David watched him carefully, then pulled the photo off the wall and turned it round to face Dan. 'What do you remember about that day?'

Dan turned and stared at David. 'Why?'

David walked back over to his desk and sat down, then gestured to Dan to take a seat, placing the photograph between them. 'It might be important.'

Dan eased himself into the chair and looked at David for a few seconds before speaking. 'I remember getting the call that there'd been activity out on the north road – you know, that single lane track out of town. So they sent us to investigate. Two in the front of the Warrior, four of us in the back. You, me, Terry, Mitch, Dicko and H.'

'Go on.'

'We reached the location, radioed in and got out. There was no sniper activity – we put it down to the lack of building cover. There was a house on the left side of the track – mud and bricks, a low wall keeping in a goat and some chickens. There was an old couple staring at us from the house. You shouted to Terry to get the old lady in the doorway to move away from the area.'

Dan pulled the photograph towards him and held it in his hands before continuing. 'Me and Mitch began the routine – you, Terry, Dicko and H began to cordon off the area and watch out for snipers. I remember you sending Terry off in the direction of the house to make sure the old couple weren't hiding anyone. Dicko and H began to walk along the track. That kid on the bike – he cycled into the middle of the road. Dicko and H ran to him, sent him back. Then they went to check out the dunes to the side of the road to make sure we weren't ambushed from there.'

He rubbed his hand across his face, remembering too well what happened next. 'Mitch saw something – a movement, I don't know, something made him look up to where Dicko and H were walking and then over to the house. Then he turned to me and Christ, his face was so pale. He said "this isn't the one" and then it all turned to shit.'

Dan carefully put down the photograph. He remembered the noise, the screams; Dicko – where was he? H lying there in pieces crying for help, knowing he was dying; shouts in a foreign language; and then, darkness. He looked up at David.

'I don't remember anything else.'

David nodded. 'You were out of it for a couple of days straight. I think they thought it'd help with the trauma more than any injuries.'

Dan snorted. 'Yeah, well it didn't. I'd trade anything to lose the nightmares.'

David leaned over and picked up the photograph. He glanced down at it, and then looked up at Dan.

'What if I told you Terry didn't die?'

THIRTY-EIGHT

Dan felt his jaw drop open.

'What?'

David said nothing and watched Dan as his brain processed the information.

'T-that means – *fuck* – we left him there?'

David nodded slowly. 'After we got you and Mitch onto the helicopter, we searched the area. There was a lot of mess, obviously, and it was too hard to make out if any of the clothing was ours. That blast knocked in one wall of the building opposite, the far end of our patrol line.'

'Where Terry was,' added Dan.

'Yes. Well, we searched that area too – all we could see was rubble, bricks, dust, blood and some scorched clothing. No sign of Terry. We had to assume he'd come out of the building and been in the way of the blast when it went off.'

David stood up and, picking up a remote control from

his desk, wandered over to a small television in the corner. He turned to Dan. 'Come here and watch this.'

Dan wandered over to join him, standing in front of two armchairs. 'What is it?'

'A few weeks ago, I started wondering whether we were missing a link in this whole mess. How on earth did someone like Delaney get involved in bomb-making? We know he's a megalomaniac and obsessed with protecting his assets but who else is involved? Someone's got to be helping him finance it – all that research and development would be too easy to track if it was just being operated out of his companies. But who's building the bomb for him? It's almost as if he's got outside help – which doesn't make sense because Delaney doesn't trust anyone.'

'So you reckon someone's got a grudge against the UK government and Delaney's taking advantage of that?'

David nodded. 'What if Delaney found someone who had his own agenda and turned it to his advantage?'

'What are you saying?' asked Dan, frowning.

David smiled. 'Watch.' He hit the 'play' button on the remote and the television began to run a news item. 'This is from three years ago,' he explained, pointing to the screen. He turned up the sound, the male reporter's sombre voice cutting in.

'... bomb disposal squad turned up at the location and began to defuse the device using a robot. Unknown to them, the bomb they were defusing was a decoy...'

The camera panned out. Behind the reporter, dust and smoke churned the air from the explosion, a ruined house teetered to the left of the screen while people milled about behind the reporter, shouting and crying as they stepped over the rubble searching for family and friends. The reporter ignored them and continued filing his report.

'… A second bomb exploded while the soldiers were working, killing at least five civilians and two army personnel. Two soldiers remain in a critical condition at a hospital at an undisclosed location …'

'Jesus,' said Dan, sitting down heavily in one of the armchairs. It was the first time he'd seen any news footage of the aftermath of the explosion. The hairs on the back of his neck stood up on end as he watched the scene.

The camera panned round to the left, taking in the sheer devastation of the blast, while the reporter continued. '…the UK government has pledged it will keep on reducing troop numbers here, despite the ongoing problems, saying that this was an isolated case and attacks on troops are decreasing. The local populace is asking who is going to protect them from internal threats once the Western coalition forces have gone…'

David stopped the tape. 'Did you see it?'

Dan looked up at him. 'What?'

David smiled and hit the rewind button. He stopped the recording when it reached the part where the camera began to pan away from the reporter's face and over the scene of the blast. Then he hit the play button again, the reporter's voice continuing over the scene.

'…reducing troop numbers here, despite the ongoing…'

David hit the pause button. 'There.'

He pointed at the screen and went through each frame of the film, one at a time.

Dan got up and walked closer to the screen. From behind the ruins of the house, a figure appeared. Dan squinted. 'It's too hard to make out.'

'Keep watching.'

Tall, ragged, silhouetted in the weak sun filtering through the dust-laden breeze, the figure seemed to waver, before turning and disappearing back behind the building.

Dan stood up and looked at David. 'No way.'

David held his gaze. 'How close were we to the border?'

Dan wracked his brains. 'About fifteen miles. He'd never make it, not after surviving that.'

David walked back to his desk. 'You're assuming he was injured in the blast.'

Dan nodded, following him. 'He must've been. All of us were, one way or another. I remember him being next to that building before Mitch yelled.'

'Yes, but did he stop when Mitch yelled, or did he expect the worst and run for cover?' David mused.

Dan shrugged. 'I suppose it's possible. But, to me, it doesn't give him a big enough motive.'

David reached down to a file on his desk and flipped it open. He sifted through the papers on the top and lifted out a two-page document, then slid it across the desk to Dan, who turned it around and began reading.

'Holy shit.'

'Exactly my thoughts. The Military Police were about to arrest Terry for drug trafficking at the base. They just didn't have enough evidence to take it all the way to court martial so they were biding their time,' explained David. 'Terry must have found out and planned his escape, taking advantage of the confusion after that roadside bomb.'

Dan leaned back in his chair. 'But he'd have been incredibly lucky. There's no reason to believe he made it through the desert on his own. We don't even know if he survived the blast, so all of this is conjecture.'

David nodded. He picked up a photograph from the folder and flicked it across the desk. Dan picked it up and looked at it, then back at David. The photograph was a still shot taken from the news report, enlarged by computer and sharpened to bring the figure into focus.

'Shit.'

David nodded. 'Indeed.'

'That was three years ago though – not enough to prove he's Delaney's bomb-maker.'

'True,' David conceded. He reached back into the file of papers. 'Try this.'

He tossed another photograph across the desk to Dan. 'This one was taken in December at Bangkok airport.'

Dan looked at the photograph. 'Jesus – he hasn't even bothered to disguise himself.'

'He doesn't need to – he's dead, remember?'

THIRTY-NINE

Oxford, England

Sarah turned to Dan and shoved her hands into her jacket pockets. 'What the hell are we doing here?'

Dan locked the car and walked on ahead of her before turning on to the track leading to the River Cherwell. Looking around at the stalactite-like ice on the trees, he sighed. 'I miss Peter as well, Sarah. I just thought if we came here, I might be inspired – that's all. I just don't understand why he didn't tell the authorities what he really knew while he still had the chance. I mean, it's a lonely place to die here, isn't it?' He shrugged and turned, stomping off into the trees, away from the path, careful not to slip on the ice-covered puddles.

Sarah lowered her head and blew into her jacket, desperately trying to create some sort of warmth. Despite her boots and warm socks, she could feel her toes slowly turning to ice. She raised her head and squinted at the bright sunlight streaking through the empty trees and began to follow Dan, her footsteps crunching on the ice-strewn undergrowth. She stamped her feet as she walked, trying to get the circulation flowing through her veins again.

Dan had stopped a few metres ahead of her and was standing, staring up at the tree branches, lost in thought.

Sarah slowed as she approached him, then stopped. 'What now?'

Dan lowered his gaze and looked at her, almost startled to see her there. 'Sorry – lost in thought.' He scuffed at the frozen earth at his feet before speaking again. 'Did Peter ever mention being contacted by anyone from my old army unit?'

Sarah frowned. 'No. Well, not that he mentioned to me – why? Why on earth would someone contact Peter about you?'

Dan grunted to himself and continued walking.

Sarah threw her arms up in exasperation, and then followed. 'I'm sorry – that came out wrong. Wait.' She jogged to catch up with him and grabbed hold of his sleeve. 'Wait.'

Dan stopped and turned. 'It's okay – I know. Why would someone I used to work with want to speak with Peter? But someone did – I'm sure of it.' He ran his hand through his hair.

Sarah folded her arms. 'Okay – there's something

you're not telling me. Out with it.'

Dan grinned. 'Is that how you journalists approach potential interviewees?'

Sarah shoved him, hard. Dan slipped on the frozen path and grabbed a sapling to steady himself.

'Hey – watch it!'

'Stop changing the subject – what do you know?'

Dan took hold of her hand and pulled her over to a large fallen log. Brushing the frost off the surface, he sat down, gesturing for Sarah to join him. As she sat down, he turned to her.

'I met with David Ludlow when we got back here last week.'

She stared at him. 'Was that wise?'

He smiled. 'I didn't think so at the time, but let's face it – who else is going to help us?'

Sarah nodded. 'Go on.'

'He thinks one of the guys in our team we thought was killed in Iraq actually survived.'

Sarah's breath was reflected in the winter air as she exhaled deeply and considered the consequences.

Dan looked around the icy woodland. 'If he's right, I think we might have found a motive – at least from the bomb-maker's point of view.'

Sarah wrapped her arms around herself. Her eyes flickered as she took in the scenery around the clearing while she processed the information. Finally, she spoke. 'Why on earth did you go there, Dan? To Iraq, I mean. It just seems so unlike you.'

Dan smiled. 'I just had to get away, do something a bit more meaningful than just do what everyone expected me to do. I suppose it was my own sort of rebellion. A bit later in life perhaps, but I don't regret it.'

Sarah glanced over at him. 'What about the recurring nightmares?'

'How did you know?'

Sarah reached out and took hold of his hand, noting it was much warmer than hers, despite the freezing temperatures. 'I could hear you crying out in your sleep again last night. Sorry.'

Dan squeezed her hand before letting his slip out of her hold. 'It's okay.' He stood up and stretched. 'Are you cold enough yet?'

Sarah smiled. 'Bloody freezing.'

He grinned and held out his hand. 'Come on – let's find a pub with a nice open fire.'

Sarah stood up and brushed off the back of her jeans. 'That has to be the best idea you've had all day.'

Sarah looked up as Dan walked over from the bar, a drink in each hand. Approaching the table, he put a wine glass down in front of Sarah.

'There you go – mulled wine. That should thaw you out.'

Sarah held the glass in both hands, warming her fingers. 'Oh, that's great – bliss,' she breathed.

Dan grinned, sitting down on the cushioned bench seat next to her. 'You're such a wimp.'

'I know. But I'm happy being a wimp.' She took a sip, the cinnamon flavours mixing with the red wine, warming her from the inside. She loosened her scarf and put it with her gloves on the seat. She glanced at the window, condensation running down it while outside, the sun ducked behind ominous clouds. She sighed. 'I can't help feeling we're being manipulated.'

Dan took a swig from his pint before putting the glass down on the table. 'I know. I had a good talk with David – almost friendly really. The problem is, he's spent so long playing the political game, it's hard to know if he's being honest or not.'

Sarah leaned back, stretched out and tapped her foot along with the pub's sound system gently playing in the background. 'I don't want to give up now, Dan. I know you'll just say it's my journalism background but it's more than that – I feel like I owe it to Pete. And myself.'

Dan nodded. 'I know. You don't have to explain yourself to me.' He squeezed her hand.

Sarah felt herself instinctively pulling back from his grasp, then relaxed.

'What are you thinking?' he asked.

She smiled to herself. 'Just that I think we need to keep going. We have to stop this guy. I know we're completely out of our depth but I've got this gut feeling we're on the right track. We can't give up now.'

FORTY

London, England

Dan gestured to Sarah to follow him through the door, walked over to David's desk and pulled out a seat for her. Sarah stood at the threshold, and cocked an eyebrow at Dan before stepping towards him. As she approached the desk, Dan made the formal introductions. Sarah held David's proffered hand briefly and then sat down. Dan shut the office door, pulled out a chair next to Sarah's and gestured to David to begin.

David held Sarah's gaze and slid a sheet of paper across the desk to her. 'Before we begin, I'm going to have to ask you to sign this.'

Sarah glanced down at the document. 'Official Secrets Act?' She slid the document back towards David and stood up. 'I don't think so, thanks.'

'Sit down.'

She looked down at Dan. 'What?'

'Sit down – and sign it.'

'Wh…'

'Just do it – please.'

He nodded at her. *It's okay.*

Sarah sat down and began reading the document.

'It's a formality,' explained David. 'I just need to be able to control what you tell the general public. Before, during and after the event. The last thing we need is mass hysteria. You can sign it now and continue to be part of this investigation, or I can have you imprisoned until after this is over. It's up to you.'

Sarah nodded. Then signed the document.

'Thank you,' said David, taking the pen from her. His face softened. 'A few months ago, I don't think you'd have done that.'

'A few months ago, I didn't have a dead ex-husband, a dead friend nor the sneaky suspicion you know a lot more than you're letting on,' said Sarah defiantly. She folded her arms and glared at David, then at Dan. 'Now we have the pleasantries out of the way, are you going to bring me up to speed on what you two have been discussing behind my back?'

David reached out for a file on his desk and slid it towards himself. Opening it, he brought out a large photograph then spun it around to face Dan and Sarah.

What is it?' asked Sarah.

'Forensics from the explosion in Singapore,' he said.

Sarah stared at him.

David shrugged. 'We were still close by. I could've given you a lift to the airport if you'd waited another ten minutes.'

Dan picked up the photo and studied it before staring at David. 'What the hell did they use?' he asked. 'I've never seen anything like this before.'

David flicked through the notes in the file. 'Nothing conventional. Tech nerds reckon it's a new form of propulsion. They're still investigating. Which to me,' he said, throwing the file shut in disgust, 'means they haven't got a clue.'

David stood up and beckoned Dan and Sarah to follow him. He pushed open the door and walked across the open-plan office to a separate room.

'You can set yourselves up in here,' he explained. 'If you need anything, ask Philippa – she's quite resourceful.' He turned to Dan. 'Meet me back in my office in five minutes. Let's see if you can help fill in some of the gaps we have in our investigation.'

Dan nodded, sank onto a sofa in the corner of the room and began to read the report provided by the technicians about the car bomb. It was woefully short on detail. He wondered if he'd have found anything more, if he'd had the chance. His first priority had been to get Sarah to safety.

He glanced over while she set up her laptop on the empty desk, unravelling wires and checking phone lines were working. He smiled – she was tougher than he'd first thought, her mind always on the new story she hoped would propel her into journalistic stardom.

Dan re-arranged the photos in the file, then clipped them back together and stood up. 'I'm going to get a coffee then go and see David,' he said. 'Back later.'

Sarah nodded. 'Okay. I'll catch up on some work emails, then have a dig around to see what I can uncover about shipping movements out of Singapore to see if I can find that car.'

David looked up as Dan entered the office, stood up and walked over to the incident board. 'Come here and take a look. See if you can fill in any of these other gaps for us.'

Dan put his coffee mug down on the desk and joined David. He scanned the evidence David's team had managed to collate so far. Suddenly he pointed to a photograph on the wall – a man, stocky build, wearing a dark grey suit and glasses.

'Who's he?'

David took a closer look. 'A rather nasty character by the name of Charles Moore. Hired gun we reckon, although we've got nothing to prove it at the moment – why?'

'He's the one who destroyed Peter's house. We saw him outside Sarah's house before we went to Australia. My bet is he was responsible for the deaths of Peter and Hayley too.'

David unpinned the photograph and handed it to Philippa. 'Organise a few copies of that, would you?'

She nodded and left the room.

David turned back to Dan. 'Anything else?'

'I reckon Delaney's hired him – he's a contract killer. Very clever. Seems to have a knack of making his hits look like accidents most of the time. When Sarah's friend Hayley was killed last month, it was meant to look like a car accident while we were in Brisbane. She'd been helping us find out more about Delaney and he obviously didn't like us poking around.'

'What do you think Delaney's up to?' asked David.

Dan rubbed his chin. 'Looking through Peter's research notes, I reckon it's something to do with that white gold powder he was lecturing about. It appears to have the capability of being the future of energy. More environmentally friendly than nuclear or any fossil fuel and pushes out four times the power.'

David studied him carefully before continuing. 'Delaney has been getting more and more obsessed with protecting his coal business against any environmental legislation. We know he's been lobbying politicians here in the UK and using his contacts to do the same in Australia. Let's face it, he's not the only one.'

Dan nodded. 'He's just more extremist about it.'

'To put it mildly,' David agreed. 'He seems to have become fanatical with the thought that white gold powder is going to wreck his empire – it's already being used for fuel cell technology because it uses a lot less power than oil-based fuels. When the UK Defence Department started putting out feelers for how that power could be harnessed to drive military aircraft at supersonic speed, the Government also began to look at how white gold powder could fuel power stations instead of coal.'

Dan grinned. 'Bet your lot are kicking themselves for selling off the UK's gold bullion in the nineties then.'

David ignored the remark and continued. 'The last couple of winters have proved our existing gas supplies can't cope without us buying in more. Oil supplies are a lot lower than we're telling the public. Of course, that information has somehow leaked out to Delaney and he appears to be doing all he can to protect himself.'

Dan picked up his coffee and took a sip. 'So – what do you think he's up to? Are you going to tell me?'

David sat back down at his desk. 'We've got reason to believe Delaney's been buying up gold mines over the past five years specifically to refine the method of producing this white gold powder so he can defeat the science we've been investigating. If we're right, he's managed to find a way to create radioactive material when turning the white powder back into metallic gold.'

Dan looked at David. 'Are you saying he's managed to create a weapon with this stuff?'

David nodded. 'We think he's been successful too. If he can prove to the world that white gold powder is too dangerous to consider as an alternative fuel source, he's going to buy himself a good number of years to exploit the coal and oil markets. No-one will go near the white gold powder. Look at hydrogen – no-one's designed an aircraft using that fuel since the Hindenberg disaster – you'd never get enough passengers to make it a viable project.'

He paused. 'In the meantime, he's using profits from his coal mining ventures to buy up gold mines. In twenty years' time, he'll probably begin to sell the idea of white gold powder as an alternative energy source and start reaping the rewards himself.'

Dan frowned. 'How does he expect to get away with it?'

David shrugged. 'Come on. It won't take much for the media and public to assume any attack on the Western world would be made by the usual extremists. Why not just pin it on them? Unless you and I can track down this weapon and prove it's Delaney behind it before it goes off,' he said, 'we haven't got a hope in hell.'

FORTY-ONE

Brisbane, Australia

Morris Delaney threw the whiteboard pen onto the desk and grinned at his guests. He took a long swallow of the twenty-year-old single malt in his glass and savoured the warm burn in his throat.

'You're absolutely sure this is going to work? We won't have a second chance,' asked Petrov.

Delaney nodded. 'We built a smaller one and detonated that down one of the mine shafts to test it.'

Uli smiled. 'I like your thinking. I presume it was remote?'

'Yeah – middle of nowhere.'

Pallisder looked at the photograph in his hand and quickly put it down on the desk, realising his hands were beginning to shake. 'How did you design the chamber?'

'It's easier if I show you rather than describe it,' Delaney explained and gestured to Pallisder to sit down. Taking a marker pen, he drew the rough shape of the canister on a pad, and then added a smaller box shape with a series of dots around the frame.

'The super-conducted precious metal – white gold powder in this case – is currently housed in a borosilicate glass cylinder. The glass cylinder sits in one side of this panelled housing. On the other side sits the timing device.' He drew in a rough circuit system and connecting wires. 'Once the timer begins its countdown, you've got about nine minutes to get clear of the area – otherwise you're toast. The cylinder itself is just there for protection. The more we package the glass cylinder, the better protected it is and we can control the explosion with the timer.'

'Why the glass cylinder?'

The other man grinned.

'It's the only way to stop the white gold powder from quantum tunnelling its way out and into the atmosphere before we're ready. We're the first to create a weapon using this stuff – most people are more interested in converting it back into gold because it generates a higher yield. Both the British and American governments are trying to build aircraft which will use its anti-gravitational capabilities. Using it as a weapon probably hasn't crossed anybody's radar.'

He threw the pen on the desk and sat down opposite Pallisder and Petrov. He pointed at the sketch of the glass cylinder. 'During those nine minutes, we instigate a chain reaction which will begin to turn the white gold powder back into metallic gold.'

Petrov looked at him and raised his eyebrow. 'When I agreed to help fund this project of yours, I said I wanted to create a major impact – lining the streets with gold wasn't exactly what I had in mind.'

Delaney chuckled. 'We're a long way off from achieving that on any great scale, so you don't have to worry. When we tried to turn white powder gold back into metallic gold, it created radioactive material. Now we've just increased the quantities so when the two electrodes in the canister begin to burn...'

'... you've got the equivalent of an atomic bomb,' finished Pallisder.

Delaney nodded. 'A small one compared with some, but it'll get us the impact we're after.'

Pallisder studied the drawing carefully. 'What's the radius of the blast?'

Delaney flicked through some notes. 'Here you go – we added a bit more than the test device. I reckon you ought to hold fire buying any real estate within a twenty mile radius.'

Petrov laughed with Delaney. Neither man noticed Pallisder's face go pale.

'It's the superconductivity created by this stuff that's the threat to the coal, gas and oil industries,' said Petrov. 'If anyone works out how to generate power using this white gold stuff on a large scale, we're finished.'

Delaney laughed and stood up, slapping the other man

on the back. 'I don't think you need to worry there. By making an explosive device out of super-conducted heated gold – white gold powder – we can derail any further research into its viability as an alternative energy for years – probably decades.'

Uli shuffled in his seat. 'Yes, but will it have the effect we want?'

'Absolutely. Remember the old black and white film footage of that airship disaster? That was decades ago and people still won't reconsider hydrogen as an alternative fuel on a large scale. When people think of hydrogen, they immediately think of the Hindenberg or hydrogen bombs.'

Pallisder glanced out the window. The sun was high over the city, reflecting the river traffic onto the windows of the skyscraper opposite. He stood up and stretched, trying to appear relaxed in front of the other two men.

'Well,' he said, 'You appear to have it all under control Morris. When do you think you'll be able to give us another update?'

Delaney walked the two men to the reception area. Pallisder blinked in the bright open space. He could feel the beginning of a headache starting to pulse in his temples.

'I'll know more in a few days,' smiled Delaney. 'I'm just waiting for confirmation from a contact to make sure our plan is still safe, then I'll let you know.'

Pallisder nodded and, shaking hands with the two men, headed for the elevator.

He stepped out through the atrium of the office block

and walked across to the waiting limousine. The driver stood next to the passenger door, waited until Pallisder was ready, then opened the door for him. Pallisder climbed in and savoured the cool air-conditioning. It was proving to be a hot summer.

'Take me home,' he said, and settled back into the leather seat for the ride.

London, England

Dan turned as Sarah appeared in the doorway of David's office, her face flushed. 'Both of you – come and look at this.'

She disappeared again. Dan looked at David. They both shrugged and hurried to where Sarah sat at the spare desk, a series of printed documents in her hand.

'Okay, sit down,' she said. 'I want to run a theory by you.'

Sarah waited until Dan and David gave her their full attention.

'What have you got?' asked Dan.

Sarah handed them each a copy of the paperwork. 'I was just having a flick through the stories on one of the news wires, catching up, when I came across this one. There was a house invasion at the beginning of January in Ramsgate in Kent. Nothing was taken but the place was trashed – presumably to make it look like a burglary.'

Dan opened his mouth to interrupt but Sarah held up her hand.

'Hang on. There was a woman in the house at the time. The police think there was more than one intruder. By the time they'd finished with her, there wasn't much left intact.' She shivered. 'The police report states she probably died as a result of blood loss.'

Dan leaned forward. 'What's it got to do with us?'

Sarah looked at him, a grim expression on her face. 'I did a bit of digging around,' she explained. 'It turns out the woman is, sorry was, married to the captain of a freighter called *World's End.*' She paused. 'He and the ship haven't been seen since it left Singapore in January.'

David frowned. 'I hate coincidences. The ship should have a transponder fitted to it – we should be able to track its current location with that.'

Sarah nodded. 'I already thought of that.' She turned back to her laptop. Her hands flew over the keyboard, a staccato string of commands flowing into the computer. She brought up two websites, and spun the computer monitor to face the two men.

'Okay, we have couple of ways to track the ship. One, Lloyds Register – this will tell us who owns it and what it's being used for. Two, we can use the transponder manufacturer's website to track its progress.'

Dan scrolled through the screens. 'This is a good start,' he conceded, 'but it only tells us where the ship is. We know Delaney's using a car and it might be in a container, so how are we going to track that?'

Sarah smiled. 'You've just voiced the concerns of western civilisation.'

She swung the keyboard back to her side of the desk and hit a couple of keys. 'Here, look at this. A couple of years ago, several western governments worldwide demanded the maritime industry provide a better way of monitoring shipping containers. Through a Singapore-based financing initiative called the MINT Fund, several systems designers developed and manufactured tracking devices for containers.'

She flicked through various web pages. 'All the devices in use now are reasonably effective at preventing theft of goods from container ships, as well as trying to stop them being used by terrorist organisations to move weapons and explosives.'

Dan stood up, stretching his back. 'How do they work?'

Sarah swung her chair around to face him as he paced the room. 'From what I can gather, the devices have sensors which monitor temperature control – you set it up just as the container is sealed and any fluctuation – whether warm or cold, or the container being opened before it's timed to do so, or the angle of the container changes –an alarm is set off.'

'On the ship, or at a remote location?' asked Dan.

Sarah glanced at the screen. 'According to this, it's designed for electronic tracking, so it looks like most devices feed information via satellite up to a central database these shipping companies subscribe to and it provides them with real-time data, so remote would be my guess although I'd expect the ship's bridge to receive notification of the same time. That would make sense in, say, cases of piracy – it would give the crew time to arm themselves, or get to a safe room on the ship.'

Dan sat on the edge of the desk and looked at the computer screen. 'I wonder how reliable it is?'

Sarah tapped her forehead with her pen as she continued to scroll through the web pages. 'I guess it's fine – unless it gets switched off.' She threw her pen down on the desk.

'Okay,' said David. 'Here's the plan. Go through the manufacturers' websites. They should have subscriber databases you can log on to. Enter the ship's name and search to see if there's a transponder signal available for the freighter or each container they're carrying.'

Sarah nodded. 'I'll do my best.'

David pointed at Dan. 'You and I are going to start planning what to do when we find this bloody ship. Come with me.'

It was late, the office cleaners had nearly finished their rounds and the coffee machine had broken down two hours ago.

Sarah pushed her hair away from her face and

continued her work, long fluid keystrokes creating strings of data on the computer screen, illuminating her face. Stopping, she sighed, ran her fingers through her hair – realising it needed a cut last month – then stopped and stared at the screen. She exhaled loudly.

'What the…?'

She typed in the data string again, more slowly this time, then sat back and watched as the screen refreshed. She shook her head in disbelief and flipped her phone open. Hitting the speed dial, she got up and stretched.

"lo?' a voice answered.

'Dan, it's me, Sarah. We have a problem.'

'What do you mean, it's gone? Where?'

Dan sat at Sarah's desk, re-arranging data on the screen and re-checking her work.

'If I knew where, I would've said so on the phone – and don't look at me like that, I've already double-checked the information before I phoned you. Look – no transponder signal anywhere. The hijackers must've destroyed it.'

She pointed as the computer screen once more filtered through the search strings and stopped. They both looked at the screen – nothing. Dan threw his pen down on the desk and sighed. 'We're screwed.'

'Maybe not.' Philippa walked into the room and

wandered over to Sarah's desk, looking at the computer screen. 'There are ways to find out.'

'Right,' said Sarah, sounding unconvinced. 'Well, if you can find a missing freighter, she's all yours,' she added, and pushed the computer keyboard towards the other woman.

Philippa sat down at the desk and cracked her knuckles. Sarah glanced at Dan and rolled her eyes. He smiled, and put a finger to his lips.

'You two get some rest – I'll do this,' said Philippa. 'The thing is,' she explained, 'what you get on subscriber websites is filtered information. What we want to see is everything recorded by the tracking system and uploaded to the satellite.'

'How do you do that?' asked Sarah, now intrigued.

Philippa grinned. 'Dial up the satellite and ask it – nicely, of course.'

FORTY-TWO

Arctic Ocean

Brogan took a gulp of coffee and leaned against the side of the ship. The sun gave the grey clouds streaks of white and caught the waves in places, casting shadows across the sea. He squinted and glanced up at the ice-breaker in front of them. So far, they'd been making good progress but he guessed the ships would slow down once they reached Severnya Zemlya. He turned as the door next to him opened.

One of the hijackers stepped onto the deck and lit a cigarette. Brogan ignored him, took another sip of coffee and contemplated the endless grey scenery.

Brogan stepped through the studded metal doorway and into the cargo hold, the freighter's engines rumbling through the soul of the ship and resonating through the walls.

The cargo hold resembled a large underground car park. Vehicles had been parked tightly together by the stevedores at Singapore. Four steel rope lashings held each car securely – two at the front and two at the rear of the vehicle to prevent any movement during the voyage.

Brogan walked between the lines of cars, occasionally stopping to check the tautness of the steel ropes. If the cars came loose in rough seas, they would move in the cargo hold and the combined shift in weight could sink the ship. The lashings creaked with the motion of the ship. Brogan nodded to himself, satisfied.

He made his way slowly to the front of the cargo hold, near the loading doors. As he walked around each of the vehicles, he bent down and checked the floor beneath them.

'What are you doing?'

Brogan jumped. Another one of the hijackers stood behind him, an assault rifle resting across his folded arms. Brogan stood up.

'I was just going around checking we didn't have any fuel leaks. All these were loaded onto the ship with a full tank of petrol. We don't want any accidents.'

The man grunted and left Brogan to carry on with his checks. The captain made his way over to the sleek black sedan parked on its own across two bays. He checked over his shoulder once more, and then bent down next to the vehicle's front wheel arch.

Reaching under his thick sweater and into the waistband of his jeans, he drew out a small flat object. Sliding a switch on the side of it, he checked as a red LED light began to flash next to the switch. He reached forward and felt with his hand into the wheel arch until he found a lip of metal on which to place the object.

He withdrew his hand and untied his bootlace. He shuffled slightly in his crouching position and re-tied it to kill some time, then stood up slowly. He risked a glance around the hold, and saw one of the hijackers watching him.

He nodded, acknowledging his presence.

'Can't risk loose bootlaces round here,' he shrugged. 'Too many trip hazards.'

The other man nodded, then held up his gun and gestured for Brogan to move along. Brogan worked his way back through the rows of cars, back to the main staircase. The ship's transponder might have been destroyed, he thought, but if anyone's looking for the ship, they would now find the signal from the sedan somewhere in the middle of the Arctic.

Brisbane, Australia

Stephen Pallisder closed the door to his study, sat in the leather chair behind his desk and closed his eyes. Outside, his two children played in the garden, the sound of their shouts and laughter filtering through the window. He opened his eyes and reached out for the family portrait he kept on his desk. He held it carefully in his hands and smiled. It had taken half an hour just to get the kids to sit still and even then, the photographer had been relieved when the ordeal was over.

Placing the photograph frame back on the desk, he opened a drawer and pulled out a business card. The Englishman had said to call him if he wanted to talk. Pallisder ran his hand over his face, feeling the damp from the sweat emanating from his cool skin. His hands shaking, he pulled his mobile phone from his jacket pocket and began to dial. *Too late to turn back now.*

The call was answered within seconds.

'Mr Pallisder, I trust you're well?' said the man at the end of the line.

'We need to talk Mr Frazer,' said Pallisder. 'Now. Before I change my mind.' He breathed out, and tried to stop his heart beating so hard.

'I'm listening,' said Mitch.

'I need to know my family will be safe.'

'We'll move them until all this is over. What do you know?'

Pallisder took a deep breath and threw the business card on the desk. 'He's made a bomb. I-I had no idea it was going to get this serious. I thought we were just going to organise a few anti-environment rallies, scare a few people so they'd support us – I never would have given him the money if I knew what he had on his mind. He's mad – he's not listening to anyone any more. You've got to do something!'

'Calm down,' said Mitch. 'You're no use to us if you have a heart attack.'

Pallisder closed his eyes and gulped for air. He loosened his tie and threw it on the desk.

'Who else knows?' asked Mitch.

'I don't know – he won't tell me who else is involved. But I think he might know someone in the government.'

'Yours or ours?'

'Yours.'

London, England

David stalked through the office, glowering. Agents changed direction and did their best to avoid his gaze, just in case it was their backside about to get a kicking.

Philippa glanced up over her glasses as he approached her desk. 'Problem?'

'Come with me,' he ordered, as he walked past her without breaking stride and headed for his office.

Philippa stood up, locked her computer screen and picked up her notebook. She followed David and closed the door behind her. David was pacing the room. Suddenly, he stopped and turned, grabbed the cord for the window blinds and pulled them shut, shielding them from the prying eyes of other staff in the outer office.

Philippa calmly wandered over to the two-seat sofa and sat down, crossing her legs. She flicked her long hair over her shoulder and looked up at him. 'What's going on?'

He leaned against his desk. 'We have an informant.'

Philippa paled. 'But I screened all those agents out there myself – they're solid. They're...'

David shook his head. 'It's not one of them.'

'Who is it?'

David sighed and ran his hand over his face, exhausted. 'The Minister for Energy. The fucking Minister for Energy.'

'Holy crap.'

David nodded. 'You said it.'

Philippa slouched back on the sofa. 'Who else knows?'

Standing up, David walked round his desk and sat down in his leather chair. 'So far, the Prime Minister, the Home Secretary and the head of the Ministry of Defence. They'll be keeping it contained of course until this is all over, one way or the other. We're arranging to take the Minister out of circulation – we'll move him up to a safe house at Brecon tonight. With any luck, they'll chuck him in a room and throw away the fucking key.' David banged his fist on the desk.

'How much does he know?' asked Philippa. 'We haven't used Dan or Sarah's names in the briefing papers so surely they haven't been compromised?'

David shook his head. 'No – but Delaney will know we're onto him now.'

Philippa drew small flowers on a page of her notebook, deep in thought. 'What are you going to tell the media about the Minister? We can't just make him disappear.'

'There will be a press release issued at five this morning stating the Minister has been diagnosed with cancer and has been ordered to rest.'

Philippa studied David's face. 'Is it a terminal case?'

He nodded grimly. 'Very. He's unlikely to make it to the end of the month.'

Brisbane, Australia

Delaney slammed the door behind him. He bit his knuckle to stop himself from screaming out loud. Three years of planning and it was all in danger of falling apart.

He stalked across the room, reached his desk, then stooped down. He picked up the wastepaper basket and threw it across the room. It hit a painting on the far wall and tore a hole through the million-dollar masterpiece. The wastepaper basket fell down onto a mahogany side cabinet, smashing a crystal decanter and six glasses before falling to the floor, where it rolled to a stop, the painting crashing down on top of it.

Delaney glared at it, and surveyed the damage,

panting. He pulled a handkerchief from his trouser pocket and wiped his forehead, then turned and threw himself into the desk chair. He could feel his heart beating in his chest. He ignored the pain behind his ribs and concentrated on breathing heavily, pushing the oxygen into his system. He pinched his nose and closed his eyes. *Think.*

He had expected the Minister's aide to tell him the politician was busy when he called. The message that the Minister was no longer at work and his whereabouts unknown had thrown Delaney off track. No-one could tell him where the Minister could be found.

He switched the television on in the corner of his room until he found the national twenty-four-hour news channel for the United Kingdom. The ticker-tape headline running across the bottom of the screen confirmed his fears. The Minister had made a mistake. Someone had found out.

He picked up the phone, dialled a series of digits for the UK and tapped his foot on the rug, waiting for the call to connect. A voice eventually answered. 'Charles – are you watching the news? Right, get on a flight to Severnya Zemlya,' said Delaney.' I want you to board the ship there and make sure it arrives on time.'

He paused, listening.

'Well, tell them you're going on a cruise,' he growled. He slammed the phone down, stood up and looked out his office window at the river below. No way would he let the plan fail now.

FORTY-THREE

Near Denchworth, Oxfordshire, England

Dan woke, sweat beading on his brow. His heart was racing. He ran his hand over his eyes. *How much longer?*

He realised the lamp next to the bed was switched on, and frowned.

'Are you okay?'

He jumped at the sound of Sarah's voice. 'What?'

She stood at the end of his bed, concern in her eyes. 'Same dream?'

He nodded. 'Sorry if I woke you.'

She shrugged, her arms folded across her chest. He noticed she was shivering. The t-shirt she was wearing was no match for the cold winter night.

'Here, get in before you get cold again,' he said, pulling the blankets back.

She rolled her eyes and smiled. 'I've heard some excuses…'

Dan shuffled over and Sarah curled up next to him. He pulled the blankets up around them and propped himself up on an elbow. Sarah gazed up at him. His blue eyes pierced through the gloom. Dan lowered his face to hers, and she tilted her head up.

Sarah hesitated, unsure. 'Dan – I don't know if I can do this.' She put her hand on Dan's chest, closing her eyes.

He rested his chin on her forehead, breathed in her perfume, then leaned back and took her face in his hands. 'It's okay.'

He leaned down and kissed her on her neck, his lips caressing her collarbone.

She groaned and leaned back. 'Dan…'

He wrapped his arms around her, pulling her towards him. She kissed him frantically, desperately searching out every part of him.

'God, Sarah, you feel wonderful,' Dan slid a hand down her body, caressing, touching.

Sarah dug her fingernails into his shoulder blades, relishing his touch. She pulled at his hair, desperate to get closer to his skin.

Then her mobile phone rang.

They both jumped. Sarah bit her lip. She sat up, torn between staying and finding out the identity of the caller. She pulled away.

'Bloody mobile phones,' said Dan under his breath, and let her go.

He could hear her padding about in the guest room as she switched on a light and tried to find her mobile phone before it stopped ringing. He groaned and let his head hit the pillow. Talk about bad timing. He heard Sarah answer the phone, then the murmurs of a short conversation before he heard her coming back to the room.

'That was Philippa,' she said, as she stood in the doorway and balanced on one leg, pulling on a pair of jeans. 'David wants us back in the office. Now. She says they've found a trace of where the hijacked freighter's been.'

Dan pushed open the door to the conference room and strode across to where Philippa sat staring at her computer screen. 'Where?'

'The Kara Sea, north of Russia. Turned up in an historical report on one of those satellite databases I told you about.' Philippa handed him the report and glanced pointedly at Sarah, who blushed and sat down.

'And,' Philippa continued, 'we just got a report in from the Japanese Coast Guard. They found the freighter crew. Well, what's left of them anyway.'

'Whereabouts?' asked Sarah, leaning forward on the desk.

'Orono-Shima – a small island off the coast of Japan,' said David. 'The bodies washed up two days ago – not much to go on after the fish had a go at them but our people in Singapore identified the second in command through his dental records – it seems logical to assume the remaining bodies are the other crew members.'

Dan glanced at the fax over David's shoulder. 'What about the captain?'

Philippa shook her head. 'No sign of him – we're assuming they've held on to him.'

'He's still useful to them,' added Sarah, regaining some of her composure.

Philippa nodded. 'Exactly my thoughts.'

David stalked across the room and threw the door open. He stopped and turned. 'Pip, get us into a bigger ops room within twenty minutes – one with an electronic tracking map. Get two analysts to help us. We're running out of time.'

David rapped the surface of the table, bringing the varied conversations around it to a halt. 'Okay people. Let's have your full attention.'

Five faces turned his way.

'Let's get down to business. It's now confirmed Delaney has taken over a cargo freighter.' He picked up a remote and hit a button. One side of the conference wall was bathed in white light. David pressed another button and a map appeared. He dimmed the lights, and then turned to Dan. 'I'll let you run with this.'

Dan nodded, stood up and turned to face the room. He

hit the remote and fired up the live satellite feed. The screen on the wall flickered, and then a series of dots and lines appeared across the top section of the map. 'Okay, everyone listen up,' he said. 'Let's see if we can spot our freighter.'

He typed a series of keys on the keyboard in front of him and the satellite picture changed. It swooped down to the surface of the Earth and showed the northern coast of Russia.

'We know the ship left Singapore in December and has been travelling north. Thanks to Philippa's intelligence report, we now know the ship passed Busan in January. We then have a reported sighting from Severnya Zemlya on the north coast of Russia. The freighter seems to have travelled through the Arctic Ocean.'

Sarah stopped writing in her notebook. 'How on earth did a freighter go through the Arctic Ocean at this time of year?'

'The sea ice doesn't freeze like it used to,' explained Philippa. 'It hasn't been as thick over the winter months during the past couple of years. Delaney's still taking one hell of a chance though.'

'So from there, he could be headed anywhere,' said David. 'At what point do we tell our American friends they might be the recipients of a potential atomic weapon?'

Dan shook his head. 'I don't think Delaney has sent it there,' he said. 'He hasn't got any business interests there and he wouldn't want to jeopardise a potential future market.' He turned to the screen as the satellite's camera began to zoom out. 'I have a feeling it's coming here,' he murmured.

He faced the team. 'The transponder signal stopped two weeks ago. We don't know whether that's because it's been found, or if the captain's using a battery-powered version which may have gone flat. So, ladies and gentlemen, the only way to do this is the hard way.'

The group gathered around the conference table fell silent as they watched the progress of the satellite images on the screen. It moved along the coastline and then slowed as it approached the surface of the planet, and then Dan hit a key to tell the computer to stop the zoom. He punched in a series of commands and a list of data appeared on the left-hand side of the screen. It provided coordinates, date and time information and temperature data.

'Right,' said Dan. 'This is the first in a series of historical images, gathered daily for the past three months. We know it would have taken the freighter at least four weeks to get to Severnya Zemlya from Busan, so we can discount those dates.' He typed in a search string of data and hit the 'enter' key.

'Starting from the middle of January,' he continued, 'we'll work our way along the coast until we see the ship. We'll then plot its course. David – can you hand everyone one of those library images of the freighter so they can see what we're looking for?'

David reached across the table to a manila file, flipped

it open and distributed an eight-by-twelve inch photograph to each person.

Dan looked at the familiar image in his hands. He felt like he knew every corner of the ship already. He wondered where in the cargo hold the black sedan was parked. He turned his back to the screen and addressed the familiar faces in the room.

'This isn't going to be easy, I know. However, we believe that even with the unusually warm winter sea temperatures we've been seeing recently the freighter will still need an ice-breaker as an escort through these waters. There's no way Delaney's going to risk losing this freighter just to cut corners. So keep your eyes open for anything which looks remotely like our ship – just call out and we'll zoom in to get a better look and see if it's got an escort in front of it.'

'Alright, let's get on with this. Starting in January, we'll concentrate on the shipping lane north of the Kara Sea – they have to go through there so we can't miss them,' he said and hit a key. Six faces stared intently at the screen as the satellite images slowly changed from date to date.

FORTY-FOUR

Barents Sea, Norway

Brogan checked his watch and looked out to the starboard side of the freighter. He shivered and instinctively pulled up his collar around his neck.

As far as he knew, no-one had found the transponder he'd fixed to the wheel arch of the black sedan. If they had, he knew he'd have joined the rest of the crew. Now they were safely out of the Arctic waters, he realised his time was limited. He felt angry, frustrated he couldn't do anything more. And alone. Despite risking his life placing the transponder, it seemed no-one had heard his call for help.

When they had docked briefly at Severnya Zemlya to re-fuel and leave their escort behind, Brogan had been shocked to see the man with the glasses being led on board. He had grinned when he saw Brogan's expression.

'How's my car?' he had asked, before stepping into the cargo hold with the leader the other men called Terry.

Brogan had feared the worst then – surely, they would check the car and find the transponder. But the man with the glasses and Terry had seemed pre-occupied with something *inside* the car instead and had appeared an hour later looking satisfied.

The ship had left the port half an hour later, the man with the glasses taking over one of the old crew member's cabins for the remainder of the journey.

Brogan risked a glance at the hijackers' leader, who was bending over the chart table, intent on making sure every step of the journey went to plan.

He jumped involuntarily as the man spoke.

'How long until we reach the target?'

Brogan looked at his watch again and did the calculation in his head. 'We'll be there late afternoon on Saturday if we maintain this speed. We'll have to slow her down approaching the coastline, then it'll take about an hour to get to the dock.'

Terry grunted, satisfied. 'Good. Right on schedule.'

'Are we going through the lock?'

Terry nodded. 'And it goes without saying you don't say anything to the pilot when he gets on board.' He smiled maliciously. 'Just remember your daughter.'

Brogan shivered and turned away.

London, England

Dan walked around the conference table and looked at the handwritten plans the team had been drafting up. Philippa had located where the ship had been. Now all the team had to do was try to find it, predict where it was going, and when it would arrive at its destination.

'Given the current speed it's been keeping since leaving the Russian ice-breaker behind, the freighter should arrive in the North Sea very soon.' Dan paused.

He held up his hand to silence the sudden murmurs. 'Let's keep this focused – I don't want to miss a single suggestion.' He paced around the table, five heads turning to follow his progress. 'What's his target?'

Dan stopped and looked at each person individually. 'Think about it. What's Delaney's objective? What's he trying to prove?'

He continued to pace, thinking out aloud.

'We know he's organised a like-minded group of people to finance all sorts of research to counter scientific studies into global warming. We know he'd do anything to protect his organisation, and anything to stop anyone investigating their current project. And we know it's going to culminate in some sort of demonstration of power which could have catastrophic consequences.'

He reached his own chair, sat down and placed his

hands on the desk before looking at each of the attendees in turn. 'So – what's the target, and how is he going to get to it from the ship?'

One of the analysts raised his voice. 'We've got the Olympics coming up at the end of July. That would get everyone's attention, if he attacked that.'

Dan turned to David. 'What do you think?'

The other man shrugged. 'There are a lot of security measures in place given the high potential threat status of the event. But Delaney doesn't fit the profile of the sorts of organised terrorism we've been watching, so an attack like that would definitely make us sit up and take notice.'

Dan frowned. 'He's going to have to hide the ship somewhere for the next four months. I can't see him risking bringing it all the way here now.' He turned to the analysts in the room. 'Get onto your colleagues bordering the North Sea. Find out if they've got anything they can give us.'

He watched as the agents hurriedly began filing out of the conference room back to their desks. He waited until they'd gone, walked over to the door and closed it, and then looked at the others. 'You realise we're grasping at straws?'

David nodded. 'Part and parcel of the job, Dan. Get used to it.'

Forty minutes later, they all jumped as an analyst burst through the door, waving a fax at them. 'Found it!'

He handed the document to David. The others watched anxiously while he read the fine print. And then began to smile. 'Our friends in Norway have located the *World's End* in real time,' he grinned.

'How did they manage that so fast?' asked Sarah.

The analyst spoke. 'We gave them the coordinates of the last historical data Philippa obtained. They've got a satellite system which can track automatic identification system transponders – the same the captain must've placed on the ship.'

Philippa nodded. 'That makes sense – Norway has the largest sea area to manage in Europe.' She looked at the fax David passed to her. 'Even with the transponder going flat, it looks like they've perfected the software so it can trace the signature of the ship,' she explained. 'With the system they've got, they can give us the position, course and speed of the freighter.' She smiled. 'We're back in business.'

'The captain must've been the one who activated the tracking device,' said Dan. 'He's obviously worked out for himself that Delaney's up to no good and someone, somewhere will be looking out for that ship.'

'Not to mention the fact he knows what happened to the crew will probably happen to him once the ship reaches its destination,' said Sarah.

The room fell silent.

David stood up. 'Well, he's taken one hell of a risk, so

let's not waste the information.' He turned to Philippa. 'If we continue to plot where we know that ship's been, and what its current position is, we might be able to clarify where it's going and give ourselves some more time.'

Dan stood up and pulled one of the maps of the North Sea towards him. 'Okay – let's plot those coordinates on here and see if we can work out where it's heading.'

He and Philippa moved quickly, Dan tapping in the information as Philippa read it out. When they were done, he hit the 'enter' key and everyone looked at the screen on the wall.

Sarah gasped.

After hours of searching, they'd found the *World's End*. It was a lot closer than any of them had thought possible. After losing its ice-breaker escort at Severnya Zemlya, it had maintained a frantic pace through the northern Norwegian waters and was now heading straight towards England.

David looked at the others in turn. 'Based on what we know to date, we *have* to assume that ship is headed for the Thames Estuary.'

FORTY-FIVE

Dan zipped up his jacket and walked out through the reception doors. A bitter wind blew down the dimly lit street and the occasional car splashed through water-logged potholes in the bitumen.

He shoved his hands in his pockets and started to walk. He had no idea where he was going – he just needed to get away from the conference room for a while to clear his head.

He set himself a brisk pace and soon began to warm up. He focused on the pavement in front of him, occasionally glancing around to take in his surroundings. He missed the warm weather and wondered if he'd ever return to the city again after this. It all seemed so depressing and grey. He smiled as he thought of his father – now he understood why the man had spent so much time overseas, exploring far-flung places.

For so many years he thought his father had turned his

back on him. Now he realised it was just a bad case of wanderlust and a need for adventure. They were more similar than he'd ever realised.

Dan reached a set of traffic lights and turned left. The wind died down and Dan slowed his pace a little. He heard a flapping sound and looked up, startled. Then he relaxed. A poster hung from the street-lamp ahead of him, advertising some sort of festival. He lowered his gaze and continued on.

Frustrated, he ran through the scenarios in his head. It just didn't feel right. They were still missing something. He slowed down as he approached the steps to David's offices and pushed open the reception door. Nodding at the security guard, he made his way over to the elevators and stepped in.

When he reached the conference room level, he walked slowly along the corridor, then stopped and leaned against the wall next to the water cooler. He closed his eyes. He could hear the faint sound of voices from the conference room. He rocked his head from side to side, stretching his neck muscles and rolled his shoulders. He had left the room for some fresh air and some time out but hadn't got any closer to a reason for Delaney's attack.

If Delaney's plan was to create an impact at the Olympics, why send the freighter now? It would be months ahead of schedule. In shipping lanes and ports as busy as those bordering the North Sea, there was no way Delaney could hide the ship or the car until the time came to detonate a bomb. And given the required effort to keep the white gold powder stable... it could blow at any time, and not in a controlled way.

Dan opened his eyes. Something was bothering him. He frowned, re-tracing his steps. Then it hit him. *The advertising banners hanging from the lamp posts*!

Five faces turned as he burst through the conference room door.

'It's not the Olympics,' said Dan, striding across to the conference table and sweeping photos and documents aside. 'Where's that plan of the freighter's route so far?'

'Here,' Philippa said, pushing a copy of the printed map towards him.

Dan spun it around and beckoned David closer. 'Based on its current speed, and presuming it'll maintain that, what date would it get to the Thames Estuary?'

David picked up a permanent marker and wrote some calculations on the map before drawing a line from the Norwegian coastline to Tilbury. He threw the pen on the table when it was done and looked at Dan.

'Twenty-seventh of March.' David looked back at the satellite map. 'That's this Saturday.'

Dan nodded. 'It's not the Olympics – he's too early.'

Sarah looked at each of them in confusion. 'Then what is it?'

Dan looked at her. 'Earth Hour.'

A shocked silence fell on the room.

'Earth Hour?' asked Sarah. 'Where did you get that idea from?'

Dan nodded to the door. 'I went for a walk to clear my head – the posters for it are hanging from the street lamps outside.'

'Why Earth Hour?' asked David. 'What's your thinking behind that?'

'The impact would be immense,' said Dan. 'If Delaney uses a bomb derived from powdered white gold, he'll put back alternative energy research fifty years or more.'

'How?'

Dan sat down and ran his fingers through his hair. 'I thought he was transporting the bomb using a car because the white gold powder was so unstable. It is, but I think the car is meant to look like it *is* the bomb. This white gold powder stuff is already being incorporated into fuel cell technology in vehicles and companies are spending a lot of time and money researching its potential on a large scale as a future wonder-fuel.'

David nodded in agreement. 'So if Delaney stages an 'accident' using this technology, it's back to using oil and coal until the supplies run out for good. Not to mention his shares in European gas companies will skyrocket in value.'

Dan nodded. 'That's it exactly. What better way to get the impact he wants than by using an environmentally friendly fuel source and detonating it during Earth Hour?'

David rocked back in his chair. 'We're going to have to let them come to us – there's no way we're going to be able to board the ship in the middle of the North Sea.' He turned to the two analysts. 'Get your reports finished and have them on my desk within the hour.'

The two men nodded, gathered up the notes and scurried from the room. David watched them go then turned to Philippa. 'Get assault teams organised. Dan can lead one.'

Dan looked at him in astonishment. 'Really?'

David smiled. 'Yeah, really – think you can remember how?'

Dan nodded. 'You bet. Wouldn't miss it for the world.'

'Good. We'll need three land-based teams and one aquatic team to make sure no-one tries to leave the ship when we board her.'

Philippa made a couple of points in her notebook then rose from the table. 'We've only got a day to prepare,' she said, 'so I'll speak to Steve and see who's been in the field recently. I'll want experts – there's going to be no room for error.'

David stood up. 'Right – let's get on with it.'

FORTY-SIX

Terry looked out the window of the freighter's bridge as it powered slowly up the Thames. In the distance, he could see the top of familiar landmarks of England's capital – the Tower Bridge, the Telecom Tower, the Millennium Wheel.

He snorted, turning to Charles. 'You know, there used to be a time in history when great cities were defined by their churches and cathedrals,' he said, pointing out the window. 'Now they're defined by how big their hamster wheel is.'

Charles managed a nervous smile, unsure how to react to Terry's confidence and humour.

Terry gripped the railing and stared out the window. 'Soon,' he promised himself. 'Soon.'

Dan looked around the ops centre as the assault team

began to prepare to leave. He looked over to the conference room and saw Sarah watching him from the doorway. He smiled and walked through the small crowd towards her.

'You're loving every minute of this, aren't you?' she said.

He looked back at the assault team and smiled. He turned back to her and nodded. 'It feels familiar. And I want to stop Delaney's bomb.'

David joined them. 'Time to saddle up Dan,' he said. 'Sarah – you can go in the helicopter. I'd rather you stayed here but I know you'll just ignore that advice so I might as well put you somewhere where I know you won't get into trouble.'

Sarah grinned and began to gather her things together.

Dan laughed. 'You're going to have to travel light – there's not a lot of room in the chopper. It's not like the ones you journalists are used to swanning around in.'

Sarah grimaced and placed her laptop bag back on the table. Dan watched her glance back at it wistfully, then he pushed her out the door and into the main ops room where David was gathering his team together for a last-minute overview of the assault on the freighter.

'Okay people. Listen up. Dan will lead the assault from the bow of the ship, my team to the stern. The aquatic team won't be boarding. They'll provide cover if we need it and stop anyone from leaving the ship. The final team will cover the wharf to make sure no-one escapes down the gangways once we're on board.' David turned to make sure he addressed every person in the room. 'We know the crew, apart from the captain, are already dead so we've only got him to worry about. Okay, let's go.'

David began herding the assault team out of the ops room. As they made their way down the stairs to the underground car park, Dan pulled Sarah to one side. He nodded as David walked past them. He waited until they were alone, and then lowered his voice.

'I know it goes against your nature but you really have to do as I say tonight. This is real, Sarah. Someone's going to get hurt. I really hope it's one of Delaney's lot, not ours.'

She nodded. 'I know.' She looked around to make sure no-one could see them, and then hugged Dan. 'Stay out of trouble.'

He grinned. 'Always.' He released her. 'Come on. Can't keep them waiting.'

They jogged through the car park to where the assault teams were climbing into four black mini-vans. The windows were blacked out, the wheels painted black and as Sarah followed the pilot out to the helicopter gunship, Dan noticed none of the vehicles had licence plates.

David pulled Dan to one side. 'Here, you might need this,' he said, slipping a gun to him.

'Ah, my favourite – how did you know?' asked Dan, smiling as he tucked the Sig Sauer into the back of his waistband.

Dan followed David to the lead mini-van and clipped on the battery pack for the radio on his belt. He inserted the earpiece, tested the volume and then nodded at David. *Ready.*

He opened the sliding door on the side of the vehicle and climbed in, nodding at the men already seated. David jumped in next to the driver. Dan slid the door shut and the driver floored the accelerator, leading the vehicles out of the underground car park.

Dan watched through the tinted glass as the helicopter gunship lifted into the air, ready to offer support. He leaned forwards and tapped David on the shoulder. 'Do the police know we're coming?'

David nodded. 'We've alerted the police at Tilbury – they have their own jurisdiction at the docks.'

'As long as they're not creating a panic down there,' said Dan. 'The last thing we want is for Delaney's crew to get spooked.'

'We should be fine,' replied David. 'They're just slowly working people away from the freighter so they're out of danger. The only ones anywhere near it are going to be police posing as dock workers.'

Dan slouched back in the leather seat and watched the city go by. He turned the wire for his microphone between his fingers, unable to keep still. He blinked as the cityscape faded to desert and quickly shook his head to clear the image.

'You okay?'

Dan glanced at the man sitting next to him and nodded. 'Sure.'

The driver switched off the van's lights as they

approached the dock. The vehicle slowly crept forward, staying in the shadows.

Dan glanced behind him and saw the other three vehicles following. He tapped his microphone on. 'Don't use your brakes,' he said. 'Make sure you stay in a low gear and use the handbrake.'

A series of double clicks over the radio signified the other drivers' confirmation. Dan shifted in his seat, satisfied the brake lights wouldn't now give the team away. The mini-vans cruised to a stop under the awning of a building.

Dan looked ahead at the dock in the distance. 'Okay, the hijacked ship is the one you can see the bow of,' he explained in a low voice to the team in his van. 'We wait until David confirms the aquatic team is in place.'

He glanced at David who was staring at his watch intently with his finger on his earpiece, waiting for confirmation that the assault boat had approached the freighter. The aquatic team was approaching the ship without an engine. Sound travelled further over water and the team was communicating through a series of pre-ordained clicks and taps on their microphones, not saying a word in case they jeopardised the assault.

Dan looked up as David lowered his watch and nodded at him.

'That's it, we have a go,' said Dan, and gently slid the car door open.

He stood in the shadows and stared at the freighter. Somewhere inside, Delaney's white gold weapon was waiting for him. Arc lights along the wharf illuminated parts of the ship. Dan realised how much brighter it would have been if the police hadn't ensured that as little light as possible was used around the ship to help the assault, while at the same time trying to avoid arousing suspicion on the ship itself.

David joined him. 'Almost like old times. You remember how to do this?'

Dan nodded. 'Yeah. Second nature. It's almost like the last few years never happened.'

David nodded. 'I noticed – you're a natural leader Dan. It's good to have you back.'

Dan watched him walk away to the mini-van behind theirs and begin issuing last-minute instructions before his voice came over the headset.

'Let's get busy.'

Dan signalled his team to follow him. Using the shadows of the buildings for cover, they edged closer to the ship. Dan stopped at the last building and looked over to the gangway leading up to the bow. He could see two figures walking along but they appeared to be engrossed in conversation and weren't watching the dockside activity. The enormous stern loading doors hung open, a ramp leading down into the bowels of the ship. The police had done a good job posing as stevedores and stalling the unloading process as long as they dared without arousing suspicion.

Dan detected a salty tang in the air, a cold breeze whipping off the estuary waters outside the dock area.

David's voice came low over the radio. 'All in position?'

Dan tapped his microphone twice. He heard repeat responses from the rest of the team.

'On my count,' said David. 'Three. Two. One. *Go!*'

Dan ran fast and low, keeping his team in the shadows between the arc lights, his gun drawn. As he reached the gangway, he quickly checked behind him to make sure the team was ready. He nodded, turned and began to run up the gangway.

His heart raced, not from exertion but adrenaline coursing through his veins. He wanted to be the one to find Terry, to find out why.

He reached the top of the gangway at the same time David's team reached theirs at the stern. The entry up to the ship's bridge was to his left. Dan peered up at the windows as his team fanned out behind him. Suddenly a shout emanated from further along the deck and Dan ducked instinctively as a bullet embedded itself in the metalwork above his head. His team opened fire – careful concise shots to avoid any stray bullets hitting the wrong person.

The two men he'd seen further along the deck fell to the ground.

'Two down,' he said over the radio. 'Don't fire unless you're fired at. We want to talk to some of these people if we can. Aim low to injure, not kill, if you can.'

A series of double-clicks sounded over the radio in response.

Dan edged further along the deck until he found a doorway to his right. He signalled to his team to stand clear, and then he slowly twisted the handle and gently pulled the door towards him. A metal staircase led upwards.

Dan concentrated on his breathing, pushing his heart rate down. He pulled the door outwards and risked a glance up the staircase. He leapt back as a bullet hit the floor next to him, the sound ringing in his ears a split second later.

Dan looked at the man to his right. 'Have you got any of those flash bangs?'

The man nodded and handed Dan one of the stun grenades.

Dan grinned. 'Let's get the bastard.'

He pulled the pin, opened the door and tossed the grenade into the stairwell. He slammed the door shut and held it closed, turned his head away and closed his eyes. A loud explosion moved the door in its frame, followed by the sound of something metallic falling down the stairs.

Dan opened the door and peered in. An assault rifle lay at the bottom of the stairs. Dan stepped in through the door, glanced upwards and snatched up the rifle.

'Go, go!' he yelled to the team and led them up the metal staircase.

As they neared the top, Dan slowed and waved his men to stay close behind him. He edged towards an open door which he guessed led to the control room of the ship. He raised his gun and peered around the door. His heart sank.

The man with the glasses stood facing him, holding Brogan in front of him as a shield and pushed a gun into the man's throat.

'Drop the gun,' he said.

Dan's mind raced. He looked at Brogan.

'Are you okay?'

Brogan nodded, watching Dan carefully.

'We've got your daughter. She's safe,' said Dan.

Brogan noticeably slumped. The sudden movement threw Charles off balance. He let go of the captain to get a better grip on the man and Dan saw his chance.

He fired. Once. Low.

Charles bellowed as the bullet smashed his ankle and embedded itself in the table behind him. He dropped his gun. He let go of Brogan, falling to the floor in agony. Dan rushed over and kicked his weapon out of the way. He bent down and placed his foot on the man's throat.

'You bastard. I should use the next five bullets on your other body parts.'

He called over to one of his team, who was kneeling on the floor beside Brogan.

'Is he going to be alright?'

The man nodded. 'We'll get him to hospital. I would think he's dehydrated and in shock. His daughter's there, waiting for him.'

'Good.'

Dan turned his attention back to Charles. 'It's over. Where's the bomb-maker?'

Charles laughed. Then Dan kicked his ankle and he cried out from the pain.

'Where's Terry?' demanded Dan. 'Where's the car?'

'It's gone.'

Dan spun round. Brogan was easing himself up on an elbow, staring at Dan. 'They got it off the ship just before you turned up. The guy in charge is driving it.'

'Sir!'

Dan looked up. One of his men was pointing out the window. 'I think you need to see this, sir!'

Dan rushed over. A car, headlights blazing across the wharf, revved its engine, spun round and accelerated towards the exit of the docks.

Dan raced down the stairs, meeting David on the deck. They watched over the side of the ship in disbelief as the black sedan charged at one of the policemen dressed as a dock worker. The man leapt into the freezing cold water of the dock, narrowly escaping being run over and began to swim back towards his colleagues.

David turned to Dan, then clicked his radio.

'Helicopter!' he yelled.

FORTY-SEVEN

Dan and David turned and ran along the deck towards the gangway on the stern. Dan looked up. From the steps, he could see the car weaving its way through the dock complex. He heard a screech of tyres as it slammed through a barricade and turned towards the city.

David was already using the radio to speak to the helicopter pilot. 'Two incoming. Get us up as fast as you can.'

Dan leapt into the seat next to Sarah and fastened his belt. He glanced at her. Her face was white. He leaned over and squeezed her hand. 'Getting all of this noted down?'

She opened her mouth to say something, and then turned as David jumped in next to the pilot.

'Go, go!' he yelled. 'Get after him!'

The helicopter lurched into the air, fast.

Dan watched out the window as the helicopter banked away from the river and began to follow the car as it took one of the main arterial roads into the city, travelling fast. He heard David talking on the radio, telling someone on the other end to get the police to stay away from the car.

Dan could feel the adrenaline pulsing through his veins. His nightmares forgotten, he began to try to work out how Terry could have designed the bomb and what he would see if he got the chance. He looked at his watch, and then leaned forward. He tapped David on the shoulder and shouted to be heard over the engine.

'This isn't going to work! You need to get me on the ground so I can follow him by road.'

David turned to the pilot. 'Get us down there. Now!'

The pilot nodded. Dan looked down at the city below. He just had to get to the vehicle before Terry detonated it.

He felt the pressure in his ears change as the helicopter began to quickly descend. He looked out the window. The helicopter was hovering over a public car park, the pilot seeking out a clearing in between cars and street lighting.

Dan held his breath. The pilot couldn't tell if there were power lines or telephone cables beneath them – they were just going to have to take a chance.

'Hurry!' shouted David. 'Get this thing on the ground, or we're going to lose the car!'

Dan winced as Sarah's fingers dug nervously into his thigh. He lifted her hand off and held onto it, ignoring her nails biting into his flesh.

He glanced out the window again. To the right of the car park was a supermarket, its bright lights illuminating the silhouettes of startled shoppers staring up in amazement at the helicopter.

As the aircraft landed, Dan climbed out, slammed the door shut behind him and ducked instinctively from the down-draught of the rotors. He walked around the helicopter and opened the other passenger door.

'Are you coming?' he shouted at Sarah.

She raised her eyebrows in surprise, nodded, then unclipped her belt. Grabbing her bag, she climbed out of the helicopter. David already stood on the bitumen.

Dan turned to him. 'Mind if we leave you?'

David pushed him in the back. 'Get going – we'll follow as closely as we can and see what we can do about making sure you don't get pulled over on the way.'

'But you won't know what we'll be driving!' said Sarah.

David grinned as he climbed back into the helicopter. 'I reckon I'd spot his erratic driving anywhere, don't worry. We'll find you.'

Dan watched the aircraft lift back into the air, then grabbed Sarah by the wrist and ran across the car park. He pulled her towards the lines of parked cars.

'Come on, run!' he urged. They raced to the entrance of the parking area. Dan swerved and changed direction as he spotted a shopper putting overloaded bags onto the back seat of a sports saloon. As he drew near, Dan pulled out the gun.

'Keys!' he yelled at the shocked man, who threw the

keys at Dan and raised his hands in the air in one fluid motion.

Dan pushed Sarah into the car, and then ran round to the driver's side. Starting the engine, he gunned it, grinned at Sarah and reversed out of the parking bay. Changing gear and hauling the steering wheel round at the same time, he spun the car so it pointed towards the car park exit and floored the accelerator.

There was an audible crash from the back seat as vegetables and tin cans of food tumbled to the floor of the car.

Sarah's hands shook as she tried to fasten her seatbelt. Dan glanced over at her, a confused look on his face.

She shrugged. 'I believe David about your driving.'

Dan braked hard and Sarah was thrown forward into her seatbelt. 'Jeez,' she gasped, as she reached down to ease the tension against her chest and stomach. 'That's going to leave a dent.'

'Missed him though,' Dan pointed, then put his foot down on the accelerator again. Sarah looked back over her shoulder as they took off, a security guard madly waving his arms in their wake.

He wrenched the wheel round hard and stomped on the brake. The gearbox whined in protest as he crashed through the gears, downshifted, then guided the car round the corner and accelerated hard down the street.

Sarah hung onto her seat, knuckles white as she slid across the car. 'We're losing him!' she yelled.

'Do you want to drive?' Dan yelled back, as he

swerved to miss an oncoming truck, the driver gesticulating furiously at them as they tore past.

Dan wrenched the wheel around hard to his left. The tyres shrieked in protest as the car slid across the wet bitumen. He feathered the throttle to bring the vehicle back under control, and then slammed his foot on the accelerator. The car bucked forwards and he straightened it out, blasting past a bewildered cyclist.

'Can you see him?' he screamed to Sarah.

She pointed to a car's tail-lights at the end of the street.

'There. Going round that corner. Quickly, Dan – we'll lose him!'

Dan floored the pedal and swung the car round the junction. Turning right, he slid the car forty-five degrees and overtook a white panel van, braking hard as the road turned sharply left and then ran parallel with the Thames.

The black sedan's tail-lights glinted a few hundred metres in front of them. Dan eased off the accelerator and followed at a distance.

'Dan?'

Sarah glanced over at him, confused.

'Aren't you going to stop him?'

Dan shook his head.

'I can't – I don't know how that bomb is designed to detonate. I need him to get it to its destination in one piece.'

He broke off as his mobile began to ring. He rummaged in his jacket pocket and handed the phone to Sarah.

'Get that.'

She flipped open the phone.

'Hello?' She turned to Dan and mouthed, *it's David.*

'David? We're following him – he just turned on to the Embankment... no, he wants to wait until the car stops – he says it's too dangerous... okay.'

She hung up and held the phone tight in her hand.

'David's got a team about two minutes behind us. They'll follow at a distance. He's got a visual on us from the helicopter.'

Dan risked a look out his window and glimpsed the tell-tale lights of a helicopter at low altitude. 'Good – as long as they keep their distance. I don't want this guy to get spooked...'

He broke off as the black sedan slewed to the left-hand side of the road. Its brake lights flashed once, then again as it drew to a stop.

'Shit!' Dan sped up and overtook the car. 'Don't look at it, for Christ's sake! Let's just hope he doesn't know we were following behind him!' He continued driving along the street until he saw a left-hand turn and steered around the corner. 'Phone David back – they're going to have to tell us where Terry is heading now so we can try to get there first – hopefully we can hide before he shows up.'

Sarah opened the phone and began to dial, her hands shaking. She relayed the message and fell silent.

Dan kept the car at a slow speed until Sarah finished the call.

'David says the car's heading for a wharf off of

Wapping High Street – Philippa's tracking us and says we can pass him further along here.' She pointed ahead of him.

'Okay, just yell out the instructions as we go – and keep your fingers crossed we can beat him to it.'

FORTY-EIGHT

Brisbane, Australia

Delaney burst through the door to his office, slammed it shut and locked it. His eyes darted around the room. Sweating and out of breath, he forced himself to breathe slowly. It was all falling apart.

Delaney pulled his mobile phone from his jacket pocket and hit redial. He put the phone to his ear, closed his eyes and leaned back against the door. He listened as the same tone-flat recorded message informed him Uli Petrov's mobile number was no longer available.

He disconnected the call, and then looked up sharply as his desk phone began to ring. He strode across the office and snatched it from its cradle. 'What?'

He closed his eyes and rubbed his hand over his face as he listened and processed the information. 'When?'

He leaned against the desk. His heart raced. This couldn't be happening. 'Send the report to my private fax line.'

He put the phone down and walked around the desk. Pulling out a drawer, he felt around until he found a small plastic bottle. Pulling it out, he twisted open the lid and shook it until two small white pills fell into his hand. He shoved them in his mouth, swallowed them and threw the bottle back in the drawer. He slammed it shut and turned as the fax machine began to print.

He snatched the single sheet of paper from the machine, read the contents and exhaled loudly.

It was a copy of the latest edition of the *Moscow Times*. Uli Petrov had been found dead in his Krylatskoe mansion, the victim of a burglary gone wrong, the police said. The Kremlin had undertaken to seize control of his oil and gas assets immediately, to secure production over the European winter, and was not expected to relinquish control of the business for the foreseeable future.

Delaney tore up the sheet of paper and threw it in the wastepaper basket in disgust. He picked up his phone and dialled the number for Charles. He eased himself into his chair, breathing heavily.

No answer. Delaney held out the phone at arm's length and stared at it in disbelief. Where the hell was he?

Delaney reached down and pulled out one of the desk drawers. Tipping the contents out over the Chinese silk rug under his chair, he turned over the empty drawer. A thin manila envelope was stuck to the base of it. Delaney carefully peeled it away and threw the drawer on the floor.

He opened the envelope, looked at the carefully planned schedule, and then at his watch. It still might work. The freighter would have docked at Tilbury on the Thames. Terry would have unloaded the car and be on his way.

Delaney paused. What if Terry and Charles had been apprehended? Was he next?

He crouched down and began to gather the documents on the floor. He placed them in the wastepaper basket and pulled out his lighter. Holding the flame to the edge of the page, he noticed his hand was shaking. Rage, fear, frustration, anger – it boiled up through his veins and consumed him.

He growled – a long, low primeval sound, and then the paper caught fire. He stood up, grabbed the manila envelope and its contents and dropped them into the flames. Spinning round, he walked over to the opposite corner of the office where two filing cabinets stood. He pulled open the drawers, tearing out anything that could be used against him. He glanced over his shoulder at the wastepaper basket, then turned and began to feed the files in his arms to the flames.

He looked at the pages as he fed them one by one into the inferno – the plans, test results, land acquisitions, the covering up of accidents and fatalities as Terry had perfected the weapon.

Delaney stopped and looked at the next file in his

hand. Inside was a list of all the politicians and business associates he'd ever bribed through lobbying for his coal enterprises. He smiled to himself, and held onto the file tightly. If his empire was going to be destroyed, then he'd take down a few people with him.

He looked up as he heard a sharp crack and saw the wastepaper basket fall over. The flames began to lick at the rug at his feet. He stepped backwards, alarmed at the speed at which the flames spread across the office, sweeping across his desk. He raised his eyebrows in alarm as he saw the fire burn effortlessly towards the decanter and spirit bottles behind his desk.

Time to leave.

He strode across the room and slid a bookcase to the right. It revealed the entry to a small private elevator. Delaney held the file of lobbying activity tight to his chest and stepped into the elevator. He turned and pulled the small concertina gate across and hit the button for the underground car park. As he descended, the spirit bottles exploded, sending shards of glass down the elevator shaft.

Delaney ducked, holding the file over his head to shield himself. He snarled as a glass shard embedded itself in the back of his hand. Cursing, he lowered his arm and looked at the damage. Blood poured over the back of his hand and began to drip on the floor of the elevator. He pulled out the glass and flicked it onto the floor, crunching it under the heel of his shoe.

The elevator ground to a halt just as fire alarms began to sound throughout the building. Delaney grabbed the gate and pulled it open. As he stepped out of the elevator, he glanced to his left towards the car park exit. People were walking away from the building but then stopped and pointed upwards at the thick smoke emanating from the remains of Delaney's office.

He turned and jogged towards his car. He felt in his pockets for the keys and slowed to a brisk walk while he looked through them, selecting the right one. He held it between his teeth, then took the key between his finger and thumb and aimed it at the vehicle.

Nothing happened. He frowned. The alarm system wasn't on.

He hurried over to the car. As long as he could still get into it, he'd be fine. He'd still be able to get away.

As he approached the vehicle, he could hear sirens in the background. He smiled. The trucks would create enough of a diversion for him to slip away, drive to the house and organise a council of war with the lawyers. *Damage limitation.*

Delaney pulled open the car door, threw the file on the passenger seat and lowered his bulk behind the wheel. He pulled the door shut and held the key to the ignition.

'Hold it right there.'

Delaney jumped and looked in the rear view mirror at the face peering over the back of his seat at him.

'You broke into my house!' spat Delaney.

Mitch grinned back. 'No – we had an invite, remember?'

Delaney reached for the door handle, kicked the door

open, and then ran. A loud, short burst of gunfire broke the silence. Delaney sank to the floor, clutching his leg and growling through gritted teeth.

Mitch got out of the car and walked over to Delaney, his gun in his hand at his side. He crouched down and lowered his face to the other man's. Delaney glared at him, his skin pale from the pain.

'You bastard!'

'That was for Hayley,' said Mitch. He stood up. 'And this is for Pete.'

He kicked Delaney hard where the bullet had penetrated.

Delaney screeched, the sound ricocheting off the walls of the car park.

Mitch turned away, held up his hand and waved. A team of agents, dressed in black and carrying assault rifles, appeared from behind various vehicles and walked towards Mitch.

'Get him bandaged up, then put him on a flight to Canberra,' he said. He reached into the car and picked up the manila file from the passenger seat. 'I think we've got some mutual friends down there who will want to have a quiet word with him.'

FORTY-NINE

London, England

Dan spun the wheel and slid the car to a halt. He switched off the headlights and stared into the darkness. He lowered his window and strained his ears. He could hear the sound of a helicopter drawing closer.

'Keep your head down,' he said to Sarah, and slouched behind the wheel. Sarah took off her seatbelt and lowered herself into the foot-well of the passenger side of the vehicle, just as the headlights of another vehicle lit up the back of the car seat.

Dan threw himself across Sarah, keeping his face close to hers as the other car sped past theirs. Its brake lights flared as it flicked around the corner of the building next to them. Dan and Sarah raised their heads and peered out after it.

'Was that him?' asked Sarah.

Dan nodded. 'That was our bomb-maker. And the car we've been searching for.'

'Now what do we do?' said Sarah, impatiently shuffling in her seat.

Dan put his hand on her arm. 'Just wait. It's a dead-end – he's not going anywhere.'

They both looked up at the sound of the helicopter as it hovered above them. It began to drop closer to the ground, a searchlight skimming the road beside them.

Dan turned to Sarah. 'Phone David and tell him we'll get out the car after he's landed. I don't want to lose my night vision with that searchlight shining right on us.' He closed his eyes and looked away while the helicopter continued its descent.

Sarah made the call, and then put her phone away. 'He's here, Dan.'

The helicopter landed and Dan looked up as the searchlight died away. The rotors slowly stopped and David and his team climbed out. Dan walked over to them.

'Where did he go?' asked David.

Dan pulled up his jacket collar against the cold breeze coming off the river and pointed. 'It's a dead-end. I haven't taken a proper look yet though. I thought I'd wait for the cavalry to arrive.'

He glanced across as Sarah joined them. 'You stay right behind us. We have no idea what this guy could do.'

She nodded, zipped up her coat and shoved her hands

in her pockets. She looked to where David had walked over to his team.

'What are they going to do?'

Dan followed her gaze. 'They'll work their way along the buildings to wherever Terry's parked the car.' He glanced up, tilting his head slightly to one side. 'I can still hear the engine running.'

He walked over to where David was speaking with his assault team, Sarah following close behind. David turned as they approached.

'Right, well we're ready. You stay behind us.' He pointed at Dan. 'You too. I need you in one piece to take apart whatever this maniac has designed.'

Dan nodded and watched as David's team broke away and began to filter across the open expanse of the riverside wharf and headed towards the buildings. He walked over to their car, opened the door and reached inside for the gun David had given him. He shut the door quietly and looked up, realising Sarah was watching him steadily.

'This is really happening, isn't it?' she said. 'You've really got to stop him.'

Dan nodded. 'Any way we can.'

She walked up to him, wrapped her arms around him, and looked up at his face. 'Be careful.'

He nodded, bent down, and kissed her. 'Behave yourself. Stay out of the way when I tell you to.' He took her hand and led her down the track between the buildings, staying close to the side of the warehouses. He glanced ahead and saw the shadowy figures of the assault team methodically working their way down the line of buildings.

At the end of the track, about seventy metres away, the buildings formed a u-shape. Parked in the middle of the space, its headlights switched off and its engine running, sat the black sedan.

Dan stopped and looked at it. He felt relief, thankful they'd finally found it. He realised the adrenaline had kicked in. It felt like a lifetime since he'd felt it properly like this. He could feel his heart pounding in his chest, hard, rapid. Already, he was thinking. Imagining what the bomb would look like, how it would be wired.

He stopped dead as a shout from one of the assault team members reached his ears.

'It's him!'

Six bright torches switched on at once, illuminating a figure walking away from the black sedan.

Dan stepped out from the building into the path of the figure and stared in disbelief at the wretched form pacing towards them. He jumped instinctively as another figure loomed out of the darkness to the side of him and pulled him close to the opposite wall.

'Concentrate Dan!' said David. 'For Christ's sake, we don't know if he's armed and there you go walking out right in front of him!'

Dan shook his head in disbelief. 'I just can't believe it's him.' He peered around David and watched the figure approach.

David walked out from the shadows and yelled. 'Stay right there Terry, otherwise we shoot!'

The figure stopped and a cackle emanated from the shadow in front of them.

'Well, what have we got here? A fucking reunion?' laughed Terry. 'I hope your bomb disposal skills have improved, Dan.'

Dan made a lunge for Terry but David held him back and muttered in his ear. 'Leave it. We don't know if he's wired himself up.'

Dan shrugged off David's grip and nodded.

'It's not too late Terry,' yelled David. 'Tell us how to disarm the bomb. Tell us how we can help you.'

Terry growled. 'Help me? It's a bit fucking late for that, isn't it? You bastards – you were always going to leave me behind…'

He trailed off, rambling. Dan strained his ears to listen but couldn't make out the words. He looked at David and shook his head. 'I don't think we're going to be negotiating.'

David nodded. 'Reckon you're right.' He turned back to Terry. 'Okay Terry. Game over. We've got Delaney in custody. Uli's dead.' He nodded at Terry's look of disbelief. 'That's right – it's just you. So, raise your hands and get on the ground.'

Terry nodded. He raised his hands halfway to his chest. And then began to laugh. He turned his hands away from Dan and David's view. Dan saw something glint in the light of the torches. He saw Terry wince as if he'd been struck by something. And then David screamed.

'Everybody down! He's injected himself! He's going to blow himself up!'

The assault team ran for cover as Terry walked slowly towards them, laughing. Dan grabbed Sarah and pulled her behind an industrial waste bin, just as David landed on top of them.

'You're never going to take me alive,' Terry called. 'That's what I told them. That's what I said. They chased me over that damn desert. But they couldn't catch me, they couldn't…'

Terry's voice was swept away by the sound of a sickening explosion.

As the sound died away, Dan raised his head. There was nothing human left. Terry's body had been completely incinerated, wiped away by the force of the explosion and ensuing soundwave.

'What the hell was that?' said Sarah, her face pale in the glow of David's torchlight.

David visibly shuddered. 'The next phase in terrorism. Forget suicide bombers strapping explosives to themselves.'

Dan spun round to look at him. 'What do you mean?'

David leaned against the wall, his face tired and drawn. 'What I mean is we have reason to believe, now proved, that in future terrorists will simply inject themselves with the chemicals needed to make themselves into a walking time bomb. And we have no way of telling. They use the same sort of needles as diabetics. Can't spot them.'

He eased himself off the wall and looked at Dan. 'Ready to go and play?' He began to walk away, in the direction of the black sedan.

Dan pulled Sarah to her feet. 'I need to take a look at that bomb. Don't look at the walls. Do you hear me?'

She nodded.

'I mean it. You don't want nightmares like mine. Ever. Just keep your head down. I'll lead you past it.'

She grasped his hand tightly and squeezed. He pulled her towards him and turned, running towards the car, David leading the way. They edged around what was left of Terry and approached the vehicle.

FIFTY

Sarah hung behind Dan as they drew closer, her breathing audible in the muted silence around them.

He led in her a wide circle around the vehicle as his eyes took in every detail, every nuance of the car, trying to fathom a way forward.

'What are you waiting for?' whispered Sarah as they stopped next to the driver's door.

'Look.' He pointed.

Sarah peered through the back window and shuddered. A silver canister perched on the back seat of the car. Half a metre in length, it was held in place by two metal posts drilled into each of the back doors of the sedan. She shuddered.

Dan scratched his chin. 'I'll have to go through the front door – it'll make it more awkward to defuse it though.' He studied the canister. 'I can't see a timer from here – it must be inside that panel there.'

He stood back, crossed his arms. Closing his eyes, he recalled every scenario he'd experienced before, desperately trying to think of a solution from his catalogue of memories. He squatted on the floor, taking in the details of the car, how to gain access and how to defuse the bomb.

One of the team members ran over, placing a small tool kit next to him. 'Sorry sir, it's all we could find.'

Dan opened the lid and looked through the contents. 'It'll have to do – thanks.' Standing, he stretched and cricked his neck muscles.

'Everybody out,' he commanded, picking up the tool box.

The group of people milling about the car began to run out of the enclosed space, making as much distance between themselves and the impending explosion.

'I'll stay,' said Sarah.

He shook his head and gave her a slight push. 'No – get going. There's nothing to be gained by playing hero around a bomb. I want everybody out of this area – including you. Follow the team to their muster point and wait there.'

Sarah nodded, knowing he wouldn't change his mind. She put her hand on his shoulder and squeezed gently. 'Good luck.'

Dan looked up at her briefly and smiled.

'Well, look at it this way – whatever happens, you're going to have one hell of a story to write.'

She didn't return his smile, but turned on her heel and walked away.

Dan watched her go until she was out of sight, and then reached out for the front door of the car. He rubbed his thumb across his fingers, took hold of the handle and pulled the door slowly open.

Nothing happened. He breathed out slowly. He climbed in, pulled the tool box in with him and placed it in the foot-well of the car. He leaned behind the front seat and looked down at the silver surface of the canister. Taking a small screwdriver from the tool box, he began to gently remove each of the screws holding a small panel in place. Once each screw was halfway out, he placed the screwdriver on the front seat and began to gently remove each screw in turn, careful not to let the panel drop from its slot until he was ready.

As the last fastening came away, Dan used his left hand to hold the panel in place. Then, slowly, he placed his fingernails under each end and carefully lifted the panel away.

He breathed out as it cleared the canister, and dropped the panel onto the front seat. Turning back to the bomb, he surveyed the layout.

The timing cavity was the space of a man's hand, with four alloy posts supporting a small digital timing display and a series of switches. Wires protruded from the timer display in the top left-hand corner, wound their way through the alloy posts to the switches then out again, disappearing into the hulk of the canister in the bottom right-hand corner. Dan had never seen anything like it.

His hand twitched, once, as it hovered over the wiring.

The timing mechanism was complex – if his team hadn't apprehended Charles on the ship, the device could still have been deployed remotely by mobile phone. Sweat ran down his face as he considered his options. If he worried about what could have happened, he'd never focus.

Dan concentrated on slowing his breathing, desperately trying to lower his heart rate. He wiped his face with his sleeve, rubbed his fingers together and shuffled to try to get a workable position in the cramped quarters of the back seat of the car.

Dan ran his fingers down the wires, testing their thickness. He raised his gaze to the timer, now showing five minutes and twenty seconds. Three years ago, he would have considered that a luxury. He let go of the wires and turned to the front of the car, where he'd placed the tool box. He rummaged around until his fingers found the pliers – small, compact, and perfect for working in small spaces. He removed them and sorted through the contents of the box until he found a small pen-like torch. His fingers wrapped round it and he turned cautiously back to the bomb.

Shining the torch directly onto the wires, he cocked his head to one side, trying to get a look under the switches. He nodded to himself, convinced.

Cutting the blue wire, Dan eased himself back onto his haunches.

Suddenly, hell broke loose. Dan jumped as the car alarm shrieked. He looked down at the timer – at that instant, two minutes dropped off the countdown.

'Shit!' Dan tried to block out the noise from the alarm, concentrating desperately and went back to work on the timer – only two and a half minutes now remained. He growled loudly in frustration. So much for luxury. He bound the two ends of the broken blue wire together and the alarm stopped.

A noise at the end of the row of buildings made him stop and look round. A shadowed figure was walking towards him. Dan drew the gun from the waistband of his jeans. Raising it, he sighted it on the figure as it drew closer. 'Hold it right there.'

The figure froze. Then slowly raised its hands. 'Dan, it's me.'

Dan lowered the gun. 'Sarah?'

She came running then, tears streaming down her face. 'I couldn't leave you!'

Dan extracted himself from the car and caught her in his arms. 'I don't need to tell you how stupid you are, do I?'

She sniffed and held back from him. 'No, not at all. How long have we got?'

He looked back at the timer. 'Just over a minute and a half.'

Sarah managed a weak smile. 'Better get to work then.'

He nodded and climbed back into the car. Reaching over to the canister, he ran his fingers gently over the remaining wires. Red, white, green. Red, white, green. Which one? *Which one*?

He wiped the sweat from his eyes and noticed his hand was shaking. Breathing hard, panting, his mind flashed back to the desert, the dust in his eyes, a friend looking at him desperately, pleading, defuse the bomb! He couldn't do this, it wasn't possible –

'Dan!'

He blinked, looked up at Sarah.

She nodded at him. 'You can do this. I trust you.'

He closed his eyes, re-focused, then looked at the wiring array below him. And then somewhere, in the back of his mind, he realised he wasn't going to be able to defuse it. He desperately pulled at the wires, separating them between his fingers. It was no use, Terry had used an illogical pattern. No way of telling which wire would stop the bomb. It was impossible.

He realised his hands were shaking. He tried to think, tried to remember…

Then it hit him. Hard. The fuel cells weren't hiding the weapon. They *were* the weapon. He turned and shoved Sarah out of the way.

She stumbled, tripped and fell onto the ground. 'What are you doing?' she demanded.

Dan ignored her. He ran around to the driver's door and wrenched it open. Sliding in behind the wheel, he pulled the door closed, shoved the gears out of neutral and spun the wheels on the wet bitumen. He flicked the lights on and they illuminated the sides of the buildings.

He floored the accelerator and the car shot forward. Sliding the vehicle past what was left of Terry, Dan steered the car between the buildings, the speed increasing with every metre. He glanced in the rear view mirror at the silver canister on the back seat, gleaming in the moonlight. He smiled to himself. There was only one way to do this.

So be it.

As the car shot out from between the buildings, it swept past David and his assault team. They watched in disbelief as the car skidded past the helicopter, accelerated once more and hit the side of the wharf.

Time seemed to slow down as the car lifted off of the wharf, became airborne, then slewed into the dark waters of the Thames below.

FIFTY-ONE

David rushed to the edge of the wharf and peered into the icy waters. The roof of the black sedan was lurching in the tidal flow, slowly sinking. He turned as he heard footsteps running up from behind him.

'Dan!' screamed Sarah.

David caught her as she ran to the edge. 'Careful! We don't want you falling in as well!' He held her tight, aware tears were streaming down her face.

They stared at the black sedan as it succumbed to the black water lapping over its roof and sank below the surface.

'Come on Dan, get out,' murmured David. 'You can do it.'

Two members of his team joined them, aiming search lights at the surface of the water. They swung the beam left and right, as everyone desperately looked for a sign of Dan.

Dan forced himself not to scream as the icy cold water began to pour into the car. He twisted and turned in the driver's seat to look back at the canister. The timer clicked over. Sixty seconds remaining.

He wriggled his legs out from under the steering column and grimaced as the water seeped through his jeans. He began to shiver involuntarily as the icy depths claimed the vehicle. He glanced at the window to his right. Water was halfway up the glass. The heavy sedan was sinking fast into the river. He could see the lights from the wharf through the windscreen.

A metallic groan trembled through the vehicle and Dan's stomach lurched as the car pitched forward into the water and the engine finally died. His heart accelerated. He turned and watched the water lapping at the back seat. It was still too low. The canister was still above water level.

Fifty seconds.

Dan began to kick at the windscreen. It wouldn't give. He shouted, pure frustration emanating from him as the water ebbed around his knees. Exhausted, freezing, his muscles screamed with the effort. He shifted his weight in the car seat, lifted his feet and began to kick the windscreen again. He glanced in the rear view mirror. There still wasn't enough water around the canister.

Forty seconds.

He hollered, shouting at the glass as he continued to

pound at it. He lost his grip and slid down the car seat as his foot went through the glass.

Water began to pour over the dashboard, cascading onto his legs and streaming over the front seats. He gasped as a fresh coldness swamped him. He reached out to steady himself as the car lurched forwards and downwards into the murky depths.

He took a final deep breath as the car sank below the surface and search lights began to probe the darkness. He turned and stared at the timer on the canister.

Thirty seconds.

He crawled forwards, out through the windscreen, then turned and held onto the front of the car as it sank further into the dark muddy waters of the Thames. He willed the timer to stop. He could hear his heart beating hard in his ears. His lungs were starting to burst and he breathed out a little to release the pressure, the bubbles escaping to the surface.

Twenty seconds.

He stared at the timing mechanism, entranced. It had to work, had to. He thought over the last three months – everything he and Sarah had discovered. It all culminated with this, right now.

Ten seconds.

Dan knew he had to let go of the car and surface, or drown. His lungs were on fire, his heart pounding. He stared at the canister, willing the system to fail.

He looked up, and jolted involuntarily. He hadn't

realised the car had sunk so deep. The faded white light of torch beams swung over the surface, seeking him out. He forced himself to focus on the canister, gleaming eerily in the faded light. The red light of the timer blinked.

Five seconds.

Dan's whole world closed around it and he watched the time slipping away.

Two.

One.

Dan instinctively closed his eyes and waited for the inevitable sound wave. And waited. Then opened his eyes.

The timer remained on zero.

He looked around him, momentarily bewildered. He was still there. The bomb hadn't exploded.

He blew the stale air from his lungs in a watery yell and propelled himself to the surface.

Delaney had failed.

Sarah pulled away from David and began to frantically pace the wharf, staring at the river and willing Dan to resurface.

Then there was a shout and everyone turned.

Dan broke through the surface, a huge grin spread across his face. He raised a fist in triumph, and then began to swim towards the wharf.

David strode over to Sarah. 'Go to the helicopter.

There are blankets and a medical kit. Hurry, or he's going to get hypothermia in this temperature.'

Sarah nodded and jogged over to the helicopter. David turned and crouched down at the top of a ladder. Dan had reached the foot of it and was hauling himself out of the water. David reached out as Dan climbed the rungs, and pulled him up towards the wharf.

Sarah rushed over with a blanket and threw it around Dan's shoulders. 'Are you okay?'

He nodded. 'Bloody freezing,' he grinned, and realised his teeth were clattering together.

'Get on the helicopter. Let's get you both out of here,' said David.

As the rotors began to turn and lift the helicopter higher into the air, Dan glanced down at the searchlights sweeping across the water below.

Sarah leaned over and kept her voice low. 'I left Peter's notes in the car we stole.'

He looked at her, smiled and gave her a hug. 'It's okay. Those are copies. I left the originals at the house,' he whispered. 'And those copies down there had *loads* of pages missing. Strange, isn't it?'

She punched him. 'Bastard. When were you going to tell me that?'

He shrugged, smiled. 'You and I need an insurance policy.' He put his finger to his lips. 'Don't tell David.' He winked.

The helicopter soon began to descend and bumped

gently onto the roof of a building. Dan looked quizzically at David.

'Ops centre,' he explained. 'There's a clean change of clothes for you at the office. My team need to debrief. And you need to tell me what the hell you were thinking.'

Dan nodded, and then sniffed. 'Warm clothes first,' he said, and climbed out of the helicopter.

FIFTY-TWO

Dan walked into the conference room in borrowed jeans, boots, and sweatshirt. The atmosphere was electric. He finished towelling his damp hair from the hot shower and tossed the towel over the back of a chair. He could still feel the adrenaline rushing through his system and he smiled as Philippa handed him a glass of champagne.

'Well done,' she said. 'I'm really impressed.'

'Make the most of that,' David called, 'she doesn't hand out compliments every day.'

Dan grinned. 'I could get used to it though.'

Philippa smiled and walked over to the table, sat down and pulled her laptop towards her.

David pulled out a seat and indicated for Dan to join them. 'Before you drink all that, we're going to need to have a bit of a debrief,' he said. 'We'll do a full one in the morning but I want to know exactly what the hell you were thinking.'

Sarah sat down next to Philippa, putting her glass on the table. 'I agree Dan – how on earth did you know that driving the car into the river would stop the bomb?'

Dan smiled. 'It was something Harry said to me about fuel cells. I don't know why I suddenly remembered but he told me that if the membrane around the fuel cell is over-hydrated, the fuel cell gets flooded, which prevents the hydrogen reaching the catalyst.' He paused and shrugged. 'I just figured if I drove the car into the Thames, it would work.'

Sarah looked over to David. 'Have they caught Delaney?'

He nodded. 'Mitch apprehended him just before we boarded the *World's End*. Apparently Delaney started a fire in his office, then tried to leave without being noticed, amongst all the commotion. They're flying him down to Canberra for questioning. I think our colleagues in the Australian intelligence service have a room ready for him.'

Sarah began to pack her bag and Dan stood up, draining the last of his champagne in one gulp. 'What time do you want us here tomorrow?'

David shrugged. 'I think we all deserve a lie-in,' he said. 'Make it about ten.' He followed Dan out to the elevators and they travelled down to the reception area. Dan smiled as he saw Sarah and Philippa deep in conversation at the doors with a man Dan guessed was Sarah's editor.

He turned and noticed David looking at him, appraising him. 'What are you thinking?' he asked.

'You know, we're always interested in recruiting good people.'

Dan shrugged. 'I don't know if I'm ready for that.'

David smiled. 'Well, you've earned a break. Here's my card. Contact me if you change your mind.'

Dan turned to find Sarah looking at him. He walked slowly over to her. 'Hi.'

She smiled. 'Hello. Come here often?'

He grinned. 'How're you doing?'

Sarah shrugged. 'I'm sure in a few days it's all going to hit me.' She inclined her head towards the door, where her editor, Gus, paced the floor. 'I think he's going to have me locked up until this story's finished though.'

Dan looked over her shoulder and smiled. 'He doesn't seem too bad, as far as bosses go. Although I'd hate to see his face when he sees your expenses claim for this month.'

Sarah laughed. 'Yeah – although I think I forgot to keep some of my receipts.'

Dan smiled and looked down at his feet. 'Are you going to be OK – seriously?' He glanced up at her, nervous and not sure why.

She shrugged. 'I really don't know. It's been a mad couple of months, y'know? All I want to do is get this story finished and Gus happy with it. After that – who knows?'

Dan nodded. 'Yeah. I know what you mean.'

Sarah glanced over at David, standing with his team and packing up communications equipment, forensic specialists getting ready to meet the recovery team at the laboratory to pore over the defused bomb and take it apart piece by piece.

'Did he offer you a job?'

Dan glanced at David and then looked back at Sarah.

'Yeah.' He smiled. 'I don't know if I could take this sort of excitement on a regular basis though.'

She laughed. 'Oh come on – lots of action, international travel, driving cars at mad speeds, shooting at bad guys, getting your mojo back defusing a bomb – what on earth's stopping you?'

Dan smiled, shrugged, then looked at his watch. 'Hey – are you doing anything for the next hour or so?'

Sarah shook her head. 'No – why?'

Dan grabbed her hand and pulled her across the reception area. 'Come on.'

'Where are we going?' Sarah dragged her feet, unsure what was happening.

'Don't worry – trust me.' Dan pulled her out of the door, past the small crowd which had assembled there. Gus turned as they approached.

'Sarah – where are you going?' he asked, making a misjudged attempt to grab her sleeve as she and Dan hurried past.

Sarah shrugged her shoulders. 'I don't know – I'm just following him.' She grinned. 'It seems to have worked so far.'

Gus frowned. 'Don't be long – I want you at the office so we can run through the story together. The newspaper wants this in the morning edition so we can syndicate it by the evening.'

Dan stopped and turned to Gus. 'Stop panicking. She'll be there.' He glared at the other man, who nodded, realising Dan wasn't in the mood to negotiate.

Dan began to walk again, pulling Sarah along after him into the crisp night. Their breath froze in the air.

'Dan? Where are we going?'

'Hurry – I don't want to miss it. Come on!' He headed out the doors and up Belvedere Road. He hurried along the street until they reached a high fence. Opening a wrought-iron gate, he entered a small park. He glanced around and then stopped.

'Give me your mobile phone.'

Sarah reached into her bag and pulled out the phone. She handed it to Dan. 'Why do you need it?'

He grinned, switched it off, and then put it in his jacket pocket. 'That's why.' He looked around the park. 'Perfect.'

'Thank god for that,' said Sarah sarcastically. 'I wondered where the hell we were going.'

Dan ignored her, pulled her through the narrow entrance to the park and pointed to a low wooden bench which overlooked the city stretching out below. Sitting down, he patted the bench next to him and looked up at Sarah.

'Here – quickly. Otherwise you'll miss it.'

Sarah sat down, confused. 'Miss what?'

'Shh.' Dan looked at his watch. 'Look.'

As the clock swung round to eight o'clock, Sarah raised her eyes to the skyline and gasped.

One by one, the lights in each skyscraper, office, apartment block and tourist attraction began to switch off.

'What's wrong?' Sarah turned to Dan. 'What's going on?'

Dan reached into his jacket and pulled out a small candle and a box of matches. Lighting the candle, he turned to Sarah and grinned.

'Earth Hour – I nearly forgot, with all the excitement.'

Sarah laughed and punched him gently on the arm. Dan put his arm round her shoulder and pulled her to him, kissing her gently.

'It's been a blast, thanks,' he said.

Sarah smiled and nodded, not trusting herself to speak as they sat in the enveloping darkness.

THE END

FROM THE AUTHOR

Dear Reader,

First of all, I wanted to say a huge thank you for choosing to read *White Gold*, the first book in the *Dan Taylor* series. I hope you enjoyed the story.

If you did enjoy it, I'd be grateful if you could write a review. It doesn't have to be long, just a few words, but it is the best way for me to help new readers discover one of my books for the first time.

If you'd like to stay up to date with my new releases, as well as exclusive competitions and giveaways, you're welcome to join my Reader Group at my website, www.rachelamphlett.com. I will never share your email address, and you can unsubscribe at any time. You can also contact me via Facebook, Twitter, or by email. I love hearing from readers – I read every message and will always reply.

Thanks again for your support.

Best wishes,

Rachel Amphlett

Printed in Great Britain
by Amazon